KNIGHTS OF T

Julian Atterton has a passion for early and medieval English history. He has written five adventure novels set between the sixth and the fourteenth centuries – in the ancient kingdom of Northumbria, which encompasses the part of Yorkshire where he now lives. When not writing he spends a good deal of time researching his subject. "I like my fictions to have truth," he says. His novels are an attempt "to put back together stories where the historical evidence is fragmentary – tales no historian would dare to tell." He doesn't, however, want his books to be labelled simply "historical fiction". "It is chance that determines if our imaginations are fuelled by contemporary worlds, the past or the galaxies of the future, fantasy or realism," he says. "What matters most is the magic of reading-time – the escape from our day to day cares provided by immersion in the fiction – which is as rich in any genre."

Although a complete story in itself, *Knights of the Sacred Blade* is also the first in a trilogy, the second part of which is *Knights of the Lost Domain*. The author's other books are *The Last Harper* and *Fire of the Kings* (both shortlisted for the Young Observer Teenage Fiction Prize), *The Tournament of Fortune* and three stories for younger children, *The Shape-Changer*, *Robin Hood and the Miller's Son* and *Robin Hood and Little John*.

To Rosemary Sutcliff,
a troubadour's homage.

First published 1989 by Julia MacRae Books
This edition published 1991 by Walker Books Ltd
87 Vauxhall Walk, London SE11 5HJ

© 1989 Julian Atterton
Cover illustration © 1991 Iain McCaig
Map drawn by Mark Schlesinger

Printed and bound in Great Britain by
Cox and Wyman Ltd, Reading, Berkshire

British Library Cataloguing in Publication Data
A catalogue record for this book is available
from the British Library.
ISBN 0-7445-2042-8

JULIAN ATTERTON

KNIGHTS *of the* SACRED BLADE

WALKER BOOKS
LONDON

david

SCOTLAND AND NORTHUMBRIA

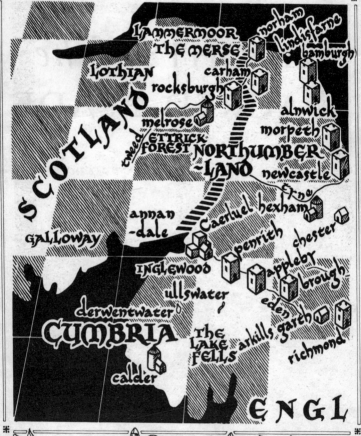

LAMMERMOOR
THE MERSE
norham
lindisfarne
bamburgh

LOTHIAN
carham
rocksburgh
alnwick

melrose
morpeth

tweed ETTRICK
FOREST
NORTHUMBER
~LAND

SCOTLAND

newcastle

tyne

annan
-dale
Caerluel hexham

GALLOWAY

penrith
chester

INGLEWOOD
appleby
brough

ullswater
eden

derwentwater
arkills garth

CUMBRIA
THE
LAKE FELLS
richmond

calder

ENGL

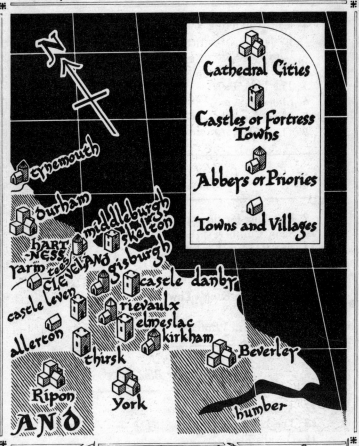

IN THE YEAR 1135

 STEPHEN

N

Cathedral Cities

Castles or Fortress Towns

Abbeys or Priories

Towns and Villages

tynemouth

durham

middleburgh

HART-NESS

skelton

yarm tees

CLEVELAND

gisburgh

castle danby

castle leven

rievaulx

elmeslac

allerton

kirkham

thirsk

Beverley

Ripon

York

AND

humber

Mark Schlesinger

CONTENTS

PART ONE
The Lords of the Waste Land
September *1135*–February *1136*

1. THE WANDERING SCHOLAR

I was leaning against the wall of Gisburgh Priory,
eating an apple and watching the market come to life.
Even though the canons were still singing the harvest
Mass, the traders had set up their stalls, and were calling
their wares. Most had come from miles away. Mother had
told me to keep an eye on the drapers, and to call her from
church if they began to sell out. Father had told me to keep
an eye on the twins, my younger brothers, and I was trying
to when I first caught sight of the scholar.

He came walking down the northern track like someone half asleep, wearing a long black cassock with the sleeves
rolled up, his hands clenching the strap of a calfskin
shoulder-bag. The darkness of his eyes, and the raven colour
of his thick, straight hair made him stand out like a black
lamb among the Norse folk of Cleveland.

He stopped to gaze up at the priory church. I saw from
the softness of his face and his lack of beard that he was no
older than me, and that from the ankles down, his sandalled
feet were brown with dried mud.

When his eyes met mine, he nodded cautiously.
Pushing my hands behind me to show I was not a beggar, I
nodded back.

"Peace be with you," he said haltingly, with an accent that showed English came hard to his tongue.

"And with you," I answered in French, and at that he grinned from ear to ear.

I had words of French because my father had taken it into his head that I should. Once a week for almost a year, I had come to the priory to be taught by one of the canons, and suddenly I was grateful.

"I am lost," said the stranger. "Can you tell me where on God's earth I happen to be?"

"Gisburgh."

"Gisburgh," he repeated glumly. "I was hoping it might be York."

I pointed to the hills behind the town. "York is several days of road to the south."

"And Durham?"

"Durham is several days to the north."

Pulling a face, he set down his bag and leaned against the priory wall, and I noticed him giving the apple in my hand a look of longing. When I offered him one, he tore into it with delight.

"Have you eaten today?" I asked.

He spread his hands. "I have no money."

I had three farthings, and knew Mother would pay me back if I spent them on charity. I went over to the stalls, bought a barley bun and a cup of ale, and pressed them on the stranger. As he sat down to eat, I saw the top of his head was shaved in the round tonsure of a man of the Church, so when he finished, I waited for him to say me a prayer, but all he did was grin and ask my name.

"Simon Aldredson," I told him.

"Aimeric," he introduced himself. "Aimeric of Chartres."

I nodded knowingly, though I had never heard of Chartres.

"Do you always travel without money?" I asked.

"Only when I have just been robbed," he replied. "I took ship in Rouen, with a company of Vikings, and they swore they would take me right up the river to York. When we sailed past the river-mouth, I thought I was going to die, but they threw me ashore last night in some demon-infested marshes to the north of here."

"That will be the Tees."

"An evil place, full of the cries of lost souls." He shivered. "I could hear them all night."

"Those will have been the seals," I told him. "They live in hundreds on the sandbanks."

"Ah, perhaps," he said doubtfully. "So where am I now? What is the name of this region?"

"This is Cleveland. Most of the land you have walked through belongs to Robert de Brus. His brother is the prior here. If you are Norman, they will make you welcome."

It was hard to say that without a bitterness creeping into my voice. The Normans had ruled England since my grandfather's day, and no one loved them. In the tales I had heard as a child, they were crueller than demons, but only the old men spoke of fighting them now. The folk of my village belonged to Robert de Brus and that was that.

"Have you come here for land?" I asked.

Aimeric only laughed.

"I have come for what the land can tell me," he answered. "My road lies to the cities, to the places of learning, and they were places of learning long before the Normans came and built their castles and bright new churches."

"Are you a priest?"

"No," he said, "just a wandering scholar. I am a clerk and a poet. I travel to learn, and I learn by travelling."

"If you are a poet, would you sing me one of your songs?"

"It would have to be in French or Latin," he warned me.

"In French then."

Closing his eyes, he took a deep breath, and sang, conjuring a melody that was strong enough to rise over the chattering heads of the market-place. He sang of the city of Chartres in its sea of corn, of the orchards of Normandy, of the bird-skimmed marshes of Poitou, and he left each place with a cry of refrain.

> *"I must touch the edges of the earth,*
> *Crow on wind, I swoop to catch the words.*
> *There's no town, there's no door,*
> *There's no land, and there's no shore*
> *Where I stay."*

It was a song from a world far wider than the one I knew, but while he sang it was mine.

"Is that your own song?" I asked.

He bowed his head, looking almost regretful.

"It was magic," I told him.

"No, just words," he said teasingly. "Words in a pattern I found for them. If you liked it, that means you could find patterns as good of your own."

"Oh no," I said. "I have nothing to sing about."

He took me seriously, and thought a moment. "Perhaps not yet," he agreed, "but all of us have things in our heads that would be better set free in a song. Only poets and women at the washing-trough have the time to find their songs, but that is the only reason they are the ones who sing for us all."

I pointed my thumb over my shoulder towards the stone-muffled chanting in the priory church. "And the canons," I said. "They sing for us all."

"True," said Aimeric, "but is it our lives they sing about?"

He settled his bag back on his shoulder. "Mine is just a song I sing to keep me walking," he said. "Tell me as much as you can of the way to York."

"Follow the road that leads west along the foot of the hills. That will bring you to Stokesley, and then – then you must ask someone else, for that is as far as I know."

"It may be enough for one day. I thank you for your kindness, Simon Aldredson."

A moment later, he was no more than a tonsured head bobbing through the crowd. He had sung about the edges of the earth, and left me wondering how far away they were.

At the end of the Mass, the worshippers came chattering out of the church, and I made my way back into the priory yard. It was a warm day, but my parents walked as if they were fighting a cold wind.

Mother, who was a woman not easily shaken, had a face as white as the linen of her head-dress, and when she saw me she looked away, as if I made her ashamed. My father looked the same as ever, but he was not smiling.

"I am taking your mother home," he said, and gave me some coins from his wallet. "Stay here with the twins, and keep them out of trouble."

They walked on, hurriedly, and as they passed through the gateway, my mother gave a backward glance: not towards me, but to a group of nobles who had gathered talking around Robert de Brus and his brother, Prior William.

The tallest of them was a knight in a blue surcoat, his hair cut in the old-fashioned Norman crop, and he was staring after my parents. When they were gone he turned to Father Matthew, the canon who taught me French, and he looked to be asking him questions. Then, as Father Matthew answered, the knight turned to stare at me.

I ran out of the priory yard as if there were demons on my trail. It was a feeling I had not had for years.

When I was small, I often caught the women of our village looking at me sideways, whispering as I went by. Mother said it was nothing to do with me: it was just that I had been born at a time of ill omen.

For I was born in the same winter moon that saw the White Ship splinter on the rocks of the Normandy coast.

They say it sailed at dusk, the deck lit with lanterns and crowded with nobles, and the folk of Barfleur stood watching it glide out to sea. They saw it strike the rocks, and they watched as one by one the lanterns went black.

In the morning the dead were washed ashore, and among them was Prince William, grandson of the Conqueror and true-born heir to the kingship of England.

The fate of the White Ship has shaped the lives of many who never sailed in her. It was about to shape mine.

Our village lay halfway between Gisburgh and the sea, on a broad slope above a wooded ravine. As the twins and I climbed up from the bridge, the stones of the little church were amber with evening light. The oxen had been turned loose to graze the stubble of the harvested fields.

Tethered in my father's yard were two magnificent horses with Norman saddles, and sitting by our door was a broad-shouldered man with a stomach the shape of a barrel. His face was wrinkled as bark, and tanned as the old leather jerkin he wore over a shirt embroidered with a pattern as tangled as a thicket of brambles. As he looked up, there was a flash of gold from an ear-ring, and I saw that in his hands he held a stick he had been carving into the likeness of a dragon.

"Come for your suppers?" he asked, and as he looked us over, his eyes, too, came to rest on me. The twins went wide-eyed, and asked to touch the carving, but I hurried by into the house.

Sitting at the table were Mother and Father and the knight in the blue surcoat.

"Ah, Simon," said my father. "Come and greet our guest, Jordan de Falaise."

I fumbled for the right words of French to greet a Norman knight, but he simply held out his hand. When I reached out to grasp it he held me fast. Above a long, broken nose his eyes were deep-set and blue, while his skin was tanned and freckled, as if he came from a land without clouds. He studied my face, and his mouth curled ever so slightly downwards, as if I troubled him.

Father patted the table and rose to his feet, and the knight released my hand.

"Let me be the one to tell him," said my father.

He drew me out of the house, leaving Mother face to face with the knight, then led me quickly past the others into the lane that led up out of the village. He said nothing until we had crested the hill and could look out to sea, and the dark sweep of the water seemed to soothe him.

"It's a small enough thing, really," he said, half to himself.

"What is it?" I asked. "What have I done?"

"Nothing," he said. "It was none of your doing. Listen. Would it trouble you to know you are not my son?"

At first I could not even take him seriously.

"Your true father," he said grimly, "is the Norman you have just met."

I waited for him to chuckle, to give himself away, but he just stood there, watching me. Then I felt as if the ground were turning to water.

"I do not believe this," I said. "Are you telling me I am Norman?"

"As Norman as our dear lord de Brus."

On the far side of the valley I could see the torchlit castle of our lords and masters. How could I be one of them? I started laughing so wildly I took to coughing and shuddering, and Father had to thump me between the shoulders to make me stop – only he was not my father. He took me in his arms and I clung to him. I had never thought I would leave him. I had always thought we would work the fields together until the day came for me to be the one who led the plough.

"What can I call you?" I asked him desperately.

"Call me Aldred," he said. "That's my name."

"And me? Who am I if I'm not Simon Aldredson?"

"Simon de Falaise, or Simon FitzJordan, whichever you choose."

I looked down at our house, where my mother and the Norman would still be face to face.

"Why has he come back?" I asked.

"God knows," muttered Aldred, "but now he has seen you, he will want you."

"He has never seen me before?"

"He left when your mother was heavy with you," said Aldred bitterly. "In those days there was a lot of shame when a Norman took an English woman. He could have lived with it, but he chose to go, and leave it to your mother: and in all these years he has never once sent word. We thought he must be dead."

"Yet you have always known he might come to claim me?"

"Why else," said Aldred, "would we have had you learn French?"

"Why should I care who he is?" I asked. "I will not go with him. He cannot make me."

"No," said Aldred, "but think what it may mean. Jordan is a knight, so he will have land, and if he has come to offer you a son's place in his household, that means a right to inheritance, and as a Norman, a free man. It will be more than we can ever give you. But you can always come back. Remember that."

When we got home, we saw the horses and their riders had gone. The twins had tumbled off to bed, but Mother was working by the light of a butter-lamp she had placed on the waxed oak table, chopping herbs to add to the bowl where she was pasting onions and wood-pigeon. Beside it on the board stood the carved wooden dragon.

Mother held out her arms and I ran to her. She called me names she had not called me since I learnt to walk, and it was as if she were reciting a spell. I relaxed, certain now that nothing was wrong. It was only that the ground had moved. We were all still there.

"You could have told me," I reproached her.

"Could we?" she asked. "What if he had never come? Could you have worked the fields knowing you were as Norman as the Conqueror?"

"What did Jordan say when he left?" asked Aldred.

"That he will be back in the morning to speak with Simon."

"Is that all?"

"Oh, you know the Normans," said Mother. "They

always want the earth. He told me it was not only Simon he had come back to claim."

"And what was your answer to that?" asked Aldred breathlessly.

Smiling, my mother untied her linen head-dress to let her hair spill out into the lamplight.

"I told him he was my youth," she said, "while you have been my life, and always will be."

It was the look that passed between them then which told me I was free to go. They could spare me.

I went to bed, and lay awake, frightened of Jordan and all he might be, but thinking also of Aimeric. That was what I wanted to become: a scholar wandering from corner to corner of the earth, and if I were Norman, a free man, there would be nothing to stop me. In the morning I told the twins I was setting out for Jerusalem. Neither of them believed me.

It was a morning like any other. Breakfast done, Aldred and the twins set out for the fields, only without me. Mother packed my clothes into a shoulder-bag like Aimeric's, told me to keep myself clean, hugged me one last time, and hurried after them. I was left alone to wait for Jordan de Falaise.

He came riding up the track from Skelton with his barrel-shaped companion at his side and two mules trotting behind on a tether. At the gate of our yard he drew rein, and we looked searchingly at each other. I saw his face was gaunt, and his hair thinning as it greyed. Either he was older than my – than Aldred – or he had led a harder life.

"I am glad to find you again," he said, in flawless English. "Were you waiting for me?"

The words of greeting I had prepared dried on my lips. In the end I said simply, "If you wish, I will ride with you."

He gave no sign it was what he wanted. Instead he pointed to the house.

"Are you certain?" he asked. "Why leave your hearth for me?"

I had an answer to that, thanks to Aimeric.

"I am not," I said. "I wish to travel to learn, and to learn by travelling. Our roads may be the same."

That pleased him, or at least it made him smile.

"The further I travel," he said, "the less I wish there was to learn. Have you met my companion, Orm the Axe?"

The stout man winked. "Do not be fooled by the name," he told me. "I may carve dragons, but it is Jordan who eats them alive."

"Until we tame you one to ride," said Jordan, "you will just have to make do with a mule."

I chose the taller of the two mules, and folded a blanket to make a saddle, but even then when I was mounted my feet almost touched the ground.

The women at the washing-trough stared as we rode by, and the gossip broke out behind our backs. I knew now what they had whispered about me when I was a child. In the fields, the twins were waving. Aldred put his arm around my mother, and they stood watching, and I kept waving until our horses had dipped down the bank to the bridge by the mill. Then I told myself to stop crying and keep my eyes on where we were going, so that one day I could find my way back.

2. JORDAN

JORDAN and Orm rode at ease in the comfort of their tall, padded saddles. I bounced along behind. They were high above me, and the little they said was hard to catch.

We were past Stokesley, where the hills fell behind and the forest grew thick, when they stopped to graze the horses, and at last I was able to dismount.

"How far are your lands?" I asked.

The two men exchanged glances of amusement.

"I wish I knew," said Jordan. "The truth is, we are on our way to find out. You must know Robert de Brus?"

"The lord of Cleveland?"

"Not only of Cleveland. He is lord of Hartness, north of the Tees, and far to the west, of Annandale, a domain he holds for David, the king of the Scots. He tells me Annandale is wild, with room enough for me and mine if I want it that way. So we ride to Scotland. I hold nothing in England, and I doubt I ever will."

So the bundles in the baskets of the mules were all he owned, and I had been expecting him to have a castle and a household.

"Where, then, is Falaise?" I asked.

"In Normandy," he answered. "It is the town where my father was born, which he left to follow the Conqueror to England. He made his fortune here – and lost it."

"And have you never made yours?" I persisted.

Jordan smiled patiently. "I have never tried," he said. "Christendom has been my domain, from Normandy to the Holy Land, from the Empire to Sicily, wherever it has seemed good to take my sword. I have served some fine lords, but none have I loved enough to want to be tied to them by a gift of land."

"Until now," growled Orm.

"Until now," agreed Jordan.

"So, how far is Annandale?" I asked.

"No need to look alarmed," Jordan told me. "Today we ride no further than Castle Leven."

The road led through forest. For some distance we saw no one. We passed a clearing where saplings and gorse grew where once had been the fields of a steading. Jordan made the sign of the cross.

Soon afterwards, we heard the tolling of a bell some way ahead.

"Early in the day for Vespers," remarked Jordan, turning to me. "Is there an abbey in these parts?"

I could not say. Ever since we passed Stokesley, I had been outside the land I knew.

"It sounds to me," said Orm, "as if someone is calling on the saints."

They heeled their horses into a canter, and at the end of its tether my mule was jerked into a trot that all but sawed me in two.

The bell had stopped tolling by the time we came out of the trees onto the autumn-ploughed fields that ringed a village of some ten or so houses and a small stone church.

The door of the church stood open, and inside we could hear voices, and chief among them, a woman's voice raised in anger or fear.

"It must be someone claiming sanctuary," said Jordan, and we dismounted and went in.

By the altar steps, a woman was kneeling on a stone slab set into the floor. Around her were seven men, six in the dress of villagers, and one with the tonsure of a priest. As we entered, they looked up, startled.

The priest came towards us, spreading his arms to keep us away.

"No," said the woman hurriedly. "He is the sign, the answer to the prayer."

She was staring at Jordan and the sword that hung from his belt. He bowed.

"Lady, you may be mistaken," he said. "We were passing by chance when we heard the bell."

"I prayed to Saint Cuthbert," she said.

"Saint Cuthbert?" repeated Jordan, with a reverence that surprised me, for I had been told the Normans sneered at English saints.

The woman touched the slab on which she knelt.

"This is his place," she said. "Here his bones rested on their flight from the heathen."

"What was your prayer?" Jordan asked her.

The villagers muttered to her to be quiet.

"Think, Ulrica," begged one of them. "He will be a friend of FitzWalter's."

Orm's nose went up like a hound on scent. "This reeks of trouble," he whispered in French, but Jordan's eyes never left the woman. Even though she was barely in the middle of age, her hair was already white as silver; but her skin was rosy, and her eyes a bright blue even in the gloom of the church. She rose to her feet, and tucked her hands into her sleeves.

"I prayed for a champion," she said. "I have been challenged to trial by combat."

Suddenly, the villagers were all talking at once.

"FitzWalter wants Ulrica's land to add to his hunting-chase," said one.

"When she refused, he told her the land was his to use as he wished," said another. "He told her to find a champion, for trial by combat, and to find him in seven days. Tomorrow is the seventh day."

"All of us are with her," said the first, "but who could hope to fight a Norman, and live? Whatever we do, Ulrica will lose her land, and FitzWalter will say it was all within the law."

"They are talking of Pagan FitzWalter," explained the priest. "He is lord of the manor. It is true he often steps beyond his rights."

"And the land is yours?" Jordan asked Ulrica.

"I have it from my father," she replied, "and he had it from his."

"So that if I were your champion," said Jordan, "you trust that God would give you justice?"

"Your sword would be blessed," said the priest, "and the killing would carry no guilt."

Jordan's eyes went from the woman to the slab in the floor.

"I have met Pagan FitzWalter," he said thoughtfully, "and tonight I hope to be his guest. If I cannot change his mind, then tomorrow I will stand as your champion."

The villagers said nothing. It looked as if none of them believed him. Jordan bowed to the woman, and made for the door.

"Tomorrow morning," he called over his shoulder, "be at the castle gate."

We had only to ride down a bank beyond the church to find ourselves in a deep and narrow valley, and see above us on the far slope the towered motte and spiked palisades of Pagan FitzWalter's castle.

"Forgive my asking," said Orm, "but what if he refuses to even listen to you?"

"I fight his champion," replied Jordan.

Orm looked as if he were struggling to keep his temper. "You know what I mean," he said. "Two days ago, you gave your oath of loyalty to Robert de Brus, and now you want to quarrel with one of his men! De Brus will spit fire when he hears this."

"He may well," agreed Jordan, "but I'll take that chance." He nudged his horse down into the waters of the ford. "After all," he said, "you would not ask me to forget the vows of knighthood?"

"Why not?" muttered Orm. "You seem able to forget everything else."

All at once, they burst out laughing, and spurred their horses into the river, sending spray in all directions. I was dragged in with the mules, and drenched.

Jordan had only to name himself to the guards at the castle gate to win entry.

We rode into a wide bailey, with stables and workshops on one side, a hall and lodgings on the other. At the far end, perched above the river, a wooden keep towered on its motte of stamped earth like a giant's beehive.

Jordan and Orm rubbed their horses down themselves before they gave them to the grooms to be fed, then we washed and made our way to the hall which was filling for supper.

A steward had given us places at one of the long side tables, when Pagan FitzWalter made his entrance amid a flurry of family and servants. Like most Normans, he was tall and well-fed, and he took his time walking up the hall. When he caught sight of Jordan, he greeted him by name.

"But you cannot sit there," he protested. "Your place is at my side."

Jordan bowed, and moved to join the lords and ladies in their procession towards the high table at the tapestried end of the hall. One of the daughters glanced at me, but when I smiled, she looked insulted. She had seen my clothes, and judged me a peasant.

After that I shrank a little, and kept my eyes on those near me, and on the food. The main dish was goose roast with sage, and there was more than we could eat. Now I knew why so much of what we grew in our village went straight to the castle at Skelton.

We were sitting with two foresters, so the talk was of where to hunt and the best horses to ride. Orm and Jordan had caused a stir in the stables. Everyone wanted to know how they came to be riding Arab stallions bred in Castile.

When the supper was over, the ladies swept out in their gowns that trailed through the rushes, and the hall began to empty as folk left in twos and threes. The fire smoked, and the hunting-dogs stretched out to chew the scraps they had been thrown. While Orm diced with the foresters, I moved along the bench to where I could overhear what they were saying at the high table.

There were only three left sitting there: Jordan, FitzWalter, and an older man with a bald, freckled head. They looked in good humour, and FitzWalter was telling

Jordan with a gleeful disdain about the wildness of Annandale.

"It would be fine if it weren't for the people," he said. "The men of Galloway are half Irish and half Viking. Can you think of anything worse? They like stealing cattle, and women, and they'll steal from anyone, Norman, English, or Scot. You'll find they need a strong hand."

"But not too strong a hand," suggested the older man.

FitzWalter chuckled appreciatively. "Well put," he said, and leaned towards Jordan. "When they make trouble, it's mostly for King David; and even though David is a Norman, we always like him to have one or two thorns in his side."

"You call David a Norman?" asked Jordan with surprise.

"Never to his face," said FitzWalter, "but he did grow up an exile at the court of our good King Henry. We formed him. He thinks like us. Robert de Brus is one of his closest friends, and we are the ones who have gone to David's help whenever there has been trouble among the Scots. He owes us his crown."

"My father would have laughed to see it," said Jordan. "He spent half his life fighting the Scots."

"And the other half fighting the English?" asked the older man. "Those days are long gone. The Scots are our friends, and the English know their place. Northumbria in your father's time was the bloodiest pit in Christendom, but we have cut it into pieces, studded it with castles, and these days you can have a longer life here than in Normandy."

"And what would you say," asked Jordan, "that we have given Northumbria in return?"

"King Henry's peace," said FitzWalter.

"And justice?" asked Jordan.

"Even justice," agreed FitzWalter.

Jordan sat forward. "On my way here," he said, "a woman named Ulrica begged my help. She said you have challenged her to trial by combat."

"Indeed I have," agreed FitzWalter.

"I was surprised," said Jordan. "I thought King Henry frowned on the old ways of trial by ordeal, and that sworn juries of local men were now the judges of such disputes?"

FitzWalter spread his hands. "So an English woman clung to your stirrup and wailed?" he said dismissively. "She is nothing. I challenged her to trial by combat because I knew she would never find a champion. We killed them all long ago. Put her out of your mind."

"Let me ask you," said Jordan, "as a favour, to leave her be."

"It is out of my hands," said FitzWalter amiably. "The old laws are the best for Northumbria, and once invoked they must run their course."

Jordan shrugged and sat back. "It may amuse you," he said, "to hear I am standing as her champion."

FitzWalter stared at him in disbelief.

"Why?" he asked. "What is this old witch to you?"

"She has prayed to Saint Cuthbert," said Jordan, "and what she asks, it is the duty of a knight to perform."

"Remember what makes you a knight," suggested FitzWalter. "Robert de Brus stands by his men, and he looks to his men to stand shoulder to shoulder. I can see the witch cast a spell over you, but your first duty is to your lord, and through him to me."

"You are the one who ordered trial by combat," Jordan replied quietly. "You could have set your claim before a jury, but you set it before God. So be it. What difference can it make if I am the lady's champion? It is God who will decide whether Ulrica or you, my lord, are in the wrong."

FitzWalter said nothing, but the look in his eyes showed a mind on fire. Jordan rose smoothly to his feet, bowed, then glanced round to nod to Orm and me. We followed him out, the eyes of the hall scorching the backs of our necks like dragon's breath.

"Well, you handled that with your customary tact and charm," remarked Orm. "Where are we going to sleep?"

"Somewhere safe," muttered Jordan. "Is there a chapel in this snake-pit?"

We found one at the foot of the motte, built in wood, and draughty, but with saints painted on the walls.

On the far side of the bailey, a glow of torchlight moved in the stables. Horses were led out. The castle gate was opened, and two men mounted and rode away into the night.

Orm gave a chuckle.

"It looks as if de Brus will be woken before daybreak."

"Let's hope so," said Jordan.

He wrapped himself in a fur-lined cloak, and fell fast asleep. Orm did the same. They certainly knew how to snore.

Jordan was not in the least what I had expected him to be. He had nothing to show for his life, and none of the greed I had always thought went with being Norman. Instead, he was driven by some strange sense of purpose he called knighthood, so strong he was willing to risk his life for whatever rang true. I had heard stories about trial by combat. To fight in one was to ask for the judgement of God. If Ulrica had lied, Jordan would die. How he could know that, and still sleep, was far beyond me. I was scared out of my wits.

*   *   *

We were up with the dew. Jordan stripped to the waist and walked over to the washing-trough. A few of the men of the castle were already there. They gave him no greeting, but I could see them counting the scars on his ribs and shoulders.

I thought it best to keep my mouth shut, and watch.

Jordan emptied his saddle-bags on the grass, and laid out his gear like a trader spreading his wares. He pulled on a coat of white silk, and over it a hauberk of ring-mail lined with quilt. Orm laced and buckled it for him, while Jordan fastened his sword-belt and drew on a pair of blue leather gauntlets. He laid ready a mail coif, a steel helmet and a long Norman shield shaped like a birch leaf; then he bundled everything else back into the bags.

"Saddle the horses," he told Orm. "We won't want to linger when this is over."

We had a long wait before it began. A shout came from the gate; we guessed that Ulrica and the villagers were outside; but the gate stayed closed. The castle folk had gathered in the hall, and they seemed in no hurry to come out.

At last, we heard hoofbeats. The gate was opened, and into the bailey, on horses shining with sweat, rode Robert de Brus and half a dozen others. FitzWalter hurried out of the hall to hold de Brus's stirrup as he dismounted.

"My lord!" he cried joyfully.

Jordan gave us a nod, and we walked over to join them.

Robert de Brus, despite his age, was giving every appearance of having enjoyed his ride. He was clapping men on the shoulder, joking, smoothing his beard; and when Jordan bowed in greeting, de Brus raised a laugh by reaching out and pretending to brush a speck of dust from the shining coat of ring-mail.

Then he set a hand on Jordan's shoulder, and the other on FitzWalter's, and peered into each of their faces in turn.

"I hear my dogs have been quarrelling," he said. "I ride up to one of my castles and find peasants standing idle at the gate. What am I to think?"

"That Jordan is bewitched," said FitzWalter, and he poured out a story that made it sound as if Ulrica were the cause of it all.

De Brus turned inquiringly to Jordan.

"I have given my vow," said Jordan. "I stand as the woman's champion."

"When you gave it," de Brus asked him, "did you know it was FitzWalter you were challenging?"

"Yes."

De Brus frowned.

"Then you were careless," he said, and took his hand from Jordan's shoulder. "Pagan is the lord of this manor. We must trust him his law."

"I trust him," said Jordan with a smile. "FitzWalter ordered trial by combat. He is the one who asked for the judgement of God."

That made de Brus narrow his eyes. He studied Jordan's face a moment, then turned to FitzWalter and began to speak softly and earnestly. "Pagan, my advice is that you let this fall. Let the woman keep her scrap of land, and rest content with all you have."

FitzWalter looked bewildered and uneasy. His men were gathered round him, and to change his mind now would be a sign of weakness that his pride refused to let him make.

"My word must be the law," he said bullishly.

"Have it your own way," said de Brus. "Who is your champion?"

FitzWalter's mouth sagged open.

"Yes," said de Brus, "for that is what this means. Who is willing to fight Jordan de Falaise?"

His voice began to rise, putting the question to each man in the bailey.

"He has fought in the Holy Land. He has fought for King Roger of Sicily. Even the troubadours of Arles sing of his prowess..."

Beside me, Orm broke into a smile. FitzWalter's men were too frightened even to cough.

De Brus let a long moment go by.

"Do I take it you have no champion?" he asked.

FitzWalter held out his hands. "My lord," he begged.

De Brus shook his head and turned towards the villagers who were watching us from the gateway. "The lady Ulrica has the land," he announced, and took their cheers with a wave as if he had earned them himself.

"You should have taken my advice," he told FitzWalter, "but I'll forgive you if you do something about my empty stomach."

FitzWalter nodded gratefully, and fled towards the hall. Robert de Brus waited until his men had followed, then turned furiously on Jordan.

"I misjudged you," he told him. "I thought you had the wits to see beyond knighthood. Men like you will always be trouble, and I have no use for anyone with higher loyalties. Be off my land by sunset."

As de Brus walked away, Jordan took a long look at the sky.

"I never learn, do I?" he asked.

"No," agreed Orm, "but at least it makes you predictable."

As we made for our horses, I moved to hold Jordan's

stirrup for him to mount. He looked me in the eyes. "Go home, boy," he said. "I have nothing to offer you now. Our roads cannot be the same."

Yet that was when my heart first went out to him. This was my father. I wanted to follow him to the ends of the earth, even if it meant riding the mule.

3. ULRICA'S RIDDLE

U LRICA was waiting for us at the gateway of the castle. She unwound the veil that covered her face.

"Tell me how I can thank you," she asked.

"You could find us a pony," said Jordan. "I'll give a mule in exchange."

"I have a garron," she said, "none so fine as your stallions, but a hardy little brute."

She led us along the lip of the valley to a toft set against a sweep of trees. In the yard were two cats and a flock of geese. The pony was grazing a patch of fallow, and as we dismounted, he came trotting over to look at us. He was as shaggy as a sheep in May.

"What do you call him?" I asked.

"Loki," said Ulrica, and Orm burst out laughing.

"He is all you have," said Jordan. "We cannot take him."

"He is all I would have, but for you," replied Ulrica. "Now come and eat."

Inside, the toft smelt like home. Fruit and herbs hung in baskets from the rafters. We pulled a painted chest up to the table to serve as a bench, while Ulrica brought a bowl of curds seasoned with chives, malt bread to scoop it out with, then pewter cups and a jug of barley beer.

Orm feasted his eyes on her. "If Loki weren't the god of mischief, I'd be shy of asking this," he said, "but how does a woman like you come to be living alone?"

"It was a choice," she said, a smile at the edges of her mouth. "Since the Normans came there are fewer good men than there used to be."

"True," said Orm, "but there are still a few good useless ones, like me."

"Are we far," Jordan asked, "from the edge of de Brus's domain?"

"No more than a mile," said Ulrica. "It ends where the fields meet the high-road. Beyond is the parish of Allerton."

"And you only have to cross it to reach the Honour of Richmond," said Orm, "and there you find the high hills and the road to Cumbria."

"Is that the road you suggest?" Jordan asked him.

Orm nodded, licking curd from his fingers.

"Cumbria is where we want to be," he said. "I have kinsfolk in the eastern fells, and they might be willing to give us a roof for the winter."

"How could they be anything else?" asked Ulrica, but her eyes were on Jordan. "Yesterday, you surprised us," she told him. "Why should a Norman wish to answer a prayer to Saint Cuthbert?"

"My father used to pray to him," said Jordan.

"And your father was Norman?"

"Oh yes," said Jordan, "one of the first to hold Saint Cuthbert's land for the Conqueror, one of the first to ride north. He loved all he found here, but he was fated to live through what followed – the Great Rising, the Burning, the making of the Waste Land. He came to love Saint Cuthbert because he saw him as the only man who had ever lived here and done nothing but good."

"There have been others," said Ulrica, "though Cuthbert was surely the strongest in spirit. He is a good saint for men. They love him for the shape of his life, a life they dream they had the strength to live themselves – without women, without speech, alone on an island in search of a truth they can never know for they are no more than men."

"He should have had a wife like you," said Orm, raising his cup.

Setting her elbows on the table, Ulrica rested her chin on her hands, her eyes still on Jordan. "Can you see a shape to your own life?" she asked.

"I have nothing to sing about," he said hesitantly. "When I was young, I chased glory, but now I search only for knighthood – for its meaning, for its fulfilment. It tests me in the things I understand, honour and courage. I succeed or I fail, I grow or I shrink. That is all, but I suppose you could say it has given a shape to my life."

"Then perhaps," said Ulrica, "you are the man I have been waiting for."

Jordan's eyebrows arched upwards. Ulrica smiled and shook her head. "I mean the searcher I have been waiting for, though I never thought he might be a Norman."

"Why not?" asked Jordan quietly.

Ulrica reached for the jug, and refilled our cups with ale.

"When the Normans came," she said, "my father, like his father before him, was a canon of Saint Cuthbert's minster in Durham. He served Bishop Aethelwin, who joined the Great Rising and died in one of the Conqueror's cells. To take his place came Bishop Walcher, with a hundred knights; and everyone knows how he met his end.

After him came a monk named William, who as soon as he was bishop, turned to the canons of Saint Cuthbert's church – the descendants of the men who carried the holy body on the flight from Lindisfarne – and told them they must either live as Norman monks, or leave. My father was one of those who left."

"There's nothing like a Norman for arrogance," remarked Orm.

"Or a Viking for starting trouble," retorted Jordan. "It was your forefathers who burned Lindisfarne and caused Saint Cuthbert to be dug up in the first place!"

"So my father brought his family here," continued Ulrica, "and this is where I was born. I was the youngest, the daughter they kept at home. On the day he died, my father called me, and talked. He was feverish. He taught me a riddle, and told me to recite it each day among my prayers, until the person came who would take it and use it. He told me the riddle was a light for the searcher, and that the searcher would come in the hour of need."

"And you believe," Jordan asked her, "that I am the searcher?"

"You must be," said Ulrica. "I prayed to Saint Cuthbert for more than just a knight to stand for me against Pagan FitzWalter."

"We were passing by chance," said Jordan.

"You came in the hour of need," insisted Ulrica. "Listen. A week ago, five strangers came and questioned our priest. They said they were searching for the Sacred Blade, and that the secret of its keeping lay with Saint Cuthbert. Father Edward could tell them nothing."

"Where were they from?" asked Jordan.

"They spoke like Scots, but they would answer none of the questions Father Edward put to them; and when they left, they swore him to secrecy."

"What is the Sacred Blade?" asked Jordan. "What does all this have to do with your riddle?"

"It is a sign my father told me to look for," said Ulrica. "He said the time for the riddle would be when men again spoke of the Sacred Blade, but that the first who spoke of it would be the ones who wished to use it for evil."

"But I have never even heard of it," protested Jordan. "How can I be the searcher?"

"Take my riddle," Ulrica begged him. "Make it your quest. Find the truth of it, quickly, and use it, before others can use it for evil."

Jordan turned to Orm. "I suppose I should start to listen to your advice on things like this?" he said.

"Why break the habit of a lifetime?" said Orm.

Jordan did not turn to me, but I nodded eagerly just in case he looked my way.

"I will take your riddle," he told Ulrica.

She closed her eyes. The lines of age seemed to fade from her face, and I saw a girl saying her prayers. She spoke slowly, and the words made a melody.

> *"Over me the thunderstorm,*
> *Search for me beneath the earth*
> *Where the water flows like mead.*
> *Arkill's Garth shall hide the key but*
> *Long the trail that hides the blade,*
> *Dark the day that I be raised."*

Over and again she repeated the riddle, until the words spun a cobweb in our minds.

"It means nothing to me," confessed Jordan.

"Nothing?" asked Ulrica.

Jordan shook his head.

"That is because you are Norman," Orm told him. "One line is as clear as daylight – '*Arkill's Garth*'. Any child can tell you where that is." He stopped and fingered his beard. "Or perhaps not, nowadays. It used to be the name of a steading in a valley off Swaledale, but it will have gone up in the Burning. Now it will be part of the Honour of Richmond."

"Then we are near?" asked Jordan.

"Near enough – a day's riding."

Jordan smiled.

"Then we might as well be on our way."

"Just a moment," said Orm, frowning at Ulrica. "You say your father taught you this riddle. How many more of the canons of Saint Cuthbert will have passed it on when they died?"

Ulrica spread her hands.

"How should I know?" she asked.

She helped me set a bridle on Loki, and soon I was mounted on the garron's broad back. He was so content to be with the other horses that I could see the only trouble I would have with him would be holding him back.

"Keep the mules," Jordan told Ulrica. "We will travel faster without them." He strapped the bags behind our saddles.

"If nothing comes of this," said Orm, "at least we are on the road to Cumbria."

"Saint Cuthbert will guide you," said Ulrica.

Jordan looked at her curiously. "When I was a boy," he said, "I was told that Saint Cuthbert allowed no woman to enter his churches, and that if any broke his law, they lost their wits. Yet you were in his church, touching the stone where his body lay, and no harm has come to you."

Ulrica tossed her long white hair and laughed. "That

Saint Cuthbert hates women is a lie told by the monks of Durham," she said. "He had too deep a heart for hatred. Never believe what Norman monks tell you of English saints."

Our way led west, through a desolation of forest and marsh. In the heart of it, we came to clearings where the fields had gone to heath and the villages were dead. Nettles grew in the ruins that had once been houses. There were no dogs to bark as we passed, no smells of cooking to tighten the stomach, no girls to catch the eye: only the damp smell of the autumn earth.

"Is this it?" I asked. "Is this what you call the Waste Land?"

Jordan made the sign of the cross. It was Orm who answered.

"This is it," he said, "the Conqueror's Waste Land."

"How did it happen?" I asked.

"Why talk about it?" asked Jordan.

"Because the boy should know," snapped Orm, but he said no more, and we rode on, through the wreckage of what had once been villages like my own. The silence was full of ghosts.

When night fell we were guests in the castle of Richmond, perched above the valley of the Swale. Jordan sat with the lords and ladies at a high table beneath round-arched windows looking out over the river below. Around the walls were richly-worked tapestries that told the story of the Crusade and the taking of Jerusalem. It seemed the Normans' favourite tales were all tales of conquest.

I nudged Orm out of a dream he had fallen into watching a serving-girl.

"The land we rode through today," I said, "how long

has it been like that?"

"Since before I was born," he said. "It was the Conqueror's work, and I was born in the time of his son, William Rufus. Then came our cold King Henry. So the Burning must have been well over a lifetime ago."

"Then why are the fields still barren?" I asked. "Why have folk not gone back?"

"These things take time," said Orm. "When I was your age, half Northumbria was like that. If you had seen it then, you would not be groaning now."

He was telling me the tale of the Burning when Jordan came to rejoin us. Jordan listened, his eyes on me, until the tale was finished.

"It's true," he said quietly. "All wars bring fire and famine, but the Conqueror made them his weapons. He had his purpose. He had been fighting for over three years, and he wanted to make an end of it."

I wondered why he was explaining it so gently, and then I realised that his father – my grandfather – had been one of the men who had ridden with the Conqueror.

"They do say that before he died," said Jordan, "the Conqueror begged God to forgive him."

"Aye," said Orm, "but they never tell you what God replied."

I could see why Ulrica had never dreamt that a Norman would be the searcher for the Sacred Blade.

4. FOX FUR AND PROPHECY

T HROUGH heavy rain, we rode into the mouth of Arkengarthdale. A track led through a wilderness of heath and balding woodland. We startled a herd of deer into leaping rock to rock over the beck. On either side, the hillsides grew taller and steeper, rimmed along the crest by walls of white rock.

Where the valley narrowed, we came to a ruined farmstead. Orm wiped the rain from his eyelids, and pointed to an orchard where apples hung unpicked and rotting on the branches.

"Arkill's Garth," he said.

"Can this really be the place in the riddle?" asked Jordan.

"Remember the shape of the fighting," said Orm. "Each time the Conqueror came north, the Northumbrians hid in the hills. That is why he made the plains the Waste Land, so that when he had gone and they came out of hiding, they starved. If I were living in those days and had something I wanted to hide from the Normans and the Scots, I would choose a place like this."

"There may be someone living near who remembers," I suggested.

"No," said Jordan. "I asked last night. The lords of Richmond have made the dale their hunting-chase. No one lives here now."

We wandered through the rubbish and nettles of the fallen buildings. If Ulrica's riddle were true and Arkill's Garth had once held a key to the hidden Blade, then it must have been lost along with its keepers. We stood there, getting wetter and wetter, unwilling to leave. Jordan was standing in a doorway, looking out, when something made him mutter to himself.

"Simon," he said, "remind me of the riddle."

"'*Over me the thunderstorm*,'" I recited, and we burst out laughing.

"Go on," said Jordan.

"'*Search for me beneath the earth . . .*'"

"That's enough," said Jordan. "Now look up there!"

He was pointing up the hillside to where an opening had been cut into a scar of white rock. Winding up to it was a narrow path, overgrown with grass, banked at the loops with a care that showed it had been built for pack-mules.

"'*Search for me beneath the earth*,'" repeated Jordan. "What can that mean but in a cavern?"

"It looks like an old working," said Orm. "They used to mine lead in these hills."

A moment later, we were climbing the hillside.

From a doorway cut in the rock, a passage ran straight into the hill. We stepped inside, out of the rain, but it was too dark to go more than a few paces. Jordan turned to Orm. "Can you make a light?" he asked.

"What do you think I am?" growled Orm. "A wizard?"

Just then, I fell over a pile of logs that must once have been rollers for the mine. We pulled them outside.

"Stand one on its end," Orm told me, raising his axe above his head.

"What about my hands?" I asked.

He winked. "You'll keep them if you hold it steady."

I shut my eyes. There was a crack and the log split in two. Soon we had a heap of splintered wands which we gathered inside the doorway. Orm pulled tinder-flints from his wallet, then squatted down, clacking them together over the kindling while Jordan and I crouched to shelter it from the wind.

Much cursing later, we had a fire. Orm took two of the wands and rolled strips of cloth around the tips. When he dipped them into the fire, they sputtered alight.

"Good enough for an Easter procession at the Holy Sepulchre," Jordan told him.

With the torches held out ahead, they set off side by side along the passage. All I had to do was watch where I trod and keep within the light.

The passage was level, but the further we went, the lower came the roof, until Jordan was stooping. We passed smaller passages cut into the walls, but paused only to thrust a torch into them for a glimpse of their length. Most were blocked with rubble.

We were a hundred paces in when abruptly the roof arched upwards beyond the torchlight. A stone Orm had kicked rolled away with a clatter that echoed, and water dripped onto our faces from high above. Jordan walked slowly forward, and he had gone a dozen paces before his torchlight fell on the far wall. There were openings to other passages that led deeper under the hill, but Jordan stared at the wall in which they were cut.

"There is writing here."

We joined him and saw letters carved in the rock.

"Are they runes?" asked Jordan.

"Older than runes," said Orm. "They look Roman."

Jordan ran his fingers along the words. "Can you read?" he asked me.

I shook my head.

"Neither can we," he said sadly.

Orm was following the wall away to the right when he gave a grunt of surprise.

He had found a block set into the wall, so neatly that only a searcher would have noticed it had been cut out and then replaced. Chiselled on the face of the stone was a mark in the shape of a hammer.

"'*Over me the thunderstorm*,'" recited Orm. "Well, a hammer is the sign of Thor the Thunderer."

He passed me his torch, wriggled his fingers into the cracks at the edges of the block, gripped and began to pull. Rasping, the block slid out into his hands and he set it down on the floor of the cave. Behind where it had been, there was a niche, and in the niche was a bundle the length of a knife.

Jordan moved towards it, then checked himself.

"You take it," he told me. "Orm and I have blood on our hands. It is not for us to touch."

I reached in, and my fingers closed over a roll of cloth. It was light and felt hollow. As I picked it up, it crumpled in my hand.

The torches were burning through and Jordan's was already sinking to a blue glow. Orm set the block back in place, and we hurried to the passage that led back towards the daylight.

We stopped in the doorway to look at the bundle. The cloth was sealed by stitching, but Jordan had only to run his knife along it for it to part, and I peeled off the cloth to find a roll of yellow vellum covered with writing. All we could do was stare. None of us knew how to read it.

Just then, lower in the dale, the birds rose startled from the trees. Five horsemen were riding towards us, on shaggy garrons like Loki.

"Ulrica said there were five of them," muttered Orm.

Jordan took me by the arm. "Tuck that parchment away in your wallet," he said, "then forget you have ever seen it."

We had almost reached the farmstead and our horses when the riders reached us. Jordan called out a greeting. It was returned by a man with bright blue eyes and a beard and hair the red of fox fur.

"What is the name of this place?" he asked, and like Aimeric, he spoke English as though it were strange to his tongue.

"I was hoping you could tell us," replied Jordan. "I think we may be lost. We came here trusting we were on the road to Brough."

The riders looked us over. I made myself look back. They were all young men, though a few years older than me. There was nothing to catch the eye about their clothes, but they each wore a sword. Like us, they were dripping with rain. They looked tired, and in a hurry, and unhappy that we were there.

"You are on the right road," said the rider. "The way lies over the high moss and down into the Vale of Eden." He pointed to the opening in the rocks. "You were on the hillside. Does anyone live there?"

"There's an old working," replied Jordan. "We took shelter, hoping the rain would ease."

Setting a foot in his stirrup, he hoisted himself into his saddle. I reached for Loki, praying he would not smell my fear and buck.

"We must be on our way," said Jordan. "Are you also

bound for Brough?"

The rider contrived a smile. "We might rest here a while," he said. "It would ruin our good name to be seen riding with Normans."

Jordan laughed and raised a hand in farewell. We trotted away and they made no move to follow. They even seemed to be waiting for us to get out of sight.

As soon as we were, Jordan turned to Orm.

"Scots?" he asked.

Orm nodded.

"Then let's widen the chase," suggested Jordan.

It was rough riding. We had to cross brown and desolate hills, sodden with watershed, before at last we came down into the Vale of Eden. The rain had stopped, and a wide, green dale stretched ahead as far as we could see.

"So this is where Adam and Eve lived," I said, eager to impress with the little I knew.

Orm and Jordan roared with laughter.

"You may be right," Orm told me, "though the name comes from the river. Eden in the old tongue means 'gliding water'."

The dale was so wide that once we had entered it, we lost all sense of its shape. Our track twisted between hillocks of gorse and pasture, and it was dusk when ahead of us rose a castle with stone walls, and a stone tower at its western end. The windows were yellow with torchlight.

In the bailey were tethered more horses than I had ever seen. A groom took ours without even asking who we were.

Supper had already begun and the hall was full, the tables crowded with as many priests as there were knights. We stood in the doorway and waited for the steward, squinting at the light and the smoke.

"Do you see who I see?" asked Orm.

At the high table sat a man who could have passed for Thor the Thunderer. Ox-shouldered and horse-browed, he must have been a giant when young, and even now, though more than fifty years of age, he was powerfully built. Grey was just beginning to brindle his thick black beard, and when he spoke, the knights and priests on either side of him stopped to listen, as if his words were worth catching.

"Walter Espec," said Jordan, and his face creased into the nearest I had seen him come to a look of delight. He strode towards the high table.

When the bearded man caught sight of him, he uttered an oath and rose to his feet, reaching across the table to grasp Jordan's outstretched hand.

They held each other's gaze, laughing, pointing at each other's grey hairs, then Walter Espec caught sight of Orm, and gave him just as warm a greeting. Jordan gripped me by the shoulder and pulled me forward.

"My son," he said. "His name is Simon."

I bowed. Walter Espec looked at me thoughtfully.

"You always were lucky," he told Jordan, "in the things that matter."

Jordan looked at me with some surprise. Walter Espec beckoned to the servers. "We need more room at this table," he ordered.

In the shuffle that followed, Jordan and Orm were seated to face Walter, but I was led to the far end of the high table to sit among a gaggle of priests. Once I was placed, the servers forgot about me, and I was trying to catch their eyes when the fellow at my side offered to share his dish. I turned to thank him, and almost jumped out of my skin.

It was Aimeric the scholar.

"How did you get here?" I asked him.

"You are speaking," he said merrily, "to the obedient pen of the archbishop of York. When you gave me that apple, it was the first link in a chain of good luck. A draper gave me a ride to York in his wagon, and when I went to beg a meal from the archbishop's household, they greeted me with open arms. The archbishop was setting out for Caerluel, and had just learnt that neither of his scribes were fit to ride. So here I am – but what about you? I remember you saying you had never been further than Stokesley!"

I told him how on the day we met in Gisburgh, I had gone home to find Jordan come to claim me. Aimeric clapped his hands.

"So now you have lands and castles?" he asked.

"Not yet, and my father seems to have a gift for making enemies."

Aimeric pointed along the table.

"With friends like Walter Espec he has nothing to fear."

"Who is he?" I asked.

"The sheriff of Yorkshire," said Aimeric, "a justiciar of the king." He raised the wine cup. "So, this is only my fifth night in England, and already I know more than you. Here's to our travels and the high company we keep."

"Which one is your master?" I asked him.

"Thurstan is not here," he said. "When we arrived, he was spent, so he is resting. He is old, and I think his legs give him pain. His household tried to prevent him making the journey, but he is too Norman to listen, too full of his purpose."

I looked up to see that Walter, Jordan, and Orm were rising to their feet. Walter Espec beckoned to the scholar.

"Master Aimeric," he said, "we need your learning."

We followed him up the sloping bailey to the tall keep

that rose from the highest ground in the castle. For the height of a house, it was nothing but smooth stone, and to enter we had to climb a wooden stairway to a door that gave onto the first floor. The windows were shuttered, the air dank and cobwebs misted the hangings. This was a stronghold within the stronghold, a refuge for when all else failed, and it looked as if it had not been needed for years.

Archbishop Thurstan was alone in the chamber above. In turn, we knelt to kiss the blue sapphire in his ring, then Aimeric brought stools and we settled ourselves by the fire that was burning beneath a chimney built into the wall. Candles flickered on a nearby chest, their flames drawn sideways by the draught.

At Walter's bidding, Jordan told the story of Ulrica's riddle, of the searchers, and of how we had chanced to come first to the hiding-place at Arkill's Garth. The archbishop listened with growing interest, and an occasional twitch of bushy white eyebrows that sent ripples of wrinkles up the mottled skin of his forehead and into his thin, tonsured hair.

"I have never even heard of the Sacred Blade," he said curiously. "Have you, Walter?"

"Never," said Walter. "This bundle they found holds a message in writing. We were hoping your scribe might be able to read it to us."

"He may well," agreed Thurstan. "Aimeric, dazzle us with all they taught you in the schools of Paris and Chartres."

I pulled the bundle from my wallet and passed it to Aimeric, who peeled away the covering of cloth and threw it into the fire, then gently unrolled the sheet of vellum. We watched his eyes move from side to side as he followed words down the page, and the further he read, the more he frowned.

"It reads like a song," he said, "and it is written in the old script you see in books from the days of Charlemagne."

"In English?" asked Thurstan.

"In Latin," said Aimeric. "I can translate the words but if I do I will lose the rhymes."

"Give us the meaning, not the poetry," Thurstan told him.

We waited while Aimeric read the page over and over to himself, with here and there a pause to puzzle. Then he laid the vellum aside and began to recite, as if it were a song he had known all his life.

> *"Fire came over water,*
> *   the dragon prows of Halfdan,*
> *Waste was made the land*
> *   and the holy places burned.*
> *Many fell running,*
> *   and many turned too late,*
> *But where was the man*
> *   to wake me from sleep?*
> *Forgotten my coming*
> *   in the year of evil,*
> *Cutting through pagans*
> *   on Heaven's Field.*
> *I am the blade*
> *   as old as the kingdom,*
> *Waiting for a master*
> *   to wake me from sleep.*
> *Aethelfrith made me*
> *   to drink blood in Rheged,*
> *Edwin cleaned me*
> *   in the blood of Christ.*
> *Cold my hilt*

when I fell from his hand,
Waiting for a master
  to wake me from sleep.
Well was I trusted
  to the sons of Iona,
I was Oswald's blade
  till Penda cut him down.
I was avenger
  the last red battle,
Northumbria the cry
  to wake me from sleep.
Sleep beyond the tides
  ordered Oswy my master,
Sleep till you are woken
  when dragons fill the sky.
Then will a man
  find the hilt of the lightning,
Northumbria the cry
  to wake me from sleep."

When Aimeric had finished, we sat as if a spell had turned us to stone.

"What does it mean?" he asked us.

"It is a prophecy," said Walter wonderingly. "It reminds me of the Prophecies of Merlin. They were written down centuries ago, and in riddles that speak of swans and eagles and adders, they tell all that has been and is to come."

"I have heard," said Thurstan cautiously, "that scholars are divided as to their truth."

"Scholars are always divided," said Aimeric, "but this song is not of eagles but of men."

"Of men who lived," said Thurstan. "The names I recognised are those of the first kings of Northumbria. Edwin and Oswald are saints to the English."

"Names of power even now," agreed Walter.

"So the Sacred Blade was a sword of the saints?" asked Aimeric. "In the deep past?" He turned to us. "Can you still remember the riddle that led you to the song?"

I recited it at once.

> *"Over me the thunderstorm,*
> *Search for me beneath the earth*
> *Where the water flows like mead.*
> *Arkill's Garth shall hide the key but*
> *Long the trail that hides the blade,*
> *Dark the day that I be raised."*

"Cunning," remarked Aimeric. "The riddle hides an acrostic."

"What in God's name is an acrostic?" asked Walter.

"A game poets play," replied Aimeric. "Listen to the first letter in every line: O,S,W,A,L,D. Put together they spell Oswald, and the song is the song of Oswald's Blade."

"Telling us that somewhere the Blade lies hidden," said Walter. "Somewhere in Northumbria there sleeps a sword as magic as King Arthur's, and we are going to be the ones who find it!"

"No," said Thurstan sharply.

Walter slapped his knee. "But the riddle and the song are telling us to search!"

Thurstan pulled himself upright in his chair, and the sheepskin that had been wrapped around his legs slid to the floor.

"Many hidden things," he said, "are best left hidden. We have suffered quite enough from the past. The Waste Land was our inheritance, and we have spent our lives ploughing over the burnt ground, sowing new seed, all in the hope that one day a harvest will rise as golden as any in the wide fields of Christendom."

"May God so will," agreed Walter, "but the Sacred Blade is surely a relic of great power? It belonged to Christian kings."

"A sword is still a sword," said Thurstan. "The kingdom of Northumbria was born in bloodshed, and we know how it died. The last thing we need is a weapon to sound an echo in the back of men's minds."

"We are too late to stop the echo," said Jordan. "The searchers are riding."

"God brought you first to the hiding-place," said Thurstan, "and I believe it was to save us."

"Then what do you advise?" Walter asked him.

The archbishop sank back into his chair.

"Find out all you can," he said, "but do it gently, without breaking the surface of men's minds. I want no ripples. Aimeric will search the library of York to find whatever else is known of the Sacred Blade, but until we know more, the song and the riddle must be our secret."

"Jordan smiled ruefully. "Are you telling me to abandon my quest?" he asked.

"No," replied Thurstan, "only to wait a while. Where can I find you?"

"Let me answer that," said Walter Espec. "Jordan will be with me."

5. THE LAKE FELLS

As soon as the archbishop had said Mass, we left Brough by a road that ran west along the widening vale.

The clouds were still low, cloaking the hills. Jordan rode with Thurstan and Walter, at the head of the cavalcade, while I kept company with Aimeric and Orm by the pack-mules, where we could talk freely. Aimeric had hardly slept, and his face was as white as the sky.

"The song of the Blade is clear," he said, "but the riddle is beyond me."

"It ought to be clear enough," said Orm, "once you have unriddled the kennings."

"And what," asked Aimeric, "are kennings?"

"You are a scholar, and you do not know?" asked Orm. "Well then, what is yeast-surf?"

Aimeric looked bewildered. Orm gave him a moment, then chuckled.

"Yeast-surf is a poet's name for ale," he explained. "That is a kenning. What is a falcon's perch?"

"The sky?" asked Aimeric. "The cliff?"

"No," said Orm, "the fist. But you're learning. You can see how they work. You'll find the old songs of Cumbria are full of kennings."

Orm began to sing, in a voice like a saw in wood. So we rode down the Vale of Eden to the battle-song of the gods of Asgard, as they fought to hold the rainbow bridge against the wolves of Ragnarok.

By noon we were nearing the fortress-town of Penrith, where Jordan broke away from the archbishop's side, and came riding back along the cavalcade to find us.

"The road to Caerluel goes north," he said. "I think our way lies west."

"Mine does," agreed Orm.

I turned to Aimeric. I did not want to leave him, but our second meeting had been too wild a chance for me to believe it mere chance. I felt we had been fated to meet, and that we were fated to search together for the Sacred Blade.

"Perhaps when we meet again," I said, "you will know the answer to the riddle?"

"You may have to give me time to learn the art of kenning," he said with a laugh, "but I will do my best. A library is a good place on a winter's day, and Thurstan will be paying for the candles."

At the gates of Penrith, we left the archbishop's cavalcade and rode west through the woods. The land grew more broken, bones of rock jutting through the earth, while the hills ahead grew taller, then seemed to close around us like a hand.

Orm took the lead. He knew the way and rode fast.

We reached a rounded hill with a ring of old earthworks on the summit, and beyond it we came abruptly out of the trees onto the shore of a wind-rippled lake. We were only at its tip. It stretched away for miles, walled by mountainsides matted with reddening bracken.

Orm drew rein. "These are the Lake Fells," he said,

"and this is Ullswater." His voice ached as he spoke the names.

"How long is it since you left?" asked Jordan.

"Nineteen summers."

That was longer than I had been alive. My heart went out to him.

"It must be good to come home," said Jordan.

"Ask me again at sunset," replied Orm.

We took a rocky track along the northern shore of the lake, which climbed to a broad slope where the woods had been cleared. There were fields, and a large steading where steep-gabled houses ringed a long, timber-built hall.

Faces appeared in doorways as we rode up, and Orm greeted each of them by name.

"Armod! Hallgerd! Bardi! Ingirid!"

They called his name back at him with laughter and disbelief, and we were well into a swirl of greetings when from the hall appeared a man with Orm's face, but of a taller, thinner build. Orm rushed at him, and they shouted and mauled each other like bears.

"This is my brother," Orm told us, "Hoskuld Sigurdsson."

Jordan and I were named, and bowed. Hoskuld looked us over. "Are you asking me to greet a Norman?" he asked, with a manner of speech as thorny as his brother's.

"You can take my word for Jordan," said Orm. "He is as much of a brother to me as you are."

Orm was looking round, and beginning to frown.

"You come too late for our mother," Hoskuld told him. "Two winters too late. But there are young ones you have never seen. Here is Thord, my son."

He pulled forward a stocky lad of about my age, who looked like Orm without the beard.

"And here," said Hoskuld proudly, "is Sigrid my daughter."

A girl slipped through the crowd. Her hair was harvest-gold, brushed back from her forehead, and she had the best face I had ever seen.

If Orm had been working for the Church, and they had told him to carve an angel, Sigrid is what he would have carved: though her eyes had more life than any carving, and when I was named to her, a look passed between us, and that was that. I was gutted by longing, blasted by the lightning of her beauty.

There was one long table in Hoskuld's hall, and at the feast the village gave to make us welcome, I sat with Thord. Sigrid was in and out of my sight as she went back and forth between the table and the hearth, and there was no mistaking the play of eyes between us. It might only be that I was a stranger, with the interest for her that Aimeric had for me, but it was enough. She could see the longing in my eyes, and it did not seem to trouble her. If anything, it kept her looking my way.

That night, although at last I had a friendly place to sleep, and I had never been so tired, I lay awake, holding the memory of her face in my mind's eye and wondering at its power over me. Suddenly, I realised how it must have been when Jordan and my mother first set eyes on each other. It must simply have been so fierce a longing that nothing else mattered.

Jordan shook me awake at dawn and we walked down to the lake as the mists cleared.

"Why did Orm ever leave?" I asked.

"There was a killing," explained Jordan. "If Orm had stayed, there would have been blood feud, so he left, which meant that Hoskuld and his father were able to reach a settlement with the dead man's kin. It will have cost them something, but Orm has treasures in his saddle-bags that will more than pay them back."

"Have you treasures in yours?" I asked.

"Some gold," he said, "a few jewels. It would not buy much. I have never had Orm's magpie knack for the pickings of the trade."

Jordan lengthened his stride. It was the first time we had been alone, and for a while he made sure I was too breathless to ask any more questions.

We came to a few huts, where a stream flowed into the lake. Jordan spoke with a shepherd, then took to the slopes of the fell, where a leg-twisting track climbed straight towards the clouds.

We toiled up it to a high ridge of grass and bilberries, where the roof of wilderness that filled the sky to the west seemed nearer than the lake now so far beneath our feet. The wind was like the breath of the frost giants, and the only bird I could see was an eagle, sweeping the sky on wide wings and looking mightily hungry.

Jordan sat down, breathing hard, a hand pressed to his side. He pointed east, and showed me how beyond Ullswater we could see deep into the Vale of Eden, and even the hills we had crossed to reach Brough.

"Look at it all," he said. "There must still be room for someone like me."

"Will Walter Espec give you land?" I asked.

"He could if he wished," said Jordan, settling himself in a hollow with his back to the wind.

"Why did you come for me?" I asked. "Aldred said you left before I was born. I could have been a girl."

"I would still have wanted to see you," said Jordan, "to know if there could be anything between us."

"So why did you leave?" I shouted.

Jordan stared at me. I wanted to stab him with questions. I wanted him to know how it had hurt when Aldred told me I was not his son.

"I hope you never understand," said Jordan bleakly, "and may God forbid you ever make the same mistake. I look back now, and howl. I was young. Northumbria was asleep in peace. The wild days of my father's time were gone. It was not the land for the knighthood I wanted then."

"So you left us," I said bitterly.

"I know what I lost," snapped Jordan. "Believe me, Simon, it is knowing all I lost that brought me back."

He was reaching out to me with his eyes, and I suddenly saw that it mattered to him what I thought, and whether I accepted or rejected him. It mattered to him greatly. I had all I needed – Mother, Aldred, and a home to go back to – but he had only me.

"What I still cannot understand," I said, "is this life you call knighthood. What gives it such a hold on you when it has so few rewards?"

"Stay with me," said Jordan. "Stay with me, and you will see."

Orm's village was named Longthwaite. The Fell folk spoke the same blend of English and Norse we spoke in Cleveland, if with a little more Norse. Every pillar in Hoskuld's hall was carved with scenes from the old Viking tales, and Orm told me the stories to the ones he had carved himself.

Our horses made us useful. We joined in the autumn wolf-hunts, clearing the dale heads to take some of the fear out of the coming winter. Thord taught me to use a bow, and we would ride home through the early dusk to Hoskuld's hall, and Sigrid.

She taught me to play chess. She would suck in her lips as she thought each move over, and the bracelets would slide on her wrists as she moved to make it.

Game after game she outwitted me, and that was with one eye on the door; for there was a young man named Arni who farmed at the lake head and took every chance he had to come and see her.

"Are they betrothed?" I asked Thord.

"The way things are going, they will be," he replied.

"Is Arni rich?"

"No one here is rich," said Thord, "but Arni is even-tempered and reliable. My father likes him."

I made the most of the chess-games. Once, I told Sigrid how Jordan had come to claim me. She stared.

"That must have been cruel," she said. "Your poor mother! I could never give myself to a man I thought would ride away and leave me."

"I would never leave you," I said, and watched her.

Sigrid only laughed and brushed back a loose strand of her hair, but what followed was unbelievable: I won the game.

And on the night of the autumn fires, she broke away from Arni and led me out into the dance. I was clumsy, and trod on her feet, so it all became a joke as we crashed around like a pair of trolls. She slipped away, back to Arni, and the dance skirled on.

I came to a halt beside Orm.

"Do you like her?" he asked.

I let my face be my answer.

"There's nothing on earth," he said, watching her, "like a girl coming into bloom. Try not to trouble her."

"What do you mean?" I asked.

"She has almost promised herself to Arni," he said. "It

will be a good match. Try not to confuse her."

He might as well have told me to put out my eyes. There was no way I could stop looking at her. It promised to be a long winter.

Two nights later, we were all asleep when there was a hammering on the door of the hall.

"Hoskuld Sigurdsson!" called a voice outside.

Hoskuld stumbled out of his chamber. "Who is it?" he bellowed.

"You shelter a Norman. Send him out to us, and no harm will come to you."

"Go and eat dung," retorted Hoskuld.

"Send him out to us, or we burn the hall down over your heads."

Everyone was now awake, pulling on clothes and reaching for weapons. Orm took his axe, and placed himself beside the door where he would be hidden when it opened; then Hoskuld drew back the bolts and swung the door slowly back on its hinges.

Outside was a throng of men, with drawn swords in one hand and burning torches in the other. Their leader was the Scot with the beard like fox fur.

Jordan buckled his sword-belt and joined Hoskuld in the doorway.

"Do I know you?" he asked angrily.

"You know who we are," said Fox Fur. "Give us what we seek and we'll leave you in peace."

Jordan contrived a laugh. "I have nothing that belongs to you."

That was true. The song on its scroll of vellum had gone to Caerluel with Aimeric and Thurstan.

"You were searching at Arkill's Garth," said Fox Fur. "Give us what you found there."

"You talk in riddles," retorted Jordan. "I touched nothing in Arkill's Garth and brought nothing away when I left." That also was true, as far as it went.

"We followed the smoke-trails of your torches into the mine," Fox Fur said quietly.

Beside the doorway, Orm raised his axe.

From away on the edge of the steading came the blast of a hunting-horn. It was answered by another, from the houses by the hall, and another, until all over Longthwaite, horns were bellowing like maddened cattle.

"These will be my neighbours," Hoskuld told the Scots. "If you want to see the dawn, you had best be going."

Fox Fur seemed to agree. He barked an order and the Scots threw down their torches and made off into the darkness. We heard horses on the track down to the lake.

"Who were they?" Hoskuld asked Jordan.

Jordan shook his head.

"I wish I knew," he said guardedly.

The hall filled with half-dressed neighbours brandishing weapons, and Hoskuld broached a barrel of ale.

Jordan shook me awake at first light. He had packed his bags, and Orm was walking towards us, softly so as not to wake the sleepers.

"The horses are saddled," he said. "I'll go and say our farewells to Hoskuld. Wait for me by the lake."

Jordan hurried me out and down the track to the shore.

"Why must we leave?" I asked.

"To take our trouble away with us," said Jordan. "God knows how the searchers tracked us here, but from now on we can call ourselves hunted."

We waited among the trees until Orm came riding down to join us.

"Hoskuld is furious," he said, "but he'll get over it."
He grinned at me. "Sigrid told me to say she wishes you well.
She asked if you would ever be back."

"What answer did you give her?" I asked.

"I told her not to waste any thought on you."

I could have cursed him.

"Call it hard," he said, "but I would rather it went
hard for you than for her. Besides, she may still have to bury
you. Somewhere in the woods, between here and Penrith,
they will be setting up a snake-pit of an ambush."

But as we rode, we met no one, and we were soon on
the old open road up the Vale of Eden.

"I have a feeling," said Jordan, "that the man with
the red beard is not the master. The master is somewhere
else, and they have gone to ask him what to do now."

We kept our pace, and were in Brough by nightfall. In
the morning we crossed the Stainmoor into the Waste Land.

6. ELMESLAC

T HE castle of Elmeslac stood with its back to the hills and its gate to the Forest of Pickering.

It was not what I expected. There was no tall keep on an earthern motte, and of all the castles I had seen, it was the least like a stronghold. A simple palisade encircled a bailey crowded with timber halls.

Despite its homeliness, I was lonely at once. At supper, Jordan was given a place of honour at the high table, among the ladies in bright gowns, but Orm and I found ourselves well down the hall. I would have sold my soul to be back in Longthwaite.

Orm was admiring the ladies at the high table.

"Which of them is Walter's wife?" he asked the castle armourer, who was sharing our dish.

"He has no wife," replied the armourer. "On either side of him, you see his sisters, the lady Albrea and the lady Odelina."

"Why has he never married?" asked Orm. "Any other Norman in his shoes would be bent on founding a dynasty."

The armourer lowered his voice. "He had a lady," he said. "She left her hearth and husband for him, so the Church would not marry them, and she died a few years ago

– may God give her peace! The one thing she left him was a daughter. He dotes on the girl. Nothing is too good for her, though God knows where she'll go when he dies, for all his lands will pass to his sisters. I say it's unlucky to waste love on a bastard."

Orm saw me blush. "The Conqueror was a bastard," he said protectively. "His mother was a tanner's daughter from Falaise, and you can hardly say that held him back."

The talk turned to the Conqueror, and tales of the hard years gone by. I listened furiously, and vowed that no one would ever dismiss me as nothing but a bastard. The one thing the Normans revered above all else was strength, and that was why they honoured Jordan, even though he was landless. I could never be noble-born, but I could show them I was stronger than any of them. I vowed there and then that I would.

Heady with resolve, I turned to Orm. "Teach me to be a knight," I said.

He gave me a long look, waiting for me to cool. "I know nothing about knighthood," he said, "but I'll teach you to use a sword, and stand alone."

On Walter's orders, a steward led us to a small guest-lodge with truckle beds. We were to have it to ourselves.

"Walter says we must wait," said Jordan.

"Wait for Thurstan?" asked Orm. "Why should he be the one telling us what to do?"

"Walter trusts him," said Jordan.

"It was to you that Ulrica entrusted this quest," Orm reminded him, "and she must have done it because she thought you would follow your heart, not the orders of a Norman archbishop."

They argued on, but for once I was too deep in my own thoughts to care. My own quest was suddenly so clear.

Somehow, I had to win a fame as great as Jordan's, and use it to win land: for then I could ride back to the Lake Fells with land to offer Sigrid when I asked her to be my wife, and it would have to be an offer so good that Hoskuld could not refuse.

Walter Espec was sheriff, and the keeping of the law took him wherever in Yorkshire he was called to give a hearing or judge a dispute. When he rode out the next day, he took Jordan with him, and when they had gone, Orm set his carving aside and gave me a wink.

He went to the armoury, and returned with a pair of wooden swords and a bundle of quilted linen, then led me to a quiet corner of the bailey, by the timber-stack behind the kitchens. Orm threw me the bundle, which was a padded surcoat, torn and stained, with a reek of old sweat.

"It's called a gambeson," he said. "You'll need it. Folk tell me I'm heavy-handed. It's hard to have a good swing without breaking a few ribs."

The surcoat made me fatter and heavier, and my hand looked puny on the sword-hilt.

"Take the hilt in both hands," Orm told me. "Feel the weight to the swing of it."

I brandished the sword like a pitchfork; swished it through the air like a broom.

"All you have to do," said Orm, "is keep your mind on the blade, and on what you're trying to do with it. To get any force behind a blow, you need to swing it in from the side. If you want the man you are fighting alive, go for his arms or his legs. If you want him dead, go for his ribs or his neck. The skill boils down to doing it to him before he does it to you. That blade is all you have to keep his blade from killing you."

With a yell, he swung his sword at my neck, forcing me to fling mine up and hack his blade away. The jolt burned my palms.

"Good," said Orm, then he struck again, and buffet followed buffet until I was giving ground as each new blow pushed me backwards.

"Keep your guard," he said. "Keep thinking. How are you going to stop me?"

I wished I knew. He left me no time to take a swing at him. It was all I could do to parry his blows. At each jolt, my grip on the hilt weakened.

"You're getting clumsy," he warned. "Keep thinking."

His next blow knocked me flat. Chuckling, Orm helped me up and we caught our breath.

"Not bad," he said. "It took nine blows to get you down."

"What if you had been fighting with an axe?" I asked.

"You would be dead."

He had made his point. After that, we began again, but slowly.

Each day, as the winter settled on Elmeslac, we would fight. He taught me how to find strength when I was aching in every sinew and ready to drop. He taught me how to measure every blow. He taught me how to use the quickness on my feet which was the one advantage I had over him.

We became something of a spectacle. One afternoon, we were hacking away at each other in the failing light when we saw a youth and a maiden standing watching. I had seen them before, sitting at the high table.

When we paused, the youth stepped forward. "You look my age," he told me. "I'll fight you."

Everything about him was Norman, and his face was

oddly familiar. The girl looked more French. Her hair was chestnut dark, and straight like Aimeric's, only long and thick as a horse's tail. Her eyebrows could almost have been drawn on her forehead with charcoal; they had an arch like those of painted saints on church walls.

"Shall we say the first to strike three blows home is the champion?" the youth asked me.

"Whatever you wish," I replied.

He took the wooden sword Orm held out to him and tried to cow me with his stare. I had a feeling he had something to prove.

He swung the first blow, and I parried it, and the one that followed; but then he made as if to strike my right shoulder, waited until I was moving to meet the blow, and froze. Before I could react to the feint, he had spun round. His blade hacked me high on the left arm, with a force that bruised through the gambeson.

"One to me," he said; and the girl folded her arms and looked down at her shoes, as if it gave her no pleasure to see him winning.

The pain in my arm was all it took to make me lose my temper.

I parried his next swing with all my strength and rocked him backwards. Before he could steady himself, I struck him high on his right arm, below the shoulder.

Maddened, he slashed wildly at me. I had only to step sideways and he lost his balance. With a single blow, I knocked his sword from his hands, then I struck low, scything, to trip his ankles and send him sprawling.

"Three to me," I said; and when I turned to bow to the girl, I saw her laughing.

"Christ's holy blood!" muttered the youth as he picked himself up. "Who are you?"

"Simon de Falaise," I told him.

He gave a groan of relief and called to the girl.

"That explains it," he said. "It serves me right for picking a quarrel with the son of Jordan de Falaise."

He smiled, and held out his hand. "My name," he said, "is Robert de Brus."

No wonder his face had looked familiar. He was the son of the lord of Cleveland. If Jordan had not claimed me, I would still be one of his father's peasants.

He pointed to his companion. "This is the lady Adele," he said.

I had heard her name. She was the bastard daughter of Walter Espec.

"Jordan never told me he had a son," she said warmly. "You should sit with us at the high table."

"You are the first to invite me," I told her.

"Tonight you will find a place laid," she replied, and began to walk away. Robert de Brus at once lost interest in me, and hurried after the lady Adele.

"That looks promising," remarked Orm. "In France, they hold tournaments for the knights to catch the ladies' eyes. Whatever you do, don't quarrel with them. Cover your tongue with honey, and let it wag."

"How did I fight?" I asked.

"Like a sack of grain falling off a wagon."

But he winked.

So when the torches were lit in the hall, I took my place at the high table, facing Robert and the lady Adele. From his own seat by Walter, Jordan smiled with surprise.

"Tell me about the Field of Blood," said Robert eagerly.

I had never heard of it. I knew of the Burning, the Waste Land, and other gory myths of the Normans, but this one was new to me.

"Surely your father speaks of it?" he asked.

"Never to me."

"The brave keep silent," said Robert approvingly. "The Field of Blood was a battle in the Holy Land. Prince Roger of Antioch and his chivalry were surrounded, in an open plain, by a host of pagans a hundred times their number. They fought for a day, until Prince Roger himself had fallen. Only a bare handful of his knights were strong enough to cut their way free. Your father was one of them."

"Robert thinks only of knighthood and war," explained Adele. "Elmeslac is too quiet for him."

"There's no glory to be won around here," he agreed.

"Why hunger for glory," I asked, "if you are the heir to Cleveland, Hartness, and Annandale?"

"But I am not," said Roger sullenly. "My father wants his lands to pass on undivided, so my elder brother Adam will have them all. That is why I am being fostered by Walter, because my father hopes I can be turned into a sheriff, happy to spend my life collecting taxes and hanging peasants for stealing eggs."

"And you, Simon," Adele asked me, "do you want a glory to match your father's?"

Eager to impress, I borrowed the words Jordan had spoken to Ulrica.

"I seek the meaning of knighthood itself," I answered solemnly.

A smile flickered on Adele's face. She seemed to be watching the way I raised my food from my trencher to my mouth. "Then let me teach you the ways of courtesy," she suggested.

Our eyes met, and hers were golden brown in the torchlight. In the torchlight, her darkness became her beauty, and her face and neck seemed to lengthen and glow. If Sigrid were the sun, Adele was the night. She had nothing of Sigrid's carefree swiftness. Adele's most constant look was a questioning frown. One moment she would appear to be dreaming, and the next she would ask a question that went so straight to the heart it was hard to answer. She moved with an awareness of her beauty that was almost a song of yearning, but she kept herself apart from the catting and catching that were the ways of her cousins, Walter's nieces. I sometimes wondered if her wariness came from uncertainty, and her uncertainty from being a bastard, but whatever the reason, she acted as if she were a chalice of glass, that the slightest false movement would break.

Robert could not have been more different. He was always either boisterous or sulking, brash or subdued, and never somewhere happy in between. I could tell by the way he looked at Adele that he worshipped her, but he always spoke to her roughly, as if she were his sister, and she loved it.

Together, they adopted me, and we rode out every morning onto the hills north of Elmeslac, where I learnt to fly a hawk. At table, Adele taught me the ways of courtesy, until I knew how to hold my knife, how to eat with only the tips of my fingers touching the food, and how to be gentle in my speech with a lady.

Amongst the youths and maidens of the castle we made a small circle of our own. We did not do it out of arrogance: it was more a linking of shields out of need. We were frightened by the world, but when the three of us were together, we felt safe from everyone else.

Walter made it his custom to have the youths of the castle serve in turn as his squire, so I thought it no more than chance when one day he called me, said he was riding out, and that I was to go with him.

It was the season of Advent. The earth was sodden and cold. We rode briskly, and were well away from Elmeslac before Walter spoke.

"You do not ask where we are heading," he remarked.

"Wherever it please you, my lord," I replied dutifully.

"I can see Adele has been turning you into a lap-dog," he said gruffly. "Honesty goes further with me. I brought you because we are brothers in today's business."

I sat up in the saddle.

"The Sacred Blade, my lord?"

"The Sacred Blade," said Walter. "I grow restless waiting for word from Thurstan."

"So where are we heading?" I asked.

"Kirkham Priory," answered Walter. "Father Waltheof has sent asking to speak with me, and it crossed my mind that he may know something of the legend. He comes from old Northumbrian stock."

Walter had himself given the land to found a priory at Kirkham on the wooded banks of the river Derwent. From my first glimpse of the canons in their black and white robes, I thought I was back in Gisburgh, and it was odd to be welcomed with respect and ushered gracefully through the cloister to the prior's lodging.

I was expecting a grizzled patriarch with a beard as long as Walter's, but Father Waltheof was very young, slight of build, his ginger hair cropped in a tonsure. He spoke perfect French, and served us with mulled wine to chase away the chill.

"Forgive the manner of my summons," he said to Walter, "but when you hear my news you may be glad I did not trust it to a messenger. Last night, one of our canons returned from Normandy. He brought news which may only now be reaching London. The king is dead."

Walter's mouth opened, but for a moment he was dumb. Then he shook himself and sat forward.

"Where?" he asked.

"Near Rouen. It was a fever of the entrails, but there was time for him to make his peace with God."

Walter made the sign of the cross. "If Henry can make peace with God, there is hope for us all," he said. "Any word as to his will?"

"None," said the prior.

"You must think me heartless," Walter told him. "I owe Henry all I have, and I have served him faithfully, but I cannot find it in me to weep for him."

"Take no blame," said Waltheof. "It is hard to love a man who hates himself."

There was a long pause. Walter sat stunned, lost in thought, and the prior waited patiently for him to gather his wits. When at last Walter looked up, he shook his head.

"Nothing that happens now will surprise me."

"Who will take the crown?" asked Waltheof.

"Whoever moves fastest," said Walter. "God knows, there are enough of them with a claim to it – but no true-born son."

"Am I wrong," asked Waltheof, "in thinking Henry wished the crown to pass to his daughter Matilda?"

"That is the kind of wish that dies with its maker," replied Walter. "No, it will be someone else: Robert of Gloucester, perhaps, or one of Henry's nephews. All I can promise you is that here in Northumbria we will be the last to know."

They looked at each other uneasily, as if they had thoughts that neither wanted to put into words.

"I can think of some," said Walter, "who will see this

as the judgement of God."

"How so?" the prior asked cautiously.

"The White Ship," said Walter. "When the boy William died, we lost the true-born heir to the kingdom, and now the last of the Conqueror's sons is dead, with no son to follow him. It can only be God's will. He had judged the Norman kings and found them wanting."

Waltheof smiled. "As far as I can tell," he said, "however it is that God works his will, it is rarely through kings."

It was dark when we set off back to Elmeslac. As we rode through the hills, I heard a wolf baying deep among the trees. The sound carried, faint but clear and blood-curdling, through the silence of the night.

"We shall have to bring our hunting this way," remarked Walter.

"My lord," I said, "you forgot to ask the prior if he knew of the Sacred Blade."

"No," said Walter, "I chose not to. I have a feeling we may be hearing of it all too soon. All we know of the searchers is that their purpose is strong enough to make them threaten fire and murder. I doubt they want the Sacred Blade to adorn the altar of a cathedral. They want it to work evil, and with the king's death, we reach a moment where the opportunities for working evil are almost endless."

"Then should we not be searching ourselves?"

"We will," said Walter. "In a few weeks I may be free to give it all my strength. King Henry made me sheriff. Whoever follows him will want one of his own men keeping the law, but until then, it is mine to keep, and I intend to see that no one breaks the peace of Northumbria without at once being brought to justice."

As soon as the king's death was known, the bells were

tolled for the peace of his soul, and the land twittered with rumours and arguments. At Elmeslac, life was unchanged, except that Walter took an armed escort when he rode out to keep the law. Here and there, folk were taking the chance to settle old scores. Many of King Henry's men had enemies, and several died within days of their master.

It was Christmas Eve, and Robert and I were among the youths dragging the Yule log into a hall filled with the smell of spices, when a messenger reached Elmeslac with something more than a rumour. He was owl-eyed with riding through the dark, and he went straight to where Walter sat among garlands of holly.

"A message, my lord, from Archbishop Thurstan. I am to tell you there has been a crowning in London."

"Who wore the crown?" asked Walter.

"Stephen de Blois, my lord."

Walter raised his eyes to the rafters.

"Stephen de Blois," he muttered. "May God protect him!"

7. PIECES FOR THE GAME

I was in the stables, about to ride out hawking with Robert and Adele, on the morning the next messenger came. Before we could follow him into the hall, Walter came storming out, calling for the grooms.

"Mad!" he shouted. "The man has gone mad!"

Jordan and Orm appeared behind him.

"What has happened?" I asked.

"The Scots," said Jordan, "have crossed the border."

"For the first time in forty years," added Walter, beside himself with fury. "We are going to see your father," he told Robert. "You may as well come with us."

"So will I," announced Adele.

The way led north, over the top of the moors. It was a few weeks after Epiphany. The track was frosted, and good riding; there was hard snow in the gullies that cut the rims of the dales.

High in the wilderness, there was a meeting of tracks at a tall stone cross and, as we passed it, we saw the sea glinting in the distance like a blade slicing the sky. Away to the north, I could see Odinshill, the thumblike peak I had known all my life. If I wished, I could be home with my mother and Aldred by nightfall.

"Welcome to my father's lands," said Robert joylessly.

"Bitterness does not become you," Adele warned him.

"I am not bitter," he said haughtily. "I will win myself lands by prowess of knighthood, and they will be lands far wider than my father's."

It was no mean ambition, for we rode on with the de Brus domain stretching as far as we could see. The heather moor tapered to a long ridge, which we followed to its toe, where on a motte there stood a castle with a view of three valleys.

"Castle Danby," Robert told us. "A crude stronghold, but this is where my grandfather first put down his roots. It cannot match the fortress my father has built at Skelton, but he still likes to winter here."

We found de Brus taking a late dinner after a morning spent hunting, none too successfully, judging by his temper. It was his wife, the lady Agnes, who rose to make us welcome. She bid us join them at the high table. Trenchers of pork roast were served to us, and mulled wine with honey and cinnamon.

I saw de Brus looking warily at Jordan.

"So now you are with Walter?" he remarked. "I trust he is noble enough for you."

"Our parting still grieves me," Jordan told him.

De Brus seemed pleased. "Well, we were both torn by our loyalties," he said. "May we never again face so hard a choice."

"When you hear what brings us," said Walter, "you will long for days when the choices were so simple. I have just learnt that David has brought an army across the border."

De Brus smiled. "I knew he would," he said. "I knew it as soon as that little peacock Stephen gripped the crown."

"You knew it!" Walter said thunderously. "You saw it coming and did nothing to prevent it? Has the world gone mad? Why is David doing this? Why is he breaking the peace he worked so hard to make? What on earth does he hope to achieve?"

"I should have thought it was clear enough," said de Brus. "He wants Northumbria."

"Then damn him!" said Walter. "He has no claim to it."

"Has he not?" de Brus asked calmly. "I seem to recall that his mother came from the royal house of England, and his wife, may God rest her soul, was the daughter of the last English earl of Northumbria. How deep is your memory, Walter?"

"In God's name, Robert," protested Walter, "are you saying David believes that gives him the right to go to war?"

"Some would say it gives him a claim to the crown of England," replied de Brus. "You cannot deny the claim it gives him to Northumbria. I would say his claim is stronger than Stephen's."

"I do not care if he has a claim to the imperial throne of Constantinople," retorted Walter. "We must stop him. If war breaks out now, every dispossessed English grandson will come at us waving his scythe. We have to stamp this out. We owe it to Henry to hold his kingdom together. We owe it to Stephen."

"King Stephen!" de Brus said scornfully. "I give him a hundred days."

"He may be young," said Walter, "but he is noble-hearted, and he has been crowned and anointed by the Church. Whether or not we rejoice, he is our king. I say he will be a breath of spring air after Henry's cold grasp."

"I can see you are ready to throw yourself at his feet,"

said de Brus with disgust.

"I see no harm in him," said Walter mildly, "and for once, we must stare into the distance. What will you do, Robert, when he summons the feudal host to throw David and his chivalry back into Scotland?"

This, I realised by the earnestness of Walter's gaze, was the question he had come to ask, and it made de Brus twist as if his chair had caught fire.

"Nothing," he said firmly.

"Think again," urged Walter. "If we let Stephen fail, we betray the kingdom. Whatever we do will be watched by lesser men, and taken as a signal."

De Brus listened patiently.

"The trouble with you, Walter," he said, "is that you stare too far into the distance to see the ground at your feet. The question is who, in this day and age, out of all the people we know, will be willing to go to war against David? Half the knights in Northumbria have lands in Scotland as well as in England – that was part of Henry and David's grand design to bring peace to the border – and these days there are even Normans with lands only in Scotland. David's army will not be the rabble of tribesmen and English outlaws that Malcolm Canmore used to trail around with. David has chivalry. No wonder he is halfway to the Tyne." He slapped his palms on the table. "So I will do nothing to harm Stephen," he said, "but I will not take up arms against David."

Walter could not hide his disappointment, and when we rose to leave, there was little said. Robert went to speak with his father. De Brus listened, then said something that made his son turn towards us with a look of disgust of the kind I now knew ran in the family.

"Did you hear that?" he asked Adele, as we rode out

onto the moor. "He said he does not care if I fight King David or not. He can hardly wait for me to kill myself."

For once, Adele said nothing to tease him.

By the stone cross on the summit of the moors stood a trough where we broke the ice to let the horses drink. Jordan and Orm were the last to remount, and I lingered to ride beside them.

"Are we riding to fight King David?" I asked.

"We ride where Walter rides," said Jordan, but when he saw the look on my face, he smiled to reassure me.

"Remember," he said, "that times like this are more dangerous for great lords than for the likes of you and me. When Henry seized the crown, there were six years of alarms and rebellions before his grip on England and Normandy was secure. Walter and de Brus stood by him then, and you can see how well they were rewarded. They backed the right man and, in your lifetime, the kingdom has known peace, but they still remember the years when nothing was certain."

"But which of them is right?" I asked.

"I wish I knew," said Jordan. "A man can make the wrong choice for all the right reasons. I know, I have a gift for it. This time, unlike Walter and de Brus, I have nothing to lose. A king gave them their lands, but another king could take them away. If they back the wrong man now, they could lose all they have."

Not for the first time, I wished I were back in Longthwaite with Sigrid. I could feel myself getting lost in a wilder game of chess than any we had played, on a board stretching further than I could see.

In the cold winter air I could see down into the lowlands. From Pickering to York lay spread a patchwork of domains that Normans had carved for themselves out of the old land of Northumbria. All this and more was the chess-board. Far away, on its northern edge, King David had made the first move; and southwards, somewhere beyond the Humber, word of it would be reaching King Stephen.

Walter Espec and Robert de Brus were no more than chess-piece knights, forced to decide which colour to take as the game began above their heads. In this game, even Jordan could never be more than a pawn.

At dawn the next day, Walter flung open the door of our guest-lodge.

"Stir yourselves," he said. "We are going to Rievaulx."

He hurried us out of the castle. Rievaulx, like Kirkham, was a religious house that Walter had given the land to found, and it lay only a short ride through the woods from Elmeslac. We heard its bells every day, yet I had never seen one of its monks.

"Forgive my haste," said Walter, "but today there must be only the four of us, the brotherhood of the Sacred Blade. If Adele had known we were riding to Rievaulx, she would have insisted on riding with us."

"Pardon my asking," said Orm, "but what can we hope to learn from a bunch of monks who spend their days buried in the wilderness?"

"To reach the wilderness, a man must first have a world to leave," replied Walter. "Rievaulx casts a spell. Many come looking. Among them was a young man named Aelred. He came a year ago, on the urging of our friend, Prior Waltheof, and once he had seen Rievaulx, he could not bring himself to leave. I am told he is an excellent novice."

"And the world he left behind?" asked Jordan.

Walter grinned. "He was King David's steward."

We came to a wide clearing. Beside a stream stood a cluster of rough, timbered buildings thrown up to form an abbey quadrangle and, on the slope above, men in brown cassocks were at work. The ground was being levelled, and a forest of planks and poles stood like siege-towers in tapestries of the winning of Jerusalem, here against the rising walls of a church of butter-coloured stone.

As we rode out of the trees, a burst of song came from a timber church that stood by the stream, and it was made up of so many voices, singing together with such strength, that I wondered how there could possibly be any monks left over to work on the building.

"How many of them are there?" asked Jordan.

"In the beginning, there were only twelve," replied Walter. "Now there are so many I have had to give them land in Bedfordshire to found a daughter-house, and still their numbers grow."

We tethered our horses, and waited by the doorway of the church until the choir monks in their white cassocks came out from their devotions. Abbot William greeted us warmly, and there was much shaking of heads over the news from the north.

"We may soon be riding to war," said Walter. "I came to ask for your prayers, and also to speak with Brother Aelred."

"He may talk with you," said the abbot, "but do not keep him long. He has come through many struggles to find peace with us. Do not remind him of the longings he has only now learnt to master."

The monks filed away, leaving us face to face with a man who looked at us eagerly with one eye and shyly with the other. He drew back his hood to show hair cut in a tonsure, so recently that the top of his head was still white as an eggshell. Red, work-roughened hands hung limply from the wide sleeves of his coarse woollen cassock. It was hard to believe that this man had once been the steward of a king.

I had heard of the white monks. It was only a few years since they first began to gather. They set out to live a life without comfort, in the wildest place they could find, and in a silence they broke only to pray. A lad from a village near mine had gone to join them, but why a man like Aelred should do it was beyond me. If Robert or I were a king's steward, we would count ourselves lucky, and make the most of it, not throw it all to the wind.

For a moment, Walter and Aelred simply looked at each other, as if they were silently recalling old times; then Walter spread his hands in a gesture of hopelessness.

"Why has he done it?" he asked. "Why has David, of all men, gone to war?"

"How could he not?" asked Aelred unhappily. "It was his father's greatest longing, the winning of Northumbria. '

"And we know the grief that came of it," said Walter. "David knows it more deeply than anyone."

"He has his father's ghost in his blood," said Aelred. "I have seen him struggle with it, and turn it away, but always it has come back to haunt him."

"And now Northumbria lies at his feet," said Walter. "No one seems minded to stand against him. Gone are the days of the Sacred Blade."

Aelred looked puzzled, then gave a slow smile of recognition.

"So you know the old legend?" he asked, "of how the Sacred Blade will come again in the hour of need?"

"My minstrels sing me many strange tales," said Walter. "Remind me, why was it sacred?"

A smile was spreading over Aelred's face. He tucked his hands into his wide woollen sleeves and hugged himself.

"I heard the story when I was a boy," he said, "from one of the canons of Hexham. He said that long ago, when Northumbria was young, King Edwin fell in battle against the heathen, and the light of God was driven from the land. Of the royal house, only his nephews remained, and it was one of them, Saint Oswald, who took Edwin's sword and set out to drive the heathen from Northumbria. God gave him victory, and his sword became the Sacred Blade."

"And when he died," said Walter, "was the sword sealed by magic in a stone, to await the day when the chosen one should come to pull it free again?"

Aelred shook his head. "It was to come again in the hour of need, but no one knows what became of the Sacred Blade. There are so many old legends."

"Does David know the story?" asked Walter.

"I doubt it," answered Aelred. "You are the first I have heard speak of it in years."

The abbot came walking towards us along the cloister. Aelred looked despairingly at Walter.

"Remember," he said, "that not all David's blood comes from his father, Malcolm Canmore. His mother was a saint, and she has marked him as deeply. There is a war between the man and the woman in David, and the woman is the force of light. We must pray she prevails."

Abbott William gave us his blessing, and we took our leave. Aelred watched us mount, then pulled up his hood and turned back into his world of prayer.

We kept the silence of the abbey until we were among the trees.

"Well?" burst out Walter.

"From what you know of David," said Jordan, "is it

your judgement that he will have misgivings about what he is doing?"

"I am certain of it," said Walter, "and you heard what Aelred said, that David is losing a struggle within himself. The David I know is a good and wise man."

"But might there be some among his barons who want war?" asked Jordan.

"There always are."

"Then let us suppose," said Jordan, "that it is one of those barons who has heard of the Sacred Blade, and sent men to search for it. He must be trusting that if it came to light now, a God-fearing man like David would take it as a sign, and strike with all his force, without a doubt in his mind."

"If the Sacred Blade comes to David," said Walter bleakly, "it can only be the will of God."

We were startled by a sound of hoofbeats, and saw a horseman galloping towards us through the trees. It was Robert, and at the sight of us he waved and came up grinning from ear to ear.

"My lord," he cried, "I have some excellent news."

"Go on," said Walter, "I think I can take it."

Robert poured it out in a breathless babble. "A messenger from Archbishop Thurstan says that King Stephen is marching north. He has summoned the feudal host to gather at Chester beyond Durham. The Scots are to be caught at the Tyne."

He was crestfallen when none of us said a word.

"What is wrong?" he asked. "I thought it was what we have all been hoping for?"

"So Stephen can move fast," said Walter thoughtfully. "Perhaps nothing has yet been lost."

8. THE HOLY CITY

O N the morning after Candlemas, we rode out to war. Walter had summoned his knights, the men who held his land and owed him service. Some were growing old, and sent their sons. None of them had used a weapon in anger for years. The way they chattered was almost as unnerving as the practised speed with which Jordan and Orm packed their saddle-bags.

I had gear of my own to pack, chosen by Jordan from the armoury of Elmeslac. There was a jerkin sewn with ring-mail, comforting round the guts, but leaving my neck bare to stick out like a chicken's; there was a steel cap with thongs for me to tie under the chin, which though padded with quilt, pinched my ears; and there was a sword, heavier than I would have liked, but with a good edge. On Orm's advice, I took no shield.

"Carrying it will wear you out," he said, "and shields only get in the way."

As our horses were led out into the bailey, Robert came strutting over in his armour and gave me a friendly metalled clap on the shoulder. I held his stirrup while he mounted. I was about to swing up onto Loki, when Adele came splashing towards me. With her feet slipped into clogs to walk through the mud, and her gown hitched up in her hands, she looked more a village girl than the maiden of a castle.

"Watch over Robert," she whispered.

"He needs no help from me," I told her.

"I do not mean in battle," said Adele. "Keep his mind away from his bitterness."

We looked at each other with a flush of understanding.

"Is he your love?" I asked.

Adele gave me a mute look of protest.

"Forgive me," I said. "That was not a courteous thing to ask."

Smiling, she reached out and kissed me on the cheek, so hard and quickly, it was more as if she had slapped my face.

By nightfall, we were in Yarm, and the following morning we rode out onto the bridge over the Tees, the mist so thick we could barely see the water. When at last we came to Chester, we only knew it because the village was full of soldiers. Bright-coloured tents had been pitched wherever the ground was clear, and smoke rose from cooking-fires, thickening the mist.

In the corner of a field, we made our camp. The horses were rubbed down and picketed, and shelters thrown up in the ebbing daylight. Jordan had a faded tent, much in need of repair, and as soon as it was pitched, I huddled in my cloak and saddle-blanket and left it to Orm to kindle a fire. The damp wood hissed and gave more smoke than flame.

It was dark when Jordan returned from a walk he had taken with Walter, to the village.

"Well?" Orm asked him.

"Stephen himself is in Durham," he answered. "So is Thurstan. David, it seems, is still on the north bank of Tyne.

Newcastle is under siege, or taken."

"What do you make of the army?"

"The army," said Jordan with amusement, "is the best that money can buy."

Orm raised his eyebrows. "Mercenaries?"

"From Flanders," said Jordan, "almost a thousand of them, in training and well equipped – but of the northern lords who should have answered the summons to the feudal host, not a sign."

"I suppose," said Orm cheerfully, "that if Stephen has hired men to pay, at least he will not keep us sitting here long."

"How can you bear to be only pieces on a chessboard?" I asked.

Jordan looked at me in surprise, then smiled appreciatively. "In the game we are in now," he said, "the next move belongs to King David. I would say Stephen has the knights to hold him at the Tyne, but not enough to throw him back to the border. Not in the dead of winter, when David holds the castles."

It was a bitter night. I woke feeling a year older, but the first thing I saw as I peered into the murk was Walter and Jordan, striding from the village, looking at least a year younger.

"Saddle the horses," called Jordan. "We are riding to see King Stephen."

Robert's face appeared in the doorway of a nearby tent, and he scrambled out to join us.

As we rode south, the mist began to clear, revealing a high land of long, wooded hills and village clearings. Beyond each valley was another the same.

In the distance we heard bells. Across a valley filled with mist appeared a city perched on a hill. Above its ramparts and rooftops, high-roofed and pinnacled, rose the greatest church I had even seen.

The road down into the valley was jammed with farmers' wagons and soldiers. Walter could have shouted his name and frayed a passage, but instead he settled back to enjoy the bustle. Like bees in a swarm, we crossed a bridge to where a cobbled street wound up between the houses to the fortress, and so we came to the holy city of Durham.

At the top of the hill, in the heart of the citadel, a green separated the great church from the bishop's castle. It was crowded with armed men, who were eyeing each other with open distrust.

"Half these men are Scots!" burst out Robert.

"I was hoping they would be," said Walter.

He dismounted and yelled for a groom before turning to Robert.

"We heard at dawn that Archbishop Thurstan has persuaded the kings to meet and talk peace. Thanks be to God."

"Thanks be to God?" repeated Robert in disbelief.

Walter gave him a cautionary glare, then turned into the crowd, Jordan and Orm at his shoulders. Robert tossed his reins over the pommel of his saddle and stood muttering to himself. I reached out to take him by the elbow, but he pushed me away.

"Pitiful," he said scornfully. "That man has less courage than a sheep."

"He is our lord," I reminded him. "You must not talk like that where others can hear."

"Spare me the rules of courtesy," said Robert. "I want a battle, and the chance to make a name for myself. What do you want?"

"Well," I said, "I do not want to ride back to Elmeslac to tell Adele you have been killed."

"Leave that to Walter," said Robert. "If I get killed, ride and tell my father. He will fill your mouth with silver."

"Do coins taste as bitter as sorrow?" I asked.

Robert opened his mouth to reply, then shook his head, and we set off after the others.

The bells of the great church fell silent, and stewards appeared from the castle to clear an aisle through the crowd. Walter raised his oxlike shoulders, then nodded to Jordan. Together they pushed their way to the very edge of the aisle, and we wriggled through the crush to join them.

A procession was coming out of the castle, led by the bishop of Durham and his priests, in all their finery. Behind them came Thurstan, walking stiffly, with a face so calm and unblinking it looked a mask. Behind Thurstan, strolling side by side, followed by twin retinues of knights, walked two men who could only be the kings.

David FitzMalcolm was a small man with a worn face, his long beard brushed neatly to end in a point. He had a broad chest and stocky legs, that I guessed came from his infamous father, and a pair of gentle eyes that seemed as out of place in that warrior's body as his saintly mother must have felt, when in her flight from the Conqueror she found herself married to the king of the Scots.

Stephen de Blois was tall, his hair and beard the colour of straw. With his burnished mail and embroidered leather gloves, he could have been walking to take his place at King Arthur's Round Table. He was wearing a smile that burned like a brazier, as if he had no cares, and despite myself, I felt the blood-magic of the presence of a grandson of the Conqueror.

King David was the first to catch sight of Walter, and

he greeted him with a nod and a smile of the eyes. Walter bowed, and when this caught Stephen's eye, he turned and bowed to him as deeply.

"Walter, it lights my heart to see you," cried King Stephen.

"I'll bet it does," muttered Orm to Jordan.

"Sire, I came in answer to your summons," replied Walter, in a booming voice for all to hear. I turned to see what Robert made of all this, and found him lost in thought. He was staring at a young man who walked a pace behind King David. A few years older than us, he had a chin covered with a curling first beard, and he was smiling as if his wildest dreams were coming true around him.

"Who is he?" I asked Robert.

"Prince Henry," he said, "David's son."

We watched, with awe and envy, as he passed.

I was confused. I was Norman enough to have taken one look at Stephen de Blois and seen my king, but something in my heart went out to David and Henry.

The procession went by, and once the kings were through the doorway of the church, the crowd pushed to follow. Robert and I felt no yearning to stand through a Mass, so when Walter and the others moved to join the flow, we stayed where we were.

Someone tapped me on the shoulder.

"I was hoping I would find you here," said Aimeric. With his black hair, and threadbare cassock ruffling in the wind, he looked like a crow. I told him.

"And you look like a fish," he said, pointing to my jerkin of ring-mail, "or a lizard from the kingdom of Arles."

"You cannot let a clerk insult you like this," said Robert.

"He is a friend," I explained. "Robert de Brus, meet

Aimeric of Chartres, wandering scholar and scribe to Archbishop Thurstan."

Robert's eyes narrowed. "Can you tell us about this peace that Thurstan is said to have made between the kings?" he asked.

"I doubt it," said Aimeric. "I have heard so much these last few days that I can no longer tell what has been argued from what has been agreed. I can tell you all I know, but only if we go somewhere out of the wind."

He tapped the wallet hanging from his belt, and it chinked. "Last night, I sang for King Stephen and he was generous. Come and help me spend my riches."

He led us down winding alleys and flights of steps to an inn by the river. Trout were grilled for us over a hearth of charcoal, and we picked them to the bone, with a fresh loaf and a jug of bitter cider to help them down. The inn was crowded, and everyone talking.

"At the end of the Mass they are singing in the cathedral," said Aimeric, "Prince Henry will go down on his knees before King Stephen, and swear his oath of loyalty. So peace will be made in the sight of all, but it hangs on the keeping of a promise."

"Do you know what it is?" I asked.

"No," said Aimeric. "It is a secret between Thurstan and the kings, but I think it has to do with Prince Henry, and the earldom of Northumbria."

Robert was incredulous. "Oh no," he said. "You must be mistaken. Stephen would never dare give Northumbria to a Scot. The barons would go wild. He might as well throw his crown into the sea."

"Or was it Northumberland?" asked Aimeric. "Is there a difference?"

"All the difference in the world," said Robert. "Northumbria was once a kingdom, but Northumberland is only a part of it, the stretch of land between the Tyne and the Tweed. It is Northumberland that the Scots have just overrun."

"Then it is Northumberland I mean," said Aimeric. "The bargain is that tomorrow King David turns for home, handing back all the hostages and fortresses he has taken, but only because he trusts that his son will soon be made earl over them."

Robert looked disgusted. "This is shameful," he said. "We should be throwing the Scots back over the border, not giving them all they want."

"From what I hear," said Aimeric, "Stephen has trouble elsewhere in the kingdom. This is no more to him than a quarrel in the far north. He wants it settled quickly."

"Well, I say Thurstan has saved us all," I said.

"You would," said Robert bitterly. "You have your father's fame to hide behind."

Aimeric looked at him in bewilderment. "What outcome would you have chosen?" he asked.

"Robert wants war," I explained. "He wants to fight his way to knighthood."

"I see," said Aimeric. He gave Robert a smile. "Surely there are other ways of winning knighthood? You could find a quest that will win you renown, or a lady whose love will ennoble your heart."

Robert only grunted and reached for the cider jug. Finding it empty, he called for more, and when no one came he seized the jug and set off through the tables calling for service. Aimeric slumped back against the wall, and looked at me wide-eyed.

"Your friend is possessed by a demon."

"I know," I said. "He worries us all."

"Can you lose him?" asked Aimeric. "Look at the carving on this table."

He bent forward, as if to study the image of a girl someone had gouged on the board. When our heads were almost touching, he began to whisper.

"Thurstan has been waiting for your father and Walter. He has a safe place for us to meet, and now you are here, he will want us to meet tonight."

Robert returned with cider, and filled our cups.

To honour the kings, the bishop of Durham gave a banquet in the great hall of his castle.

King David had already left, but King Stephen and Prince Henry sat side by side, and Normans and Scots mixed together at the tables. I was struck by how much laughter there was between the Scots and the men of Durham. It was King Stephen's Flemish mercenaries who were the strangers.

When the feasting had given way to drinking and jugglers, two by two the brotherhood of the Sacred Blade slipped away. I left with Aimeric, while Robert was so busy talking to one of Prince Henry's companions that he never saw us go.

Aimeric led me past the cathedral and along an empty street, the abbey wall on one side, tall and well-built houses on the other. At the door of one of the houses, a servant was waiting, and he led us upstairs to a room beneath the rafters, where scrolls of parchment and wooden tally-sticks were piled beneath the eaves.

A fire burned on a hearth-stone. Beside it were Thurstan and Walter, and a man with auburn hair and large pale eyes in a florid face: our host, Archdeacon Ranulf. They were talking about popes, and places I had never heard of. Thurstan was shrivelled with fatigue.

It was a while before Jordan and Orm arrived and they came up the stairs looking furious.

"We were followed to your door," announced Jordan.

"There were three of them," said Orm. "I have a feeling that if we saw them in daylight, we'd know their faces."

"Walter has just told me what happened to you in Cumbria," said Thurstan.

"And what we learnt from Aelred of Rievaulx," added Walter.

"Do we know any more about the Sacred Blade?" asked Jordan.

"No," said Thurstan, "but enough to know why men are searching for it. When you first brought me the tale, I have to confess I thought it no more than a legend from the bottomless past. Tonight, it seems to me charged with an almost unbearable meaning."

"It does now we know David's desire," agreed Walter.

"Northumbria," said Thurstan. "Not Cumbria, or Northumberland, but everything, Saint Cuthbert's Land and Yorkshire, the whole of the ancient kingdom. He wants to throw us back a hundred years, and he believes in his right. He is ready for war."

"I thought you had talked him out of it?" said Jordan.

"The peace we have bought is a long way short of the kiss of peace," answered Thurstan. "It gives us time, but not time to come."

"It ought to be time enough," said Jordan. "David came so far so fast because the castles were unprepared. That will not happen again. Our fathers fought for Northumbria, and we owe it to them to keep it. There are worse things than war."

"How many times must I say it?" Thurstan asked him.

"This is Christendom. There must be no war."

"So, how do we stop David?" asked Walter.

"We must trust ourselves to reason," said Thurstan. "David is a civilised man, and we must keep him that way, or everything will be lost. So we must find the Sacred Blade. We must find it before it can be wrenched from the past to fill David with the fantasy of a crusade. We must find it, and seal it in our deepest crypt, bound with incantations of anathema."

I looked eagerly at Jordan, but he was frowning. "How can it be done," he asked, "if the searchers follow us every step of the way?"

"You cannot do it," said Thurstan, "but only you are known to them."

"They will not be following me," said Walter.

"No," agreed Thurstan, "but you and I have the kingdom on our shoulders. Stephen will want you to remain as sheriff. Our task is to win over the men with torn loyalties, like Robert de Brus." He gave a pained smile. "And the men who are waiting for a sign from heaven to tell them which side to take."

For a moment, no one spoke. I knew what Robert would say if he were me. I knew what a Norman boy who wanted to be a knight should say. Aimeric glanced at me, and raised an eyebrow, as if he were reading my mind.

"I will make this my quest," I announced.

No one laughed, though Orm pulled a face, and scratched one of his ear-lobes. Thurstan's gaze came to rest on me.

"May God protect you, Simon de Falaise," he said gratefully.

"Will you let me have Aimeric?" I asked.

"Of course," said Thurstan, "though you cannot have

him yet. We have travelling to do, and I will need him myself. I will send him to you in May. Let your quest begin then, with the spring."

I turned to Walter. "Will you let me have Robert?"

He thought it over for so long that we all turned to stare at him. "No," he said finally. "He could never keep it secret, and his father is too close to King David. We cannot trust him."

In that magical moment, before the doubts and fears took hold of my mind, I felt only the force of the trust they were willing to place in me. I glanced at Jordan, and saw in his eyes a look of pride and concern that, in the heat of the moment, I took to be love.

PART TWO

The Quest
February *1136*–December *1137*

9. REACHING FOR THE PAST

WHEN Jordan and Orm had left noisily, Archdeacon Ranulf raised the latch of one of the window-shutters, and looked outside.

"Quiet as a crypt," he said, "but someone could still be out there keeping watch."

Walter helped Thurstan to his feet.

"Keep Simon and Aimeric here until daybreak," Thurstan told Ranulf. "Let them out only when you are sure it is safe."

When he had seen Thurstan and Walter to the door, the archdeacon brought a venison pie, ate most of it himself, then bid us goodnight. Aimeric fed a log to the fire on the hearth-stone.

"Naturally, I was flattered when you asked for me," he said, "but why do you want me with you?"

"Because I do not know Latin," I said. "I do not know how to read. I do not even know where to start the search."

"We have the song of the Blade."

"Is that all? I thought you were supposed to have been digging the secrets out of the library of York?"

Aimeric smiled ruefully. "The library of York," he explained, "is not the wonder of the world it was in the days of Charlemagne. The Vikings burnt it. Everything was lost. They say Archbishop Aldred spent a fortune starting a new collection, but it was burnt by the Normans. I did find one book ..."

"One book!"

"One wonderful book. It is a history written by a monk. His bones are here in Durham. Do you remember the names in the song?"

"There was Oswald, and Edwin ..."

"There were six names," said Aimeric. "Halfdan, Aethelfrith, Edwin, Oswald, Penda and Oswy. Of Halfdan I can find no trace, but the history tells of the other five. They were kings in the earliest days of Northumbria."

"Does it speak of the Sacred Blade?"

"No," said Aimeric thoughtfully, "which is odd, for the monk who wrote it never missed a chance to tell of a miracle. If he is to be believed, Northumbria in those days was a startling place. But I must admit, I finished it wondering how much of any of this *is* to be believed."

"What do you mean?" I asked.

"These kings lived long, long ago," said Aimeric. "Who remembers them now? If the Sacred Blade fell from the sky tomorrow, would anyone in Northumbria know what it was? Would anyone believe in it?"

"Ulrica would believe in it," I said. "She believes this is the hour of need, in which the Sacred Blade must be found and used for good or evil."

Aimeric looked unconvinced.

"I still have my doubts," he said. "King Edwin died almost exactly five hundred years ago. Think of the tides of invasion that have swept the land since then. Where was the Sacred Blade when the Vikings came? Why was it never drawn against the Conqueror? It has had its chances to save Northumbria."

"But now we have the song," I said, "and the riddle."

"We also have a choice," said Aimeric. "We can spend a summer trailing round Northumbria, asking here and there if they have ever heard of the Sacred Blade. There is nothing I would enjoy more. Or we can decide that it does not exist, and spend our time tracking the searchers, and finding out who they are. That would be too dangerous to be enjoyable, but it might be more purposeful."

I was beginning to feel uncertain.

"Which do you advise?" I asked.

"No, no," he said. "It is for you to choose."

"First we search for the Sacred Blade," I said, "because that is the best way to find out if it exists, and if it exists, we must find it before the searchers."

"There is a certain logic to that," agreed Aimeric.

"There must be other riddles," I said. "Riddles like Ulrica's, which have somehow been passed down the years."

"There must be other books," said Aimeric. "We could certainly search for them. When May comes, we could start here, in Durham, where Ulrica's father must have learnt the riddle she gave to you."

The decision made, but the danger still a comfortable margin of months away, we lay down and slept.

We were woken at dawn by the bells of the cathedral, and Archdeacon Ranulf led us from the back of the house through a skein of alleys to a postern gate in the wall of the citadel. There we parted. A steep and muddy track led down through the trees to the riverbank, which we only had to walk along to appear innocently at the city gates as they were opened.

In the great hall of the bishop's castle, we found Robert staring into a bowl of porridge, somewhat bleary after the banquet.

"So there you are," he said, sitting up with a jolt, and looking not at me, but at Aimeric. "Was it the truth you were telling me yesterday?"

Aimeric frowned. "About the kings?" he asked.

"About knighthood," said Robert. "You said a man can be ennobled by his love for a woman."

"Ah, courtly love," said Aimeric. "It is what the troubadours sing in Toulouse and Arles, and their songs are now the creed of the young knights of the north. They say that love is the greatest test of chivalry, the noblest quest of all. What is tested is your devotion to one lady – to one lady and no other – and the faith with which you serve her. The lady must be worthy of your love, and only she can tell you what will make you worthy of her."

Robert grinned. "What would you say?" he asked me.

"Adele?" I asked. "I say she is worthy of your love."

By dusk the next day we were in Elmeslac, less than half the number who had set out from there, for most of Walter's liege-men made straight for their homes.

We were welcomed as if we had taken Jerusalem. Walter's sister, the lady Albrea, came from the hall bearing a wide silver cup brimming with wine, from which we each drank in turn to toast the homecoming.

At supper, Robert gazed at Adele the way Aimeric had once gazed at the apple I was eating, as if without her he would starve.

"I forbid you to leave me again," she said. "My aunt Albrea will not allow me to leave the castle without an escort. I have missed our hawking."

"So have I," said Robert.

"Are you sure?" Adele asked gaily. "The day you rode

out to war, you could not even find me a backward glance."

Robert was chewing his bottom lip. When he raised his hands, clasping them, they left their shape behind in sweat-damp on the table.

"Give me a year and a day," he asked her. "Let me prove my love by the devotion of my service, and at the end of a year and a day, be my wife."

He had never looked so serious. Adele looked as astonished as if one of her favourite hawks had without warning begun to sing like a nightingale.

"What is all this?" asked Walter. "Is my foster-son making trouble again?"

Robert turned to face his lord. "I am asking for a year and a day," he repeated, "to prove my love for Adele and show I am worthy to be her husband."

Walter glared at him, and the whole high table fell silent. In the eyes of the lords gathered there, Robert was nothing, a mere landless boy, and his asking for Adele was as good as declaring to Walter's face that she was a bastard, and could hope for nothing better.

When Robert saw how his words had been taken, he looked down as if he wanted to crawl under the table. Walter saw his misery, and contrived a chuckle.

"So be it," he said jovially. "I will give you a year and a day, and if at the end of it, Adele wants your love, you will have my blessing."

Hearing all this, Adele had flushed crimson, then frozen over. When Robert turned to her, the look on her face chilled him to silence. It was not a lucky omen for their love.

The laughter had gone out of the meal. I was glad to escape to the guest-lodge and sit with Jordan and Orm, unpacking by the light of a butter-lamp.

"What is the best use I can make of the months

between now and May?" I asked.

"If I were you," said Orm, "I would go home."

"Yes," agreed Jordan. "Go home and gather your strength, and go now, before we make you too much of a Norman. It is the Englishman in your blood who may know how to find his way to the Sacred Blade."

"What will you do?" I asked.

Jordan gave a rueful smile.

"We will be guarding Walter wherever the task of sheriff takes him," he answered. "So our roads are no longer the same. Yours must be the way of the quest."

"Besides," said Orm, "your mother must be wondering if we have eaten you."

He rummaged under the truckle-bed and threw me an elm-wood bowl, around the rim of which he had carved a forest with birds and squirrels on every bough.

"Give her this," he suggested.

With the bowl and my belongings slung over Loki's broad rump, I set off alone across the moors, like a knight errant or a wandering scholar.

It was a good homecoming, to long winter nights when there was nothing to do but sit by the fire and talk. The whole village wanted to hear where I had been, but I watched what I said, and I never spoke of the Sacred Blade. Instead, I let a week go by, then I began asking folk for any old tales they knew about the days before the Normans came.

Not one of them spoke of the Sacred Blade, and it deepened the doubt in my mind. Aimeric had wondered why the Sacred Blade had never been found to save Northumbria from the Conqueror, and it was a question I asked myself more and more.

One evening by our hearth, I turned to Aldred. "Do you remember the Great Rising?" I asked.

"I am not as old as I look," he warned me. "It was long before my time. For all that, I remember it. What do you want to know?"

"I was wondering why it failed."

In answer, he told me the whole terrible story, from the massacre at Durham that was the spark, and the taking of York as the city burned, to the coming north of the Conqueror, at the onset of winter, and the tumble of retreats and surrenders and betrayals that brought Northumbria to its knees, when the Conqueror ordered the Burning, so it might never trouble him again.

"Why did the Scots not come to our help?" I asked.

"Malcolm Canmore gave his word he would," said Aldred bitterly, "but he never came. He stood back, and watched us fall, and starve. Then he came the next summer. He brought a horde over Stainmoor to plunder all that was left. First they burned their way down the Tees, then they burned their way back up the coast to Northumberland and the border. By the time it was over, my father had lost half his family, most of them in the famine that followed."

So David's father had betrayed us. The Scots, I knew now, had no claim to the Sacred Blade. But how was I to believe in it, when in the Great Rising, the folk of Northumbria had stood shoulder to shoulder, to hold their land, and in their hour of need, the Sacred Blade had failed them?

A few days later, I rode to Gisburgh Priory and asked to speak with my old teacher, Father Matthew.

They told me I would find him in the marsh villages, at the mouth of the Tees. So I rode along the causeway that led from dune to dune to Middleburgh, where a priory was perched on a gravel bank it shared with a huddle of tofts, above boats keeled on the mud of low tide.

Father Matthew was in the cloister. He closed the book he was reading with reluctance, but once I had greeted him with all the courtesy I had been taught by Adele, and told him a little of my travels, he began to resign himself to the interruption.

"Your French is almost perfect," he said approvingly. "I confess I would not have expected it. You were such an unrewarding pupil."

"Last summer," I told him, "I could see no purpose in learning. Now there is so much I wish to learn. I hear there is a book, a history which tells of the kings and saints of Northumbria?"

"Indeed there is," said Father Matthew. "It was written by Bede of Jarrow."

"Could you teach me to read it?"

He smiled indulgently. "Have you any idea how long that would take?"

"I have until May."

He laughed and shook his head. "It takes years to master the skill of reading. I began my studies when I was nine years old, yet I was older than you are when I first read Bede."

My disappointment seemed to take him by surprise. "Come," he said. "Let's take a walk along the dunes."

So off we went, sinking to our ankles in the sand. "Tell me," he asked, "what do you wish to be?"

"A knight."

"Then you have chosen a path as hard as the path to learning," he told me. "There are three orders of men: those who work the land, those who fight, and those who pray. Yours is the second calling, and your task is to guard

Christendom, to be the sword of those who work and those who pray. You will be tempted by power and wealth. You will find it hard to stay true to your calling."

"I know that," I said, "and this is why I want to learn about the kings of Northumbria. Were they not the greatest knights the world has ever seen?"

"They lived in hard and holy days," agreed Father Matthew. "Let me see what I remember."

As the gulls screeched and circled, he talked of the ancient kings and their battles. I listened with a shock of recognition, for their names and deeds were exactly those of the song of the blade.

> *Aethelfrith made me*
> *to drink blood in Rheged,*
> *Edwin cleaned me*
> *in the blood of Christ.*
> *Cold my hilt*
> *when I fell from his hand,*
> *Waiting for a master*
> *to wake me from sleep.*
> *Well was I trusted*
> *to the sons of Iona,*
> *I was Oswald's blade*
> *till Penda cut him down.*
> *I was avenger*
> *the last red battle,*
> *Northumbria the cry*
> *to wake me from sleep.*

"It was King Oswy who broke the heathen," said Father Matthew, "and in thanks to God he gave the land for twelve monasteries. This priory of Middleburgh is one of the twelve."

I stared at the cluster of buildings in the heart of the marshes, as open-mouthed as if I were gazing at the wonders of Durham. Suddenly, the ancient kings were real to me. We walked the same land. I could touch what they had touched, and stand where they had been. I could reach out and touch the Sacred Blade.

I believed in it now. I had no doubts.

10. SAINT CUTHBERT'S TOMB

W HEN I rode into Elmeslac, Adele and two of the lady Albrea's daughters came out to greet me.

"Why have you been away so long?" asked Adele.

"I stayed for lambing," I told her, "then for Lent, and then for the Easter Mass at Gisburgh Priory."

It had taken the spring skies to make me leave. I pointed to the half-empty stables.

"Where is everyone?"

"My father is in London," said Adele. "He has gone to attend the king's court. Jordan and Orm are with him."

"Has Robert gone, too?" I asked.

The lady Albrea's daughters smirked at each other, and Adele sensed it.

"Robert cannot be far," she said, looking around. "Since my father left, he has been pacing the palisades, telling us each night that all is well, and that we could not be in safer hands."

"So Robert is castellan?" I asked. "He must be happy."

But at supper, I wondered. Robert spoke with a desperate courtesy, warily, like a fighter waiting for the next blow to fall. When the ladies withdrew, he slumped.

"They never leave us alone," he told me. "Since I declared my love, the lady Albrea has not allowed me near Adele unless we are watched. That's the reward you get for telling the truth."

"It shows they take you seriously," I suggested. "Tomorrow, you must ride out hawking together, and I will do the watching. It will be like old times."

"Yes," he said, staring at the table, "times have certainly changed." He looked up intently. "I have missed you, Simon. We should be sword-brothers, like Jordan and Orm."

"So we shall," I said solemnly.

The next morning, in Kirkdale, his merlin snatched a duck from the sky and brought it to ground well away from us, at the bottom of a steep slope tangled with scrub and brambles. With a yell, Robert heeled his horse straight down the slope to collect the kill.

Adele made no move to follow, and I was not about to make Loki scratch his legs for nothing, so I stayed at her side.

"He tries too hard," she said sadly, "and he is torturing himself for nothing. I have already told him that he asks more than I can give."

"I did not know," I said. "I thought . . ."

"I love him," said Adele, "but he is not my love."

"I get confused by all this talk of courtly love," I warned her. "I know friendship, and the longing for more, but in the village I come from, the songs put it simply."

Adele laughed. "What I mean," she said, "is that we may love many people, in different ways, but only one may be our true love, the one to whom we give all we have."

Looking at her, I knew it was true. I was growing to love Adele, even if she could never be Sigrid.

"Tell me, Simon," she asked teasingly, "have you a true love?"

"If I had to sing," I said, "it would be of hair gold as harvest-corn, of my lady of the lake, a sorceress at chess . . ."

"Please," cried Adele. "Spare me her name!"

Robert was kicking his horse back up the slope towards us, his hawk on his wrist, the duck hanging from his saddle.

In the first week of May, Aimeric came in the guise of a messenger. He found us at supper, and bowed to the lady Albrea.

"Greetings from the lord Walter," he said. "He sends me to tell you that he is riding on with the king, who travels now from London to Oxford. Be assured that he is well, high in the king's favour, and sad only that you must wait a while longer for his return."

The lady Albrea invited him to join us at the high table, and Aimeric soon had us enthralled with tales of King Stephen's court. After the close-fisted government of King Henry, Stephen had set out to offer his subjects a pageant greater than any since the days of William Rufus. The ladies of Elmeslac wanted to know who had been there, what they had worn, and how they had been ranked at the tables, and Aimeric answered with such detail and wit that I began to suspect he was inventing at least some of it.

One of the lady Albrea's daughters gave a sigh and turned to Adele.

"Why is it always churchmen who have the best manners?" she asked. "And the best looks?"

"Forbidden fruit?" asked Adele. "Your friend is very fetching," she told me.

"He looks too thin to hold a sword," muttered Robert.

At the end of the meal, Aimeric pulled his lute from his bag and asked the ladies if they would allow him to sing. They begged him to, and he rose to his feet, tuning the strings.

He sang of a plain covered with snow, of a city of many bells, and of a girl glimpsed in the torchlight of a procession. The words that followed were a cry to her.

> *"With the moon and with the tides*
> *may the wind of spring arise,*
> *may the rivers overflow*
> *as the bloom breaks through the snow.*
> *Then when May buds the tree,*
> *we can dance, you and me*
> *we can dance till the dawn turns aside.*
> *Then when June greens the leaves,*
> *we may come to believe*
> *in a love that cannot be denied."*

But at the end of the song, the maiden gave her love to a knight, leaving a poor scholar with no one to sing his love to but the bare winter trees.

There were some moist eyes at the high table as he finished.

"Master Aimeric," Adele asked when he sat down, "what became of the poor scholar?"

"I often wonder," he said playfully. "Perhaps he fled to another country."

"To be as spineless as a snail and sing honeyed songs?" asked Robert. "Why not give us one of the old songs of deeds, or are they too manly for you, Aimless or whatever your name is?"

Adele flushed with embarrassment.

"You shame us all," she reproached him. "How can

you ask to be honoured, if you never show honour to others?"

"To feel threatened by the likes of me," said Aimeric, "is the lowest anyone can sink."

"Let us retire," declared the lady Albrea, giving Robert a look that could have withered a nettle. She swept out with the maidens like a string of ducklings in her wake.

"You must come and share my lodge," I told Aimeric, and we hurried from the hall, leaving Robert to brood among the servants and the dogs.

"If your friend were to plunge his head into the horse-trough," murmured Aimeric, "the water might boil."

In the morning we were up with the dew to saddle our horses. As we were leading them out, Robert came towards us from the hall, looking as if he had hardly slept.

"Where are you going?" he demanded.

"On a mission for the Church," replied Aimeric. "Archbishop Thurstan has bidden me write a history of the saints, and Simon has agreed to be my escort."

"I'll come with you," announced Robert.

"I wish you could," I said, "but Thurstan says we should be no more than two."

"We will be going to holy places," said Aimeric, "places where if knights strode in chattering, it would break the stillness."

"I can be silent when I have to," said Robert. "All I want is the riding. I can sit and wait as long as you like, wherever you like – just as long as it is not here."

He looked eagerly at me, so eagerly that his eyes were almost pleading. He needed to break free of the witchcraft of love that bound him to Adele; and so, I imagined, did Adele.

"How fast can you saddle a horse?" I asked him.

Robert grinned and made for the stables. Aimeric watched him go.

"He must not know the truth," he said.

"Am I being foolish?" I asked.

"No," said Aimeric. "You have just given an apple to a stranger. Sometimes a mistake can be lucky."

In Durham the fresh leaves were gold and green on the trees below the citadel.

We had ridden well from Yarm, and arrived with the afternoon still ahead of us. In the market-place, I turned to Robert.

"Aimeric and I must visit the abbey library," I told him. "It would help if you took the horses down to the hostel by the river. Say we want supper and a bed for the night."

"Why go where we have to pay?" asked Robert. "They would make us welcome at the castle."

"Thurstan is paying," said Aimeric, "and he has forbidden me to sleep among hunting-dogs, on straw smelling of slop."

With Robert safely disposed of, Aimeric and I climbed the street leading up to the citadel.

"What are you hoping to find?" I asked.

"More than may be here," he said. "If all the monks have from the past is a copy of Bede's history, then we may as well leave. Yet they could have other books, known only to themselves, with the legends of Northumbria in their pages."

"If they have," I asked, "how long will it take you to read them?"

"A week? A month? The more they have, the better our chances."

We crossed the green and entered the shadow cast by the cathedral. A demon's head carved in bronze gripped the handle of the door-knocker between its fangs. This was a place of sanctuary, and to grasp the handle and knock was to claim it. Aimeric smiled, and rubbed the demon on the nose for luck, then reached down to open the tall door by its latch.

We entered a vast hall of shadows, a clearing in a forest of stone. Pillars thicker than tree-trunks soared upwards, branching into archway upon archway, then out into a vaulted roof where the stone hung in the air as if held there by magic. The only light came shafting down from windows high above our heads, and the air smelt of incense.

Aimeric spoke with a monk in black robes, who left by a door in the far wall through which I caught a glimpse of the cloistered courtyard beyond.

Aimeric grinned at me and rubbed his hands. We stood looking around. "Have you noticed," he said, "how each pair of pillars has its own pattern?"

"I have never been anywhere as wonderful as this," I told him in a whisper. "It must be very ancient."

"You think so?" he asked, his grin widening. "None of this can have been here the day your father was born. They finished it three years ago, and it took them forty years to build."

"Forty years!"

"That is fast for a cathedral," he said, "but Normans build for their own glory as much as for God's."

While we spoke, we were joined by a monk a few years older than us, who stood listening with undisguised displeasure. "I hear you are asking about our library," he said coldly.

Aimeric looked at him with surprise. "Are you the librarian?" he asked.

"Brother Lawrence is away," replied the monk. "I am the keeper of the key in his absence."

"The key is all I need," said Aimeric. "I wish to study your histories and chronicles."

The monk looked him up and down. "Who are you to ask this?"

"A scholar."

"Then I fear I cannot help you," the monk said, smugly. "I can only give the key to monks of my order."

"Look at my cassock," protested Aimeric. "I am as Benedictine as you are."

"A scholar is not a monk."

Aimeric was speechless.

"Where can we find Brother Lawrence?" I asked.

"I cannot say," replied the monk. "As I can be of no help . . ."

"Wait a moment," begged Aimeric. "At least answer me one question. Do you have in your library any histories of Northumbria other than the book of Bede?"

"I cannot say," repeated the monk, and he scurried away back to his cloister.

Aimeric made the sign of the horns. "I hate monks," he said. "If you spend your life shut in a cloister, your mind begins to shrivel, until one day it is no bigger than a sheep's dropping, like his."

"What about Bede of Jarrow?" I asked.

"Hmm," said Aimeric.

"Or Aelred of Rievaulx?"

Aimeric held up his hands. "Very well," he said, "I bow to your reasoning. There are good monks. One or two."

"So what do we do now?" I asked.

"I think we had better pray for help at the tomb of Saint Cuthbert."

It lay behind the altar, a huge reliquary in marble and gold, studded with jewels, that brought the smile back to

Aimeric's face. "Normans never do anything by halves," he said. "Saint Cuthbert was a simple man. I wonder how he likes having an ornate heap like this lying on top of him."

"An English heart in Norman armour," I said. "There is nothing wrong with that. What do you know about him?"

"Saint Cuthbert? He was a shepherd who had a vision and became a monk. When he found the company of other monks too hard to bear, he went off to live alone, as a hermit. And so he would have spent his life, only one day they came and dragged him off and made him bishop of Lindisfarne, wherever that is."

I knew, for Father Matthew had told me. "It is an island," I told Aimeric. "King Oswald gave it to monks from Iona."

Aimeric looked at me keenly. "An island?" he asked. "Yes, I remember it from the book of Bede. It was the first monastery in all Northumbria."

"King Oswy founded twelve others," I went on, "in thanks for the defeat of Penda, the heathen king of . . ."

"Yes," interrupted Aimeric; "when Northumbria was saved and the Sacred Blade had done its work. Do you remember the last verse of the song?

> *"Sleep beyond the tides*
> *ordered Oswy my master,*
> *Sleep till you are woken*
> *when dragons fill the sky . . ."*

Aimeric shook me by the shoulders. " '*Sleep beyond the tides,*' " he repeated. "Do you see it? When the heathen were routed and Northumbria saved, King Oswy laid the Sacred Blade to rest, for it was a weapon too holy to use for any other purpose. Where else would he leave it but in the holiest place in the kingdom – on an island beyond the tides?"

We chuckled all the way out of the cathedral and down the winding streets to the inn by the river. Robert was leaning against the parapet of the bridge.

"You look surprisingly happy," he said. "You won't have found the librarian."

"How do you know?" I asked.

"The inn-keeper told me he often sneaks in for a cup. Last time he was there, he said he was setting out for Insula Sacra, wherever that is."

"*Insula Sacra*," said Aimeric, "is the Latin for Holy Island."

"And Holy Island," I told him, "is the Norman name for Lindisfarne."

11. THE ROAD TO LINDISFARNE

W E crossed the Tyne to the fortress-town of New-castle, and rode on into Northumberland, the rump of the ancient kingdom, the land that had kept its name.

It was wide country, rough and open, where the villages were so carefully placed that at first glance there seemed to be none. This was the land where Jordan had been born, and the stories he had told me came to life in my mind.

"My grandfather will have come this way," I said. "He rode north with Robert de Mowbray."

"The de Mowbray who killed Malcolm Canmore?" asked Robert.

"Yes," I said, with pride, for I had heard enough about Malcolm Canmore to know that his death had been no great loss to Christendom. "Robert de Mowbray was my grandfather's lord."

"How unlucky," said Robert.

"What do you mean by that?" I asked.

"Think about it," he said. "If Robert de Mowbray had not quarrelled with William Rufus, and lost all he had, your grandfather would have had land here. So would

Jordan. So would you."

The thought had never entered my mind, but when Robert threw it at me, it went in like a thorn.

We were hoping to find an abbey or priory where we could ask for lodging for the night, but there were none to be seen. The first place of any size that we came to was the castle of Morpeth, on its motte above the crossing of the Wansbeck.

When we presented ourselves in the hall, the steward offered us a bench near the door.

"This is not our place," Robert told him. "We are guests for the high table. I am Robert de Brus, and this is Simon de Falaise."

As he spoke my name, one of the serving-girls by the hearth looked up from the pot she was stirring.

"My lord," she asked, "your name is Jordan de Falaise?"

"He is my father," I told her, wondering for a moment if Jordan had other bastards scattered round Northumbria, and this were one of them: but the girl only smiled, gave a curtsey, and looked me up and down with two wickedly bright eyes in a way that made my mouth go dry.

"Then you are the son of a noble knight," she said. "May God protect you."

She turned back to her tasks, and the steward was so impressed that he led us towards the high table. I was bewitched. All evening I kept looking round to catch sight of the serving-girl.

The lord of Morpeth was Ranulf de Merlay, a young man going plump around the neck and jowls. He gave us a good welcome, and a good supper, and when the ladies had left the hall, he questioned us about Walter Espec.

"Is it true," he asked, "that he has founded two

abbeys on his land?"

"An abbey and a priory," I told him.

Ranulf de Merlay looked intrigued. "If a man founds an abbey," he said thoughtfully, "it is a sign to the world that he is lord of the land – that he means to stay and be buried there, and have his sons buried there after him. Signs are important when you live in uncertain times."

Robert sat forward. "May I ask," he said, "what sign you gave King David?"

"I was careful to give none at all," de Merlay said amiably. "David never struck at me, and to have ridden against his Norman knights would have been madness. He was not burning my land, so I kept to my castle."

"King Henry would have called that an act of treason," said Robert, with his incredible tactlessness.

De Merlay only smiled. "To commit treason, you must first know who is your king," he replied. "I hear wild rumours that a man named Stephen de Blois is king of England, but I have yet to see any proof of it." He turned to me. "But as to abbeys – if I wished to found one, which order of monks should I favour?"

"The white monks," I told him. "They have more novices than their abbeys can hold."

Aimeric politely kept his thoughts on monks to himself.

Later, as we were about to spread our blankets on the floor, the serving-girl came looking for us. "My lords," she said, "let me show you where you may rest in quiet."

She led us to a chamber above the cellars, and brought us a butter-lamp and a jug of ale. I offered her a silver penny in thanks, but she lowered her eyes and left, closing the door.

Robert took a long drink, and passed me the ale-jug.

"Well, now we know how David came so quickly to

the Tyne," he said. "Ranulf de Merlay cannot have been the only one to keep to his castle."

"Can you blame him?" asked Aimeric.

I was soon asleep, dreaming of the White Ship, and of swimming through cold water in darkness. Then I was lying in shallows, in sunlight, and Aimeric was shaking me by the shoulders. Water and fish bubbled out of my mouth as he shook me harder and harder.

I sat up, and Aimeric gave a groan of relief. My head felt as if it were turning to stone.

"Wake up," he said. "The ale was drugged."

Pushing up my eyelids, I saw Robert sprawled on his back, snoring with his mouth wide open. It was well after daybreak.

"We have been robbed," said Aimeric.

It was true. Our bags had been opened, and our belongings scattered all over the floor, but as far as I could tell, nothing was missing. My wallet lay untouched beside my sword.

"I had a scrap of parchment, a copy of the song of the Sacred Blade," said Aimeric. "It has gone."

"Are you sure?"

He held up a small bundle of folded pages of vellum.

"It was here, tucked away in my copy of Ovid. Whoever did this knew exactly what they were looking for."

Slowly, clumsily, we gathered our belongings back into our bags, so Robert would know nothing when he woke; then we made our way to the hall, trying to look as if nothing had happened.

The serving-girl was nowhere to be seen. I asked the steward to find her, and he sent a boy who searched the kitchens, and then the castle, and who returned full of the news that a pony had gone from the stables.

Aimeric and I could hardly bring ourselves to look at each other. The steward only laughed.

"That sounds like Catriona," he said. "She is a wayward girl. She can vanish for weeks on end." He leered and looked me up and down. "Do you wish me to give her a message?"

"Yes," I said. "Tell her I long to meet her again."

Robert had drunk more ale than us. We had to drag him from his bed and saddle his horse for him. Then we rode on in pouring rain. It was a bad morning.

We had almost reached Alnwick when a knight with six mounted men-at-arms blocked the road. He asked our names, and where we were going.

Aimeric threw back his hood to show his tonsure.

"I travel to Lindisfarne at the command of Archbishop Thurstan," he said. "These men are my escort."

The knight seemed unimpressed.

"All travellers must have the goodwill of my lord, Eustace FitzJohn," he told us. "I will take you to him."

We knew the name. Eustace FitzJohn was lord of Alnwick and sheriff of Northumberland. Any order he gave was best obeyed.

The escort closed round us and we rode on, past the gates of Alnwick and the infamous riverbank where Malcolm Canmore met his death. In the sweeping rain, we rode in silence, through wooded land for mile after mile; so many miles I wondered if our escort were who they claimed to be. Malcolm Canmore had been lured into an ambush. It was almost a local tradition.

Then beyond the trees we heard the sea, and rode out onto dunes of wind-blown grass. We followed a wild shore, until through the squalls we saw the grey mass of a fortress perched on a crag, and I knew at once where we were. This was Bamburgh, the stronghold of the ancient kings, the castle where Jordan had been born.

Once we were inside, our escort lost interest in us. We stabled our horses, wrung out our clothes, took a look round the fortress, and at the hour of torch-lighting made our way to the hall.

When Eustace FitzJohn entered, we bowed to attract his attention, and Aimeric repeated our tale.

"Why did Thurstan give you an armed escort?" asked FitzJohn. "Does he think we cannot keep the law in Northumberland?"

"These are my friends," replied Aimeric, "Robert de Brus and Simon de Falaise. They came with me out of fellowship."

FitzJohn turned his stare on me. His eyes were grey, their lower lids sagging in fleshy folds that were the only softness in the weathered hide of his face.

"Someone by the name of de Falaise served here in the days of Robert de Mowbray," he said. "Was he any kin of yours?"

"He was my grandfather, my lord."

FitzJohn's eyes narrowed.

"Well, if you think you have any claim here," he said coldly, "go shout it to the sea. I am the lord here now. Make your pilgrimage to Lindisfarne, then get off my land."

He walked on, without inviting us to join him at the high table. As his words sank in, I was furious.

"Take it as a compliment," suggested Robert. "FitzJohn must think you are someone to be reckoned with."

"But I would never steal anyone's land," I protested.

"FitzJohn seems to think you would," said Aimeric.

"He must feel guilty about the way he came by his domain. Perhaps he should found an abbey. We live in uncertain times."

We were waiting on the dunes when the tide ebbed and the causeway over the sands rose clear of the water. At its far end lay the flat and treeless isle of Lindisfarne.

The priory was a bright new building of golden sandstone. We gave Robert the reins of our horses, and walked into the cool of the church. It was far smaller than the cathedral of Durham, yet the pillars were carved to the same patterns, and the same incense perfumed the air.

By the high altar, one of the shadows moved, and crossing a shaft of sunlight became a monk, who with a smile asked what brought us to Holy Island.

"We come as pilgrims," Aimeric told him, "but also in search of knowledge. I am told that Brother Lawrence of Durham is here, and if it is true, I would dearly love to speak with him."

"And he, I suspect, will be delighted to see you," replied the monk. "I fear he misses the city. I will tell him you are here."

He left by the doorway that gave onto the cloister.

"We may at last be about to get some answers," said Aimeric, "but only at the price of a few straight questions among the crooked ones. Do you trust me?"

"Ask as much as you dare."

"Listen harder than you've ever listened to anything in your life," he told me. "Memorise all he says, however strange it sounds."

The monk reappeared, and beckoned us into the sunlit cloister, where a squat old man was sitting at a desk surrounded by bundles of parchment, some of which came up to his knees. Rising to greet us, he gathered up the scripts that cluttered a bench and invited us to be seated.

"How can I help you?" he asked.

Aimeric told him our names, and that we travelled in the service of Archbishop Thurstan.

"May Christ protect him," murmured Brother Lawrence.

"Amen," said Aimeric. He took a deep breath, and began to lie.

"My master is worried," he said. "Everywhere he goes, he finds people who hunger for books like the Prophecies of Merlin, which speak of the world as if it were ruled by magic. He fears they will forget it is ruled by God. So he has asked me to write the miraculous truth of the saints of our northern past, in a book to give people all the wonder they desire, yet hold their minds to what is real."

"A noble purpose," said Brother Lawrence.

"I have searched the library of York," said Aimeric, "and learnt much from the history of Bede; yet of the centuries that followed his death, I can find no chronicle. Do you know of any book that tells their story?"

Brother Lawrence patted his desk. "There will soon be such a book," he said proudly. "I am gathering together all the documents of Saint Cuthbert's church, and the tale they tell will make a history as great as Bede's. I am only the gatherer; it will be written by Brother Simeon, our precentor. We live, my young friends, in a golden age of learning. The past is unfolding its secrets. There will soon be very little left in darkness."

Aimeric nodded eagerly.

"Then lend me the light of your learning," he begged. "I have heard so many tales, and I need to know if there is truth in them."

Brother Lawrence was only too willing, and Aimeric began to ply him with questions about the saints and churches of Northumbria. It was all obscure to me, but each time that Brother Lawrence answered, I whispered his words under my breath and tried to store them one by one in my memory. It was hard to keep my mind from wandering. In the cloister the air was still and warm. I watched the bees moving among the flowers and herbs of the garden beyond the pillars.

At last, Aimeric came off-handedly to our purpose. "There is another tale, that Simon was told by a monk of Rievaulx," he said, "who heard it as a child from a canon of Hexham. Have you ever heard of a sword called the Sacred Blade?"

"Ah yes," said Brother Lawrence, "the sword of King Edwin and King Oswald, that drove the heathen from Northumbria. Once it was among the treasures of Saint Cuthbert's church, but it has long been lost."

"Lost?" asked Aimeric. "In the tale we heard, it lies buried here in Lindisfarne."

"By my reckoning," the monk replied, "it lies at the bottom of the Irish Sea."

"How?" asked Aimeric. "Why?"

"When the Vikings came, and the kingdom fell," said Brother Lawrence, "the monks fled from Lindisfarne with all their treasures, of which the greatest was the body of the holy Cuthbert. For nine years they wandered Northumbria, until they settled in Chester, from which at last they came to Durham. We know from their writings that they arrived in Chester without the Blade. Somewhere in their wanderings, it had been lost, and such was their shame, they never spoke of it again. We know it is not here in Lindisfarne. It is forty years now since our monks returned, and they turned every stone on the island. They found only graves."

"But why the Irish Sea?" asked Aimeric.

"There was a moment when the monks tried to cross the sea to Ireland. They set sail from the mouth of the Derwent, in Cumbria, but a storm broke out over the sea, and they knew at once it was Saint Cuthbert refusing to leave his land. So they turned back, but in the struggle to reach the shore, many treasures were swept overboard. That is when the gospel-books were miraculously returned by the tides, but when the Sacred Blade must have sunk to the depths."

"Yes indeed," said Aimeric numbly.

Brother Lawrence frowned, and sank into thought. "And yet ... and yet ..." he muttered. He bent to rummage through the heaped scripts. "There is a reference here somewhere," he told us. "I saw it scribbled in the margin of some documents that were bundled together at the time of the Great Rising, when Bishop Aethelwin fled here for safety."

I glanced at Aimeric, who was biting his lip. We had to force ourselves to sit still as Brother Lawrence thumbed through page after page.

"Here it is," he said, pointing to some faint marks on the yellowed vellum. "Listen to this.

> *"Over fresh water*
> *Search for the blade,*
> *Where the hermit of the island*
> *Yet keeps the word."*

"A riddle with an acrostic," said Aimeric. "O,S,W,Y. Was not King Oswy one of the wielders of the Sacred Blade?"

"So he was – an acrostic it is!" said Brother Lawrence. "How clever of you to notice."

"I must certainly write of this in my book," said Aimeric.

Deftly, he turned the talk to other things, and soon afterwards, he thanked Brother Lawrence, and we rose to leave.

When we stepped out of the abbey, Robert was nowhere to be seen. Aimeric ran his fingers through his hair.

"All that for another riddle," he said.

"Are we any wiser?" I asked.

"Oh yes," he said, "wiser than Brother Lawrence. We know the Sacred Blade was not lost on the flight from Lindisfarne."

"Do we?"

"It was hidden," said Aimeric. "The hiding-place became a secret, passed down by word of mouth among Saint Cuthbert's priests – until the time of the Great Rising, when someone hid the song and laid the trail in riddles, for fear the priests were all killed and the secret lost. In truth it must only have been lost thirteen years later, when Bishop William threw the English canons out of Durham; and it was the Normans who lost it, by scattering its keepers."

"And now the keepers are all dead," I said, "and they cannot all have left a daughter like Ulrica to keep the word alive."

"It still makes no sense," said Aimeric. "If the priests of Durham knew its hiding-place, why did they not find it for the leader of the Great Rising?"

"Perhaps because there were too many leaders," I suggested, "and no one man worthy of it."

A shout made us turn. Robert was waving from a brow of rock. We scrambled up to join him, and gazed out over the bay. Away to the south, the fortress of Bamburgh stood on its crag above the sea.

"Look at those heroes over there," said Robert.

The tide was coming in, and the causeway beginning to flood, yet six riders were galloping across it from the mainland. Their horses were kicking up spray.

The rider who led the way had hair and beard the red of fox fur. I had seen his face at Arkill's Garth in the rain. I had seen it by torchlight in the Lake Fells. I had known ever since I left Elmeslac that I was bound to see it again.

12. DAVID'S KINGDOM

ONCE it was clear the riders were going to beat the tides, I began a prayer to Saint Cuthbert.

"Scots, by the look of them," said Robert cheerfully. "At least we'll have company till the tide turns."

He ran down to the priory gate to greet them. My own legs had become icicles, and the cold was rising.

"We may as well go too," I said.

Aimeric took my meaning. "There is nowhere to hide," he agreed.

The riders were dismounting when Robert reached them.

"Drustan!" he called.

One of the Scots turned, and greeted him by name. He had finer clothes than the others, and a Norman saddle, and with a croak of relief I recognised him. It was the companion of Prince Henry who Robert had befriended at the banquet in Durham.

Aimeric and I hurried down, wearing our widest smiles. Fox Fur stared at us. He knew who we were.

The Scot named Drustan pulled him forward. "Robert de Brus, meet Ruari MacGillemor," he said. "He neighbours your father's land in Annandale."

In the tight-lipped greetings that followed, I realised Fox Fur was furious we knew his name. He was as frightened of us as we were of him.

"Well?" Drustan asked him. "You were willing to risk drowning to get here. Is Lindisfarne all you hoped?"

"I came to speak with the monks," said Ruari MacGillemor, and he pushed past us towards the church, with his men at his heels. Drustan waited until they were inside before turning to us with a smile.

"No friend of mine," he explained. "He is from Galloway."

"Say no more," said Robert.

"They rode into Rocksburgh this morning," Drustan told us. "They were asking the road to Lindisfarne, and the sight of men from Galloway on a pilgrimage was so unexpected that it seemed only courteous to bring them."

If they were from Galloway, I thought hopefully, they were as far from home as we were.

"How long is it until the tide goes out, and we can leave?"

"I expect the causeway will be clear in the morning," replied Drustan.

"Only then?"

"You should be grateful," said Drustan. "The monks here are famous for their hospitality."

They certainly made us welcome. There was a guest-house with wooden cots and clean blankets, where they heaped the table with cold pies, fish in wine, cheeses, salads, beer and mead, and left us to feast while in the church they sang Vespers. Ruari Fox Fur and his followers returned, and though they showed us no courtesy, they asked us no questions.

Robert was in the highest spirits and did the talking

for the three of us. He told Drustan that my father was a famous crusader, and he told him how Aimeric was writing a book on the holy places of Northumbria. The more he chattered, the more Aimeric and I winced, for the men from Galloway were all ears.

"So where do you ride next?" asked Drustan.

"Back to our quiet little lives," replied Aimeric. "I have seen all there is to see in the north."

"How can you say that?" protested Drustan. "You have not been to Scotland. You must see the abbeys King David has founded at Jedburgh and Kelsow. They match any in Christendom. You must come to Rocksburgh, and let me take you to visit them. You must be my guests."

"Nothing would please us more," declared Robert.

Neither Aimeric nor I disagreed. Staying close to Robert and Drustan seemed our best chance of staying alive. I was beginning to believe that Drustan must have been sent by Saint Cuthbert.

In the morning, we waited to hear the monks sing Mass, but as the others went to saddle the horses, Aimeric tugged my sleeve, and we stayed in the church. We slipped into the cloister, and found Brother Lawrence settling himself at his desk, while the monks of the priory filed into the chapter-house.

"We have come to say goodbye," Aimeric told him and asked a few last questions about books and saints.

"Last night I was questioned by the young man from Galloway," said Brother Lawrence. "Do you know what he asked me?"

We tried to look as if we could never guess.

"He asked what I knew of the Sacred Blade."

"How curious," said Aimeric. "So the legend still echoes. I will certainly write of it in my book. What did you tell him?"

"All I told you," said Brother Lawrence. "He seemed delighted by the riddle."

Stepping out of the priory, we found Robert and Drustan standing alone beside our horses. Ruari Mac-Gillemor and his men were already on the causeway, and riding at a gallop.

Riding westwards, we soon came to the river Tweed in its green plain. Woods and farmland stretched away to the foot of distant hills.

We followed the southern bank, past the stronghold of Norham, which flew the banner of the bishop of Durham, and on upstream to where a deserted castle kept eyeless guard over a ford. A mile beyond the castle, the track dipped to cross a beck, and as soon as our horses were clear of the water, Drustan bid us welcome to Scotland.

I looked around with surprise. Everything was the same: the birds, the hawthorn, the smell of summer.

Drustan saw my face and laughed. "What were you expecting?" he asked. "A moat? From here, the border leaves the Tweed to run south and curve westwards along the crest of the Northumbrian hills."

"It must be pleasant to be a king," said Aimeric, "and draw lines across the world."

I wondered. It had never occurred to me that a border was no more than a line drawn in the mind; and this border was no more than the line drawn by William Rufus and Malcolm Canmore.

Ahead of us, on a huge motte, stood a castle with ramparts topped with covered walkways, and a tall keep. We were close before we saw that beside it, on a tongue of land shaped by a river flowing into the Tweed, was a trading burgh with its own ring of palisades. On the far side of the Tweed, facing the burgh, there were masons at work, high on the roof of an abbey.

From the castle keep flew the blue boar banner of the house of Canmore. A smell of cooking came over the water.

"Rocksburgh," said Drustan proudly.

"Yes, it can match anywhere in Christendom," Aimeric told him. "Every building I can see is new. Has it often been burned in the past?"

"Indeed not," said Drustan. "There was nothing here when I was born. All this is King David's work."

On the riverbank we dismounted to wait for the ferry.

David FitzMalcolm was sitting on a bench by the doorway of his hall.

As we approached, a bondsman was telling the king he no longer wished to live under the Norman lord that David had set over Liddesdale. David listened patiently, and answered with a generous cunning.

"If you wish to leave the lord I chose for you," he told the man, "it can only be to pass from his service into mine. If that is your choice, I will give you a toft for yourself and your family in the burgh of Renfrew."

The man was all bewildered gratitude. On the ferry, Drustan had told us of the trading burghs David was founding all over his kingdom. Now we knew how he filled them.

When our turn came to speak with him, David took one look at Robert, and broke into a smile.

"I see your father in your face," he told him. "How are my dear Robert, and the lady Agnes?"

"Hiding in Skelton until they see which way the wind blows," answered Robert.

"Have they sent you to me?"

"They do not know I am here," said Robert. "I am nothing to them."

"If you think that," said David, "you do not know them. So what brings you?"

Aimeric blushed his way through our tale of visiting the holy places, and the king listened with growing interest.

"Ride upstream from here, and you come to a place called Melrose," said David. "What can you tell me about it?"

"Was it once a monastery?" asked Aimeric. "I seem to remember the name from the book of Bede."

"It was a monastery," said David, "founded by Aidan of Iona, and it was at Melrose that the blessed Cuthbert became a monk."

Aimeric frowned. "But Saint Cuthbert lived his whole life in Northumbria," he protested cautiously.

"So he did," said David, "and you are standing in Northumbria, for this is Lothian, and Lothian was once a part of the ancient kingdom. Ride out of this fortress, and the countryfolk will speak to you in English."

"So Saint Cuthbert took his vows here?" asked Aimeric.

"He was born here," said David. "He was a shepherd in the hills to the north of us."

He said it with wonder and reverence, as if to him, the holy past were still close. Hearing him talk, I could believe that his mother had been a saint, and it shook me. Of all the lords I had met, David was the only one who seemed born to hold the Sacred Blade. He could see the world it came from. He would know how to use it in ours.

It made me ask myself why we were there, and if Saint Cuthbert could have brought us to him, to tell him all we knew.

"When I think of the glories of the past," said David, "it is never without hoping that one day Northumbria will be whole again."

Before we were aware of it, we were nodding in agreement, and David was studying our faces, watching his words go to work on our minds. To meet his eyes, those gentle eyes, was to doubt my whole quest.

I tried to think how Jordan would respond.

"Are you saying, my lord," I asked, "that you intend to give back Lothian to the kingdom of England?"

David looked at me merrily. "Does England deserve such a gift," he asked, "while it lets an oath-breaker wear the crown?"

I wanted to agree, and I wanted to say far more. I wanted to tell him how clear it was to me now that if ever Northumbria were to be whole again, then he or his son should be its king. Most of all, I wanted to tell him of the Sacred Blade, for I knew the light in his eyes would be blinding. He was watching me expectantly, wondering why it took me so long to reply. The others were watching me. I had to speak. I took a long breath – then in my mind's eye, I saw Aldred, staring into the fire, and my words came out in a rush before I could stop myself.

"Your father broke his oath," I said bitterly, "the oath he swore to help the people of Northumbria, at the time of the Great Rising."

Drustan stared at me in horror, and even Robert looked shocked. After all, it was neither a courteous nor safe thing to say to the son of Malcolm Canmore.

David looked at me thoughtfully. "What you say is true," he admitted, "and the words came from your heart. I will answer from the heart. We cannot change the past, but we can leave it behind. We must all try to live better than our fathers. What is your name?"

"Simon de Falaise."

"Then may you always stand so fast by the truth, Simon."

Drustan and Robert were now as envious as they were relieved.

There was more to the moment than I understood at the time. I had said what I had because I had been brought up by a Northumbrian, and shared his memory. David had answered so honestly, even humbly, because he could see further than most men.

To Drustan he was David MacMalcolm, king of the Scots. But he was also David Margaretson. Half his blood was English; and if that were not enough, he was also David FitzMalcolm, a boy brought up in exile at the Norman court, who had worked with King Henry to bring peace to the north.

He was the one man alive who could see the chess-board from every side.

"I speak of Melrose," he resumed, "because there is soon to be an abbey there once more, and this time for ever. I have offered it to the monks of Rievaulx, and a month from now, the church will be reconsecrated. If you care for the holy places of Northumbria, you must be there. It would please me if you were."

"If only we could linger," said Aimeric regretfully.

"Make Rocksburgh your home," said David. "I will be in Edwinsburgh, but you are welcome to stay here, in the castle, as my guests. In a month we will meet again."

It was our turn for bewildered gratitude. There were others waiting to speak with the king, so we thanked him, and went to stable our horses.

There was an enchantment about the month that followed. It was midsummer, and the plain of Lothian was like a green banner rippling in the breeze.

Aimeric took himself off to the abbey across the river. The monks were from Tiron, near Chartres, and to Aimeric they were a home from home. He never again spoke ill of monks.

Robert and I spent our days with Drustan, and they were full of all but trouble. Once or twice, we rode out hawking, but mostly we just rode, until we had travelled half the tracks of the hills and dales of the Forest of Ettrick. I had never seen so many deer. The people we met had only to hear we were David's guests to make us welcome. Often we slept out in the wilderness, and took it in turn to keep the wolf-watch. I wondered at the patterns of the stars.

One hot day, when Drustan was talking to a glass-maker from Flanders we had met on the road to Jedburgh, Robert at last said what for days I had felt gathering in his mind.

"Have you noticed how many places in Lothian have Norman lords?" he asked. "Most of them were younger sons, with nothing to hope for in England. Drustan tells me there is still land for the taking in the highlands of Albany. I have a mind to offer myself to David, and ask for a domain."

"And Adele?" I asked.

"At least I would have something to offer her," said Robert, "and that old witch Albrea and her daughters would not be able to say I only want Adele for the dowry of land Walter would give."

When David returned to Rocksburgh, there was a tournament on the sward by the castle gates, and Robert almost broke his neck trying to impress. The following evening, as we were idling in the bailey, thirteen white monks rode in on the ponies David had sent to bring them north. Behind them rode Jordan and Orm and Walter Espec.

Jordan crushed me in a hug, then held me at arm's length and looked me over.

"I was beginning to think you were lost," he said.

"I have been," I told him.

He put a finger to my lips. It would be days before we were free to talk.

"So you have seen Northumberland," he said. "How do you like it?"

"Folk still know your name," I told him. "In Bamburgh they told me to get back to hell."

"Yes," said Jordan, "I have just met Eustace FitzJohn myself. It was a disappointment."

Orm came up and squeezed my arm-muscles. "Soft as tripe," he said, then winked.

That night, David honoured us with seats at his high table. He and Walter were old friends. They shared a hidden grief, for David's queen had died a few years before, like Adele's mother. It meant that there was no one to keep the talk to lighter things.

It was hot, and we sweltered in the torchlight.

"How is my son?" asked David.

Walter wiped his beard. "Henry is restless," he said. "One day soon, he will come riding home, and he will be riding empty-handed."

David frowned. "Are you telling me that Stephen will not keep his pledge?" he asked.

"His barons may not let him," said Walter.

Loudly, David's barons began to offer their opinions of King Stephen. David listened, his eyes on Walter. "How many oaths am I wise to let him break?" he asked gently.

"My lord," said Hugh de Morville, the lord of

Lauderdale, "whenever you choose to defend your honour, we are with you."

"And those who love you wish you would wait no longer," said William FitzDuncan, the king's nephew.

David's eyes rested on Walter. "These are the voices I hear every day," he said. "How long can I ignore them? Until my son comes home insulted, perhaps – but then?"

After supper, he asked Aimeric to sing of the Crusade.

A few days later, I stood in a meadow beneath domed hills, listening to the white monks singing their psalms in the church where Saint Cuthbert once prayed. The land was golden with hay under harvest.

I thought how simple it must have been for Saint Cuthbert, with that one bright vision that gave him the path for the rest of his life. My own quest was filling with shadows. I had been looking to learn who was right and who was wrong, and all I had discovered was that people I loved were set to go to war, against people I loved.

We left the next morning. Drustan helped us mount, and we promised to meet again, though we all knew it might never be the same. Robert was almost witless. He hardly said a word.

We followed the Tweed downstream to the border, where the castle that a month before had been silent was now bustling. The gates stood open; sleds of timber were being dragged in by oxen. Carpenters were at work, repairing the palisades.

Walter rode into the bailey and dismounted, and I saw that all the men in the castle were from Elmeslac.

"Is this yours, my lord?" asked Robert.

"This is Carham," said Walter. "Some years ago, when David was only a landless young knight, King Henry gave him this manor, so he could gaze over the Tweed at his inheritance. Later, when David had all Scotland, he gave this to me."

He turned to Aimeric.

"Master scholar, can you write a document to be my witness?"

"Willingly," said Aimeric.

Walter drew his knife and bent down. With a twist of the wrist, he cut a clod of turf from the ground, and held it out to Jordan.

"Jordan de Falaise," he said, "I give you this castle and manor of Carham, to hold at my command, and for you and your son to call your own for as long as your loyalty is true."

Jordan reached out with both hands to grasp his piece of Northumberland. His face said so much, he had no need to speak. He had come home.

"There is more to this than love," said Walter grimly. "If the dragons take to the sky, you are the one man I can think of who might just hold the border."

13. THE DAYS OF GRACE

L ATER, I stood with Walter and Jordan on the roof of the timber keep. In the bright summer moonlight, we could see half the plain of Lothian, the harvested fields the colour of ash, the river like a snake slithering by. Below us, in the torchlit bailey, the laughter in the hall had a sound of distant birdsong.

Walter and Jordan were questioning me on everything that had happened since the day I rode out of Elmeslac.

"The next step, then," said Walter, "must be a stealthy ride to Galloway, to track down this man named MacGillemor, and find out who he serves."

Jordan saw the look on my face.

"Simon has done enough for one year," he said. "He should stay here, and help me rebuild this place."

Walter looked at me thoughtfully.

"Go to Thurstan," he said. "Tell him all you have learnt, and ask him what he thinks must be done. He may well have his own ways of finding out about MacGillemor. He has a bishop in Caerluel, and from Caerluel you have only to cross the sands to be in Galloway."

I glanced at Jordan, who smiled ruefully and gave a shrug. So I would ride south with Walter, while he would busy himself turning Carham back into a stronghold. As he had said, our roads were no longer the same.

"One last thing," said Walter. "You disobeyed me, Simon. I told you to leave Robert out of this."

"I had no choice," I protested. "He threw himself on us, but you should thank the saints he did. On Lindisfarne, he may have saved our lives."

"Does he know of the Sacred Blade?"

"No."

"Nor must he ever: and next time you ride out, leave him behind."

We went down to the hall to rejoin the others. Orm was playing Aimeric's lute, and admiring the craft of its make. Robert looked up, flushed with ale.

"My lord," he said, "you never told me you had castles to give away. When will you give one to me?"

Walter levelled a finger at him, and answered in a voice for the whole hall to hear.

"I gave you Elmeslac," he said, "to guard when I rode south to King Stephen. I thought I could trust you to guard my household and daughter, but what did you do?"

Robert blanched.

"Yes," said Walter, "you ran away to go hunting in Ettrick Forest. From now on, ask for nothing until you have shown you can be trusted with the gift."

When we rode into Elmeslac, and Adele appeared in the doorway of the hall, there was a man at her side. He was young and finely dressed, with a face straight out of a tapestry.

His name, Adele told us, was Roger de Mowbray, and even as we bowed courteously to each other, I could tell that for Robert it was hate at first sight.

"We met at Pickering Fair," said Adele, "and Roger has been a generous companion. Without him, it would have been a dull summer."

I had forgotten how in sunlight her eyes were the colour of honey. She looked bursting with spirit, as if she had bloomed the moment Robert went away.

At supper, Adele found herself with Robert on one side, and Roger de Mowbray on the other. Out of loyalty, I tried to help Robert by keeping his rival distracted.

"How do you come to share the surname," I asked him, "of the man who killed Malcolm Canmore?"

"My mother was his wife before she married my father," replied Roger, "so take care what you say of him."

Robert gave a pronounced frown. "Since when," he asked, "have Normans taken their names from their mothers?"

Adele coloured, but Roger de Mowbray merely smiled.

"Stephen de Blois claimed the crown through the blood of his mother, the Conqueror's daughter," he said. "I take the name of Mowbray because one day I will claim his lands."

Robert laughed derisively. "I would like to be there when you say that to Eustace FitzJohn," he retorted.

Adele glared at him.

"Roger has no need of the Mowbray lands," she said. "When he comes of age, he will inherit the lands left by his own father, who had as many manors and castles as yours."

Nothing could have been more like rubbing salt into Robert's wounds. He hung his head, like a hound, but Adele was almost shaking.

"I only asked," I tried to explain, "because my own grandfather served Robert de Mowbray. He fought with him against William Rufus, and paid the same price."

Roger held out his hand, as if this meant there were a bond between us. His hand had a firm, dry clasp. I liked him.

In the morning, Aimeric and I were up with the dew, but Robert found us when we were still in the stables.

"Wait for me," he said.

"This time, we cannot take you," I told him. "Your place is with Walter, as his squire."

Robert shook his head. "There is nothing for me here."

"You have a place at table beside Adele," I reminded him. "If you want her, win her heart. Are you telling us you cannot do it?"

That stung his Norman pride into a sense of purpose, and before it could wear off, Aimeric and I galloped out of Elmeslac.

Thurstan led us through his palace to an orchard in the crook of the city walls.

We sat on a stone bench, among curious statues, as far away from the world as in the cloister of an abbey. Above the palace roofs, out of the teeming city soared a white cathedral, built on the very ground where King Edwin had raised the first church in Northumbria, where kings had once prayed with the Sacred Blade at their belt.

When we told Thurstan all that had happened, he said we had done well.

"Now tell me," he said, "how it has marked you."

"I must confess," I said, "that I saw nothing but good in King David. Why should we fight him? Why fear him? If his kingdom stretched south to the Humber, it would hardly be the end of the world."

"No," agreed Thurstan, "but it would be the end of mine. Remember, I was born in Normandy. I owe all I have to the Conqueror's sons, and I have spent my life serving their kingdom. Like David, I am too old to change."

He smiled at the confusion he saw in our faces.

"It would be a simpler world if evil lay always over the border," he said, "but David believes what he will, and I believe what I must. There is good and evil in both of us, but we will be judged by what we wanted, and how we worked for it."

"If we find the Sacred Blade," said Aimeric, "will you use it against him?"

"I would tell him of it," said Thurstan thoughtfully. "If it came to me, not to him, I would put it to him as a sign that Saint Cuthbert does not choose him as the guardian of his people. This riddle you learnt on Lindisfarne:

> *Over fresh water*
> *Search for the blade,*
> *Where the hermit of the island*
> *Yet keeps the word.*

"Does it mean anything to you?"

"Nothing," said Aimeric, "except that the answer lies with Saint Cuthbert. He must be the hermit of the island."

"So we are no closer to finding the Sacred Blade?"

"Our way now leads to Galloway," I said, "to track down MacGillemor and find his master."

"No," said Thurstan. "That is out of the question."

"Even with the help of the bishop of Caerluel?" I asked.

"I have no bishop in Caerluel," said Thurstan bleakly. "David has barred him from the city."

"Why?" asked Aimeric.

"A quarrel about churches," answered Thurstan, "of the kind that would make Saint Cuthbert eat his beard. It served David's purpose."

"In the chess-game?" I asked.

"Exactly," said Thurstan, "and it means that at this moment, the last castle loyal to King Stephen is Appleby in the Vale of Eden, a long ride short of Caerluel. So I forbid you even to cross Stainmoor. It would not be safe. For weeks we have had nothing but rumours out of Cumbria."

"Unless we go," said Aimeric, "soon nowhere will be safe."

"Wait until spring," said Thurstan firmly. "By then, either reason will have prevailed or we will be at war. If it is peace, we will ride to Caerluel together."

"But we spent the whole of last winter waiting for spring!" I protested. "How much longer can we live with this knowledge and do nothing?"

He held up a hand to hush me, and his sleeve fell back to show his arm, withered by age and sickness, the veins like ivy on a dead branch.

"Do you think I find it easy to wait?" he asked gently. "All I am offering you is the winter. The days of grace are coming to an end. Make all you can of the few that remain."

The long feast was over, and almost everyone in the castle of Elmeslac was asleep.

To keep warm, I had brought my bedding from the guest-lodge to the hall, and now I lay stretched out beside Robert among the men-at-arms, the servants, and the hounds. The air was thick with hearthsmoke and the lingering scents of the Yuletide revelries. I was thinking of Carham, on its motte above the Tweed, and wondering how Jordan and Orm were keeping Twelfth Night, when Robert gave a start and rolled over onto his stomach, propping himself up on his elbows to stare into the dying fire.

"Has a ghost walked through your sleep?" I whispered.

He turned to me, his eyes shieldless and stricken. "I have lost her," he said.

"God knows," I replied, "you have had little enough chance to win her."

We had spent the autumn in a grim round of hearings and juries, riding as Walter's escort, while behind us in Elmeslac, Adele and Roger de Mowbray went hawking. Roger had taken Adele to keep Twelfth Night at his castle of Thirsk, and her cousins had gone with them. At Elmeslac we had had minstrels, but no Adele.

"She will be back tomorrow," I said, "and you still have two months to Candlemas, and the end of your year and a day."

Robert only groaned.

"Why was I so blind?" he asked. "What made me vow myself to her in front of the whole household? When she rejects me, they will laugh in my face."

"They will judge you by how you take it," I said roughly, for a part of me wanted him to fail. Watching Adele set out for Thirsk, I had been jealous, and not for Robert's sake but for mine. With Roger, Adele had somehow come to trust herself, and her every movement now was luminous and carefree.

But when in the morning they came back, Adele was subdued and Roger hurried away. When he had gone, she disappeared into the women's chambers, and at supper she sat with her cousins, not with Robert and me.

A week went by without a visit from Roger de Mowbray; then one morning, when Robert had ridden out with Walter, Adele asked me to accompany her to Kirkdale.

There was frost on every blade of grass, and the sunlight dazzled. We startled some herons, but Adele left her hawk hooded on her wrist. Her mind was far away.

"Is Roger not coming back?" I asked.

"Oh, he will come," she said, "when he can."

"Has something changed?"

"Between us, no – but his mother has forbidden him to marry me."

"Why?" I asked, angry for her. "How could she meet you and not like you?"

"I dare say she likes me," said Adele, "as the daughter of a neighbour – but she has high hopes for Roger. She will not let him marry the bastard daughter of a sheriff."

For the first time, I heard bitterness in her voice.

"You still have Robert," I suggested, but I knew as soon as it was out that it was the wrong thing to say. Adele glared at me.

"When I first met you both," I went on, "you seemed like brother and sister."

"Sometimes," said Adele, "I wish you had never come into our lives."

"That is cruel," I protested. "You cannot blame me for changing Robert."

Adele gave me a look of reproach, as if I had missed her meaning.

"No one," she said wearily, "will ever change Robert."

"You could," I insisted. "He would do anything for you. Look at the longing in his eyes. Look at the way he is suffering."

"I think I know what it is to love and not be loved in return," she said. "He will live."

Then she asked so many questions, about when and why I might ride away, that I needed all my wits to remember what I could and could not say.

I could do nothing to help either Robert or Adele. They were locked in a spell that made it unbearable to them to see each other. Adele would not look at Robert for fear of the hope he might take from it, and Robert could not bring himself to look at Adele to see her turn away. Adele was wilting, unsure of herself again, and Robert was like a bear on a chain. It tore my heart, and taught me how I loved them.

Robert began to talk endlessly of our time in Rocksburgh, and it was easy to guess the drift of his mind. He would serve out the year and a day of his vow to Adele, but when it was finished, he would not stay to hear people tell him why he had failed. He would ride north and offer himself to King David.

One morning, I rode to Rievaulx and asked to speak with Brother Aelred. He met me in a draughty passage which was one of the few places in the abbey where the monks were allowed to break their silence.

"There is nothing you can do," was his comment when I had told him of Robert and Adele.

"But it hurts so much to watch."

"Love and peace are often strangers," said Aelred, and his face flinched as if there were torment in his memory, and he spoke from bitter experience. "It is your powerlessness that hurts you most. We cannot change those we love, but we can be true to ourselves, and constant in our love for them."

When I thanked him for the talk and made to leave, he looked surprised. "Is that truly why you came?" he asked. "I thought Walter must have sent you, to ask if I know of the challenge."

"The challenge?"

"You have not heard?"

"Tell me."

Aelred looked miserable. "Abbot Richard has just returned from Melrose," he said. "He was frightened by the talk he heard in Rocksburgh. Prince Henry has ridden home, insulted by the lords of Stephen's court."

I closed my eyes.

"And King David?" I asked.

"King David has made it known that if Northumberland is not given to his son, he will take it by force."

14. BEYOND THE KING'S LAW

R OBERT and Adele were spared the ordeal of a final admission of defeat. Like so much else in so many lives, the crown of thorns their love had become was swept to the winds by David's challenge. On the night when the year and a day of Robert's vow reached its term, Robert and I were far away from Elmeslac, chilled to the bone keeping watch on the ramparts of Newcastle.

We had ridden there with Walter, when King Stephen called his loyal subjects to defend his northern border. Roger de Mowbray rode with us, at the head of his father's liegemen and household veterans, but Robert de Brus of Cleveland kept to his moors.

Once at Newcastle, there were quarrels over what to do next. To ride on would have been a challenge in itself, for David had not even crossed the border. His challenge made, he was watching us, biding his time, and even though our gathering was Stephen's reply, David made no move to take Northumberland.

So we settled down to wait, on winter rations that gave us all the gut flux. We had been there five months when Aimeric at last came to find me.

"The road to Galloway?" I asked eagerly, for I was

more than willing to face Ruari MacGillemor, if only it would get me out of Newcastle.

"Thurstan still forbids it," said Aimeric, "but he has learnt that at Malmesbury there is a monk who has been studying the past. He has written several histories, and they call him the most learned man in England. Thurstan thinks we should take him our questions."

As I said my farewells, I used the old story of the book Aimeric was writing for Thurstan. Walter guessed the truth. He kissed me on the cheeks and gave me a purse of silver.

"If you are riding south," said Roger de Mowbray, "break your journey in Thirsk. My mother will make you welcome, and you can tell her all goes well with me."

Robert was the last to say farewell. He followed us broodingly out to our horses, and only then thrust out his hand and wished me good fortune. He said it with such feeling that I knew he would not be with Walter when I returned.

"Good fortune, Robert," I said sadly. "Give my regards to Drustan."

"How did you know?" he asked in astonishment.

"You talk in your sleep," I told him, so we parted with a laugh; but I was howling inside as with Aimeric I rode through the streets of the fortress-town and down to the swaying wooden bridge over the Tyne. In his desperate way, Robert had been the truest of friends, and it hurt to think that our roads would never again be the same.

The lady Gundreda de Mowbray sat presiding over a high table of linen-swathed maidens and old men, in a castle built in the loop of a river that curled out of the moors into the great plain of York.

She was old, but with more wits than most, and a voice that crackled like burning bramble. She listened serenely as we told of the thinning ranks at Newcastle, as if she had known too many alarms in her life to feel threatened by a king of the Scots.

"So Roger has yet to cover himself with glory?" she asked. "I suppose that if David ever strikes, Roger will shine all the more if the other lords have gone home."

"Who are your guests?" Aimeric asked her, for we had been wondering ever since we walked in. At a table to themselves sat a chapter of monks, their white cassocks muddy, their faces unshaven; and they were wolfing down their supper as though it were the eve of Lent.

"They were the monks of Calder Abbey," she replied, "until the roof was burned over their heads."

"But I thought Calder lay on the far coast of Cumbria?" asked Aimeric.

"So it did," said the lady Gundreda. "They fled over Stainmoor with eight oxen and a single heaped cart. My steward saw them trailing past this afternoon, on their way to beg a new home from Thurstan."

Aimeric looked at them thoughtfully.

"Like the monks of Saint Cuthbert on their flight from Lindisfarne," he said. "I never thought to see it in my own lifetime."

"Then prepare yourself for worse," the lady Gundreda calmly advised him, "for from what they told my steward, this may only be the beginning. The men of Galloway are running wild."

After supper, Aimeric and I went to speak with the abbot. He was too shaken by the horrors of his flight to be able to tell us much. All we could do was assure him that Thurstan would be quick to help.

One of the monks seemed to be watching me intently from under his hood, as far as I could tell. When the brothers rose to file out to the chapel, he paused beside me.

"I heard you say your name was Simon de Falaise," he remarked in a low voice.

"What of it?" I asked warily.

He kept his eyes on the ground. I could see nothing of his face.

"Is Jordan de Falaise your father?"

"Why do you ask?"

"I have a message for one of his followers, a man named Orm Sigurdsson."

"Where were you given it?" I asked.

"In a village called Longthwaite."

"Give me the message," I told him. "I will see it reaches Orm."

"Tell him, then, that Sigrid Hoskuldsdaughter begs him to come at once."

The monk hurried after his brothers. Shaken, I looked around the hall. The lady Gundreda and her maidens were withdrawing and bidding us goodnight.

The message burnt a hole in my mind. Sigrid had called for help; Sigrid, and not Hoskuld or Thord. Something bad must have happened. Orm was at Carham, a week's ride away, while Ullswater, from Thirsk, I could reach in three days.

For Sigrid, I could walk it in three days.

At first light, I dressed and bundled my belongings. Aimeric poked his head out from under the blanket, his hair lying across his face like a raven's wing.

"Why the hurry?" he asked.

"Go back to sleep," I told him. "I am going to Cumbria."

He jumped as if I had pushed a thistle down the neck of his cassock.

"Wait!" he said. "I believe we should discuss this calmly for a moment."

"No. My heart tells me to go, and it is a while since my heart last told me so clearly what to do."

"What makes you think the men of Galloway have hearts?" He asked. "What will happen if they find you?"

"God alone knows," I admitted, "but Aelred of Rievaulx once told me that the only way to help those we love is by being true to ourselves – so today I follow my heart."

Aimeric glowered at me, then reached for his sandals.

"You do not have to come," I told him.

"You forget I am a scholar," he said. "I came to England hoping to find miracles and wonders, but I never in my wildest dreams thought I would get the chance to see a Norman following his heart."

Two days later, we had crossed the wilderness of Stainmoor and were riding down the Vale of Eden.

The gates of Brough were closed, but when we called up to the guards that we served Thurstan, they welcomed us in. At supper, we had to account for ourselves to Ivo the castellan. He did all he could to persuade us to go no further.

"What takes you?" he asked in exasperation. "What is so important?"

"Church business," said Aimeric.

"Well, keep to the road and travel only in daylight," said Ivo. "You may even get there."

In the morning, we rode along a Vale of Eden greening with midsummer. We were soon past Appleby, and the last castle loyal to King Stephen.

Then we came to a village that had been torn to pieces. Bodies lay in the open, swollen and speckled with flies. Some were broken and spread-eagled, as if they had fallen from the sky; others curled up as if they had fallen asleep. As far as we could tell, they had all been men. The women and children must have fled or been carried off.

We rode through, choking on the smell. The next two villages we passed were deserted. A masterless dog ran after us until it dropped to the ground, whining until we were out of sight.

"You thought you would never see monks in flight," I told Aimeric. "I never thought I would see the return of the Waste Land."

Saddle-sore, sickened, and full of foreboding, we came at last to the round hill, the wooded valley like a gateway, and the lake long and silver among fells green with new bracken.

At Longthwaite, the villagers were shearing their sheep – only where Hoskuld Sigurdsson's hall had stood, there was nothing but charred timber. The roof-pillars Orm had carved as a boy were no more than blackened stumps.

As we rode up, I recognised Armod and Bardi – and Sigrid, her hair bound in a thick plait that frayed at the end into a horse-tail of gold.

"What do you want?" called Bardi.

"Look," Sigrid told him. "It is Simon de Falaise."

There were grunts of recognition. The hostility left their faces, but nothing took its place.

Sigrid had grown tall, and her face now had a gauntness to it. Everything about her had hardened. She greeted me with no more than surprise, and even that was guarded. She saw me glance down at her hand and catch sight of her wedding ring.

She met my gaze, but only as if it came from a great distance, and her eyes gave no sign of any kind. I had to struggle to hold back a cry. For two years I had been dreaming of this moment – of all I would tell her, and how it would be – and now all my dreams were blown away with a single glance. I was face to face with the Sigrid of my longings, but not the Sigrid of my dreams.

The villagers were waiting for me to speak. I remembered who I was to them: a Norman who had ridden up with a sword at his belt, who had come once before and brought nothing but trouble. Haltingly, as if I were searching for the words of a song half-forgotten in the back of my memory, I began to speak with all the courtesy Adele had ever taught me.

"My lady," I said to Sigrid, "a monk of Calder gave me your message to Orm. Orm is far away, in Northumberland, so I came at once with my friend, Aimeric of Chartres, to offer you our help."

The way they looked at each other made me realise how ridiculous I must sound. Armod shook his head.

"We do not want help," he said. "We want vengeance, and that is for Orm to take, not you."

Aimeric slid from his saddle to the ground. "All I want is something to drink," he said. "I have never ridden so far, so fast."

Sigrid clapped a hand to her cheek.

"You must forgive us," she said. "You are welcome."

They served us ale in one of the longhouses and, as we drank, they told their story.

A month before, the raiders from Galloway had struck the eastern fells. Hoskuld had sent the women and children to shielings high in Grisedale and put out watchers, but the raiders had come over the fells from Matterdale and taken the village by surprise. There had been fighting, and when the raiders left, they dragged Hoskuld and Arni with them.

"They left three dead," said Armod, "and we lost Thord Hoskuldsson."

He spoke on, telling me where else there had been raids, but all I could think of was Thord – Orm's nephew, Thord. He had been like Orm without the beard. He had taught me to use a bow. He had been my own age and now he was dead.

"Did you see the raiders' faces?" I asked, dreading the reply.

"Their leader was the man who came hunting your father," said Armod. "He had a beard the red of old bracken."

Aimeric and I exchanged glances of horror. Thord had been killed because of the Sacred Blade. I felt guilty, and from the guilt came an anger that made me vow to see through whatever it took to find the Sacred Blade before any more of those I loved were killed. If there were any way of bringing MacGillemor to justice, I would find it.

"His name is Ruari MacGillemor," I told Armod. "When we find him, I swear you will have your vengeance."

"These two who were carried off," said Aimeric, "do you know if they are still alive?"

"That is the worst of it," said Armod. "We have been told that all over Cumbria, the raiders took folk to hold to ransom, but a month has gone by and we have heard nothing."

"Have you been to Caerluel?" I asked.

"What good would it do?"

"King David will have a constable there," I said. "When he hears what has happened, he will hunt MacGillemor down. If he refuses, we will take the tale to David himself."

"You would do that?" Armod asked warily.

"Leave it to us," I assured him. "King David is our friend."

They looked unconvinced. So did Aimeric.

We ate together, without much laughter. Afterwards, I remembered the horses and went to stable them; and returning, I found Sigrid outside the longhouse, wearing an apron and gloves to stuff the greasy shearings of wool into sacks. I offered to hold the sacks, and the work went quickly.

"Do you believe you will find Arni and my father?" she asked.

"If MacGillemor had only come for revenge, he would have killed them," I said. "I believe he took them alive to ask a ransom for them, but it is a ransom he will be asking of my father, or of me, not of you. Do not ask me to explain, but when we find MacGillemor, we will find your father and Arni alive and well. Of that I am sure."

Sigrid's eyes widened as she listened. "How do you sleep," she asked, "knowing a man like that is your enemy?"

"Life has its rewards," I said gaily. "I have land. I am the heir to a castle in Northumberland. You would like it."

"Is there a lake?" she asked.

"There is a deep river, a wide plain, and hills in the distance like these, but not so wild."

"Then I am glad for you," she said warmly, but that was all. It filled her with no longing. It changed nothing. Sigrid had her life, and all she wanted now was Arni and her father safely home. We had come to the last of the sacks. In a moment we would go back inside, and the chess-board had burned with the hall.

"I would be happy," I said, "if I could only forget you, and how we danced."

"We never danced," said Sigrid. "It was long ago, and you were still a boy with eyes full of hope and wonder. Now you look as if you are haunted by demons."

I turned towards her with a face full of longing.

"No," she said fiercely. "Do not say it." She stood there, caught in the light of a silver moon rising over the fells.

"I will never forget you," I told her.

She looked at me, shaking her head and laughing.

"And I," she promised, "will never forget that you came back to tell me."

To the north of the Lake Fells stretched the Forest of Inglewood, through which Aimeric and I must pass to reach Caerluel. For safety, we chose the wildest tracks, and rode all day through heavy rain, seeing no one. It was as much by luck as by skill that at dusk we came to Caerluel, standing at the centre of its wooded plain like a spider at the hub of its web.

With heads down, we followed the swilling gutter of the main street to the gateway of the fortress where we were challenged by the guards. I gave a Norman answer.

"Who is the constable here?" I demanded angrily.

"The lord William FitzDuncan."

I grinned with relief. FitzDuncan was King David's nephew. I remembered him from Rocksburgh. "We have business with him," I told the guards. "Let us through."

Once inside the bailey, we dismounted beneath a massive keep of blood-coloured stone. The round-arched windows of the upper floors were outlined by torchlight. Throwing the reins of our horses to a groom, we ran up the wooden stairway and in out of the rain.

We found ourselves in a banqueting-hall where shields and hunting-trophies hung from the rafters. Servants were turning a boar on a spit over a fire-place built in the wall. The tables were being set up for supper, and at the high table, knights were already gathering.

Shaking the rain from our hair, we walked towards them. I recognised the stocky figure of William FitzDuncan, and was halfway through my speech of greeting when I saw that beside him, watching me intently, a frown to his eyebrows the colour of fox fur, sat Ruari MacGillemor.

15. CAERLUEL

JUDGING by the lines that seamed his cheeks and the corners of his eyes, William FitzDuncan was old enough to be my father. A moustache thatched his upper lip, but he wore his hair short and he was dressed in the Norman fashion.

With a tilt of his hand, he signalled that we might be seated. "Whom do you serve?" he asked.

"Archbishop Thurstan," I replied, sensing that he already knew who we were. My wits were thrashing like branches in the wind.

"Then I wonder what brings you here," he drawled. "Caerluel is no longer any concern of Thurstan."

As angrily as I could, I told him of the monks of Calder, and of Sigrid's message.

"So men have been killed," I said, "and two men dragged from their homes – and it shocks me, my lord, to see the man who did this sitting at your side."

MacGillemor guffawed, and others at the table laughed as loudly. FitzDuncan ran a finger round the rim of his cup.

"It was done at my wish," he said. "Those men sheltered my enemies. If they are your friends, you must also be my enemies."

My mouth was going dry. This man was a troll. If he wanted, he could eat us for supper.

"We serve only the Church," said Aimeric indignantly. "Surely the Church has no enemies?"

"I would say that depends on what the Church tells its servants to do," replied FitzDuncan. "Perhaps there is a way you could soften my heart towards your friends. I hear you have been searching the holy places. Tell me what you know of the Sacred Blade."

Aimeric contorted his face into a look of interest and scholarly delight. "The sword of the old kings of Northumbria?" he asked. "Such a curious tale. Yes, we came across it in our studies of the past."

"What did you find?"

Aimeric gave a shrug that looked more like a shiver. "A song and a riddle or two."

"And what are they?"

"I cannot remember," said Aimeric blithely. "I had them written down on a scrap of vellum, but for some strange reason it was stolen."

"I know," said FitzDuncan. "That also was done on my orders."

We contrived to look shocked.

"But why?" asked Aimeric. "Why is an old tale so important to you?"

"Let me ask the questions," he suggested. "How did you first hear of it?"

He was looking at me. With MacGillemor beside him, who had seen us at Arkill's Garth, and tracked us to the Lake Fells on the strength of it, there was a limit to how far I could lie.

"When I was a child," I said, "my grandmother told

me a riddle about a place named Arkill's Garth. A year or two ago, I found myself there. My father and a friend were sheltering from the rain, and I went wandering in an old mine. I was groping my way along a wall when a stone fell out and behind it was a scroll. It must have been there for years, waiting for someone to find it."

Their eyebrows were beginning to rise.

"So what did you do?" asked FitzDuncan.

"That same day, in Brough, I gave it to Archbishop Thurstan. He told me it was meaningless, like the Prophecies of Merlin."

Aimeric nodded eagerly.

"Last year, I began to write a book on the saints," he joined in, "and Simon rode with me to their shrines. He told me his tale and we set out to see if we could find any more riddles. All we found was a monk on Lindisfarne who gave us a riddle as bewildering as the other, but who also told us he knows the Sacred Blade to be lost in the depths of the Irish Sea."

FitzDuncan stroked his moustache. There was no way of knowing if he believed us or not.

Just then, a steward came into the hall. "My lord," he said, "the prior of Wetheral is at the gate."

FitzDuncan abruptly lost interest in us. "Shut these two away," he ordered, "in separate holes."

We were seized from behind and pinioned. Someone unbuckled my sword-belt.

"My lord!" protested Aimeric. "We are servants of the Church!"

"Pray, then," said FitzDuncan.

Half-marched, half-carried, we were hurried down a stairway set in the walls into the vaults of the keep. In a passage lit by torches, we were separated. I was pushed through a doorway, and the slam as they closed it sent me stumbling down a flight of steps onto a heap of sacks.

The footsteps receded, and I was left in darkness with the sound of my stampeding heart.

Beside me, I heard a shuffling.

"Hoskuld?" I whispered.

No one answered. I seemed to be alone.

At least I was still alive, and they were unlikely to come and torment me while the prior of Wetheral was eating his supper.

For the first time in months, I slept without dreaming, and woke to see a thin shaft of sunlight falling from a window-slit high in the wall. Standing over me, biting the knuckles of her hands, was a girl.

"Catriona of Morpeth," I said. "I should have known I would find you with your master."

She shrank away into the shadows, but not before I saw that her cheek was swollen and bruised and her hair filthy.

"How long have you been here?" I asked.

She made no reply, and huddled against the wall. I wondered if FitzDuncan had cut out her tongue.

I looked around. We were alone in a storage vault. The walls were mossy with damp, the floor strewn with rubble.

Dropping to my knees, I gathered two dozen small pebbles; then, where the sunlight touched a slab of paving, I scratched a grid of lines. When it was finished, I laid the pebbles in place and looked up at the girl.

"My lady," I asked, "will you join me in a game of draughts?"

The evil of dungeons, Jordan had once told me, was that they were places where the first thing you lost were your wits.

It might have been noon when the door was opened for as long as it took a man to set down food at the top of the steps. There was a bowl of scraps from the hall, some trenchers of the day before's bread, and a jug of water.

We set the bowl between us on the floor and made the most of it. With the courtesy Adele had taught me, I offered the choicest morsels to my companion, and as she ate I was relieved to see there was nothing wrong with her tongue.

When the feast was over, we turned back to the game of draughts. By and by, whenever I glanced at Catriona, I caught her watching me. Her eyes were a greyish blue, and her face freckled, with a thin mouth and a sharp chin. So lank was her hair that her ears poked through like tree mushrooms.

We played draughts until the shaft of sunlight rose and faded. Not a word was said. No one came to trouble us, or bring supper. At dusk, I stretched out on the heap of sacks, but Catriona kept to a stone bench that ran along the far wall, watching, watching.

Only when it was dark did she come crawling onto the sacks beside me.

"My lord," she said, "I meant you no harm when I robbed you."

"No need to rob me now," I told her. "I have nothing worth stealing."

"It was done on my master's orders."

"FitzDuncan is your master?"

"Yes," she said, giving the word a soft hiss of hatred.

"Then what," I asked, "are you doing in this hole

with a clout-bruise on your face?"

"He has finished with me," said Catriona. "I began to see too far into his purpose."

I turned eagerly – but gently, so as not to startle her.

"Tell me his purpose," I said. "I must know."

She hesitated, and when at last she spoke I knew she had been searching for the question by whose answer she would know if she could trust me.

"My lord," she said, "do you love King David?"

"I do not love the son of Malcolm Canmore threatening war," I answered carefully. "The man I love is David Margaretson, sitting in sunlight by the door of his hall, generous to strangers, and wise."

"Then if you leave here alive," said Catriona, "you must take him a warning. Tell him that FitzDuncan seeks to destroy him."

"But FitzDuncan is David's nephew," I protested. "David shows him nothing but favour."

"My master wants the crown," she whispered, as if he were listening at the door to catch her betrayal. "His father was king. He has a claim, but David and Prince Henry stand in his way."

"How on earth does he hope to destroy them?" I asked.

"He seeks to drive them to war with the Normans. He knows it will be their end, just as it was Malcolm Canmore's."

I marvelled at the cunning of it.

"Do you not believe me?" asked Catriona.

"I believe you."

No wonder FitzDuncan sought the Sacred Blade. I could imagine him striding into Rocksburgh to lay it at the feet of his king, declaring that God had sent a sign that the

Normans were to be swept from Northumbria and that David, like Saint Oswald and with Saint Oswald's blade in his hand, was to strike from the north and win the kingdom.

"How," I asked, "are we to get out of here and warn David? Do you know what has become of the two Cumbrians MacGillemor seized? Their names are Hoskuld and Arni."

"They are here," she said, "in another of the cellars."

"So is my friend Aimeric. How do you think your master will treat us?"

She went silent.

"If you are one of us," I said, "then he has five of us to kill."

"It is always MacGillemor," said Catriona, "who does the killing."

I went cold as she said it, and then came the first sick shiver of helplessness. "No one will ever know."

Catriona gave a tiny cry and reached for me and we clung together, not out of longing but out of fear, because we needed each other's touch to believe we were alive. At sunrise, she twisted free of me, but as the morning dragged by and we waited, I only had to look into her eyes to steal a glint of her will to keep strong.

At midday, the door was opened, but it slammed again as soon as food had been set down. We took it as a reprieve, as a sign that we had at least another day to live; and when we had eaten, we began to talk. Little by little, Catriona told me her story.

The child of a serving-girl, she had never known her father. When she came into bloom, she had caught FitzDuncan's eye, and when he saw what she was made of, he had used her for her wits. She could echo any voice she heard, and speak in turn as if she came from Lothian, or

Galloway, or Saint Cuthbert's Land. FitzDuncan had used her to listen and spy and steal, and now she was used up, and frightened.

So was I, but together we were strong. As day followed day, and no one came to trouble us, a tenderness grew between us, and in its wake came shyness. We no longer clung together through the dark – until one night, I woke to see moonlight pouring through the window-slit. Catriona was crouched beside me, watching me. When she saw me stir, she reached for me, and it was not out of fear.

"If you wake me," I warned her, "I may never sleep again."

"Nor will I," she promised.

It was then, in the deep dungeon of Caerluel, that Catriona unlocked the door of love, and led me out to the fulfilment of all my longings. What we found was so much richer than anything I had ever imagined, that when I woke again, long after daybreak, to find her still in my arms, I could do nothing but smile.

The days became weeks, and the nights grew colder. We had been forgotten by the world, but in ourselves, we had never been more alive. All my senses had been quickened, even my hearing.

Through the walls I could hear nothing, but through the window-slit above our heads I learnt to guess what was happening in the bailey. I could tell when it was Sunday or market-day. I caught snatches of chatter, greetings, and orders, but never a word of King David or King Stephen.

Then one day, I heard horses and loud voices and laughter, and in the midst of it all were two voices I knew.

Jumping up, I clawed at the wall, trying to climb to the window-slit; but my toes could find nothing to grip.

"What is it?" asked Catriona.

"Help me reach the window!"

She ran and crouched beneath me and, with a foot on her head, I was able to swing my right hand high and grip the sharp sill of the window. I hung there, panting, and my fingers began to uncurl, but then Catriona grasped my feet and pushed. Lunging upwards, I got my left hand to the sill, and pulled with all the life I had left.

The window-niche was angled and the sill sloping. It thrust my elbows outward, and I had to arch like a bow, toes to the wall, to get my face to the slit. I was blinded by sunlight as my cheeks scraped the stone.

"Robert!" I shouted. "Drustan!"

I yelled and yelled until the horsemen were milling beneath me.

"Simon?"

It was Robert's voice.

"Robert, for the love of Christ, help me!"

Even as I shouted, I was falling. I landed on my feet and crumpled heavily to the floor.

I was sitting there, rubbing my heels, when the door was unbolted. Catriona shrank into a corner as one of FitzDuncan's men came down the steps and dragged me to my feet.

"Lucky boy," he said. "You have powerful friends. I trust you'll tell them how well we've fed you."

I was marched up the stairway into the banqueting-hall, and through a crowd of knights to where FitzDuncan sat at the high table, Prince Henry of Scotland at his side. Then Robert came and pushed the guard away, and behind him was Drustan.

"My God, look at you!" said Robert, and the two of them burst out laughing. "How long have you been here?"

At the high table, Prince Henry turned to Fitz-Duncan.

"Why is this man in your dungeon?" he asked.

FitzDuncan frowned and stroked his moustache. "I forget," he said.

"I came here for justice," I said, and poured out my tale of Sigrid's message, of the raiding of Longthwaite, and the welcome I had been given at Caerluel.

"Now I remember," said FitzDuncan. "I threw him into the hole because no servant of Thurstan deserves anything less."

Prince Henry gave a groan. "You should be filling your pits with the outlaws of Galloway," he said reproachfully, "not with servants of the Church."

"Well, you can have him if you wish," said FitzDuncan.

"And Aimeric," I said, "and Hoskuld, and Arni, and Catriona. They are all in your cellars, when they should be free."

Everyone was staring at me. FitzDuncan affected a chuckle. "Why not?" he said. "Take whoever you want, and get out of my sight."

"You always did keep a full household," remarked Prince Henry.

FitzDuncan gave the order, and the captives were brought up from the vaults. Catriona ran to my side, and behind her, filthy and uncertain, came Hoskuld and Arni and Aimeric. I glanced at FitzDuncan, but he merely waved us towards the door.

I knew then that he was calling off his search for the Sacred Blade. He no longer needed it. The war he wanted so much was on its way.

Squinting in the sunlight, we stood in the bailey

waiting for our horses to be brought. Drustan and Robert had followed us out, and Drustan seemed mightily embarrassed by the thought of what our treatment had done to tarnish the good name of Scottish hospitality.

"At least stay and eat with us," he protested.

"No," said Aimeric. "We must get away."

Aimeric looked frightened that at any moment he would wake up back in the dark. When he had first appeared at the head of the stairway from the vaults, I had hardly recognised him. He had grown a thick black beard, and with his large dark eyes and wasted cheeks, he looked like the emperor of Constantinople on a gold besant.

Robert, too, had changed. I had never known him look so happy in his own skin.

"So now you are David's man?" I asked him.

"I could never be Stephen's," he said disdainfully. "Nor could you, I suppose, now."

"Why?" I asked. "What has happened?"

"Have you not heard, then," asked Robert, "how he has taken to trying to ambush his own barons?"

I was not sure I wanted to. I was beginning to have my doubts about Stephen de Blois.

"These things happen," I said. "My grandfather was one of the ambush that killed Malcolm Canmore."

"At least your grandfather got it right," retorted Robert. "Stephen is doomed. He will be gone within a year. Follow your heart, Simon. Come with us."

"We serve Thurstan, not Stephen," I said uneasily.

The grooms brought our horses: Aimeric's palfrey and shaggy old Loki, and garrons for Hoskuld and Arni. Robert helped me mount, while Drustan lifted Catriona to sit behind me.

"For your own sake, use your wits before it is too late,"

pleaded Robert.

"You would be welcome," added Drustan.

The others were already trotting towards the gateway. Whatever I wanted, it was not to be left behind.

"Tell David," I said, "that FitzDuncan wants his crown and will kill for it."

Robert and Drustan looked incredulous.

"Just tell him," I said, and heeled Loki to follow the others. Catriona grabbed me round the waist to hold on. My last glance at Robert caught him staring at her curiously.

It was autumn in the Forest of Inglewood. The leaves were amber and gold, the brambles dry and brown. The world had changed while we were prisoners. It was like waking from an evil enchantment.

The horses were breathless from being so long unridden, but we came at last to the Lake Fells. In the first wide dale, Hoskuld turned to Aimeric and me.

"Your way lies west," he told us. "You'll come to Threlkeld, and then a circle of stones on a hill. After that, just follow your eyes." He looked at Catriona. "This little sparrow had better come with us."

Catriona tightened her grip on my waist, and dug her chin into the back of my neck.

"No, go with Hoskuld and Arni," I told her. "You will be safe at Longthwaite."

"Will you come later?" she asked.

"Of course he will," said Hoskuld, "and when he does, there will be a feast. I never thought I would have a Norman to thank for my life. You can tell Orm he is lucky in his friends."

Arni said much the same, and I had to admit I liked him. Sigrid had made a good choice.

We set Catriona behind Hoskuld, and twice she

turned to look back as they rode on.

"What is all this about?" I asked Aimeric. "Where are we going?"

He gave me a smile as wide as the Tyne.

"Over fresh water," he said, "to meet the hermit of the island."

I stared at him. He was quoting the riddle from Lindisfarne.

"They threw me in the same hole as Hoskuld and Arni," he explained, "and there was time for a great deal of talking. One thing I learnt is that a hermit lives on an island in Derwent Water – here, in the Lake Fells – and he is not the first. There has been a hermitage there longer than anyone remembers."

"'*Where the hermit of the island yet keeps the word,*'" I recited, and the riddle opened like a butterfly.

"God willing," said Aimeric, "we can be there by nightfall."

16. *THURSTAN IN WINTER*

DERWENT Water was no silver serpent, like Ullswater, but a lake as blue as the sapphire on Thurstan's ring. The reed meadows at its head were golden, and the fellsides a colour of weathered bronze.

There were several islands on the lake, but none looked more than a clump of trees.

"How do we find the hermit?" I asked.

"We trust a Viking," said Aimeric.

He took a track into a wood of twisted trees, where the ground was all moss and boulders, forcing us to dismount and lead the horses.

We came to a clearing on the shore, where a boat lay beached on a strip of shingle by the gable end of a longhouse. The geese saw us first and set up a honking, and a horse whinnied and came to the fence of its paddock to greet ours. Away in the trees, a sound of wood-cutting ceased abruptly, and by the time we reached the house there stood waiting for us, axe in hand, a man wearing a leather apron over a brightly-patterned tunic of wool.

"Thorald Armodsson?" Aimeric asked him.

He bowed and Aimeric told him our names.

"Hoskuld Sigurdsson told us we could count on

your help."

Thorald's eyes went from our bridles to my surcoat and sword, noting all that marked us as Norman.

"From what I hear," he said drily, "Hoskuld needs help himself."

"We have just parted from him," said Aimeric. "By nightfall he will be home."

"That's good to know," said Thorald. "So how can I help?"

"We need to reach the hermit of the island."

"Well, that will not even take me out of my way," said Thorald, and he turned to call through the doorway into the house. "Hildi, put some more food in the basket for Herbert's Kell. Skuli has guests."

Aimeric was grinning. "Herbert's Kell," he murmured. "I should have known."

We rubbed down the horses, and loosed them in the paddock, then Hoskuld rowed us out onto the lake. At first I could see down to the brown stony bed, then only the deep, dark water, that made me think of the White Ship.

"Does the hermit have many visitors?" asked Aimeric.

"A few," said Thorald. "There was one about five years ago, and another a few years before. Mind you, they were both his kin."

Aimeric looked at the island ahead. "I wonder how he bears it," he said.

"We were boys together," said Thorald. "Skuli had his heart set on a girl from Stonethwaite, but her father married her to a man with better prospects. Skuli went berserk. We took him off to Herbert's Kell, for the hermit who was there in those days to look after until his temper cooled. When we went back to fetch him, he told us he had made up his mind to stay. That was longer ago than either of you have been alive, and the hermit who was his master has been dead a good few years. Skuli is the hermit now."

We reached the island at dusk. Thorald skulled the boat alongside a rock and leaned in balance as Aimeric and I stepped in turn from the dipping gunwhale to solid ground.

"When shall I fetch you back?" he asked.

"Tomorrow, if you will," said Aimeric, and we thanked him.

As Thorald bent his back to the homeward row, we made our way into the trees. We could smell woodsmoke, but it was a moment before we made out the hut. It had been there so long it seemed to have sunk into the island. Moss had grown upwards from the ground, and now it all but covered the bark-shingled roof.

The hermit took a moment to convince we were real, but soon we were sharing a meal of mutton, bread, and ewe's milk cheese. Skuli lived rough. His long hair was tangled and knotted, his hands black with dirt. He had a strong smell, though neither Aimeric nor I were exactly scented for the bridal bed ourselves.

We had no trouble getting him to talk; it came when we tried to stop him for long enough for him to listen to the questions we had come to ask. Skuli had somehow got it into his head that we had come to join him, and when he saw he was wrong, he turned downcast and bitter.

"I will be the last," he said. "The way of solitude no longer calls to the hearts of the young. They think they can give themselves to God in the monasteries that are bursting out like boils, built by Normans with blood on their hands and the belief they can buy prayers." He looked at us disdainfully. "You are Normans," he said. "Why do you come here?"

"We are searchers," said Aimeric. "Saint Cuthbert is

our guide, and Archbishop Thurstan our master."

"We are knights of the Sacred Blade," I said.

Skuli froze, like a startled deer about to bolt.

"You know what we seek," said Aimeric.

Skuli gave us a long look. "You are Normans," he repeated. "What can you know of my kind?"

"Little enough," agreed Aimeric, "but let me tell you what I do know. The first to live here was Saint Herbert, a friend of the blessed Cuthbert. When he died, the place fell silent. I do not know when a hermit next came here, but I would guess it was two hundred and sixty-two years ago, and that you belong to a line which since that day has stretched unbroken."

Skuli looked well and truly unsettled. "Our time has never been measured in years," he said. "What gives you your number?"

"I am counting back through the chronicles," said Aimeric, "to the year the monks fled from Lindisfarne. It was here in Cumbria that they set sail for Ireland, and the saint turned them back. They were the keepers of the Sacred Blade, and that same year, they laid it in a place of hiding and spun the secret of what they had done into a web of riddles. A riddle led us here and you have the riddle that will lead us away."

"They set sail from the mouth of the Derwent," Skuli answered quietly, "and the Derwent is the river that flows from this lake. They did not know the saint would turn them back, so before they took ship, they sent one of the brothers to live here, to pray for the land of Northumbria."

"And what was the riddle to be recited each day among his prayers?" asked Aimeric.

Skuli glared at him, and began to chant.

> *"Endless madness known as man,*
> *Dig my grave to slake your thirst*
> *Where a night they let me lie.*
> *If in love you lift the stone*
> *Night and dream are both outgrown."*

The riddle had the ring of a threat. I almost wished I had never heard it.

"King Edwin is named in the acrostic," said Aimeric, rubbing his eyelids sore with woodsmoke, "but the rest is dark to me."

"It has to be," said Skuli. "It is the last riddle. Solve it and it will lead you to the Blade. What makes you think you are worthy to go so far?"

"We have to be," I said. "Others are searching, who want the Sacred Blade to use it for evil."

"Then go with my blessing," said Skuli. He laughed to himself and looked at us with watering eyes. "No need now for anyone to follow me."

We slept badly, and were on the rocks at first light to see Thorald already halfway across the lake, beneath a sky of rushing clouds.

"Not a day to go fishing," he said. "I thought it best to get you ashore before the storm breaks."

The horses had gorged themselves on grass and rye and were unwilling to leave. We led them up the hill to the circle of stones and, as Derwent Water fell out of sight, Aimeric studied the fells and turned to me with a frown.

"Can you remember the way to Ullswater?"

"Why take it?" I asked. "If we ride east, we could be at Brough by nightfall."

"And Sigrid?"

"She has no need of me now."

"Catriona?"

"Best leave her where she is safe."

"I will never understand the Norman mind," murmured Aimeric. "Eastwards then to Brough."

The storm broke as we rode, and under the cover of the rain, we made for the Vale of Eden. None of the villages we had found burnt had been rebuilt, though someone had given a burial to the bodies.

Our wits were ragged from the months in Caerluel. We had no feel for the lateness of the year and the shortening days. We should have asked shelter at Appleby, but instead we pressed on and the dusk caught us well short of Brough, in the depths of nowhere.

Turning from the road, we found an empty shieling, forced the door and made ourselves at home. Someone had stacked a log-pile ready for the lambing watch, so we left a farthing for each log it took to build a blaze to steam our clothes dry.

We spent half the night talking of Caerluel, and of all we now knew of the Sacred Blade and why FitzDuncan desired it. Aimeric unwrapped and strung his lute.

"When it began to come clear," he said, "I made a song. I wanted to make a spell to ward off evil. You must learn it, for when the time comes, you may be the one who has to sing it."

It was a true song, with a tune that tore my heart out, and words that thrust it back again. Next day, we sang it at the top of our voices as we rode over the wilderness of Stainmoor.

York had been burnt. We could hardly believe our eyes.

Whole streets had been gutted, the minster scorched, and the archbishop's palace left a ruin. When we asked some of the masons at work on the rebuilding to tell us who had done it, they roared with laughter. One breezy summer night, a house-fire had run wild to lay waste a quarter of the city.

We found Thurstan in the guest-house of Saint Mary's Abbey, which was so crowded we knew at once we would be unable to speak with him alone. Kneeling, we kissed his ring.

"Where have you been?" he asked. "The road to Malmesbury cannot be as hard as your faces make it look."

"We are aged by learning," said Aimeric. "We found the tree of knowledge, but not in Malmesbury."

"And God told Adam the fruit of one tree in all the garden was forbidden," intoned Thurstan, but with a glint in his eyes. "To save time, I forgive you. You can tell me all about it when the chance comes, as it surely will, somewhere along the road."

"The road?" asked Aimeric.

"Tomorrow," said Thurstan, "we ride north to meet King David. Go and get yourselves steamed and shaved."

A fire of logs crackled on the hearth-stone I remembered so well from the night I made the Sacred Blade my quest. We were once more in the upper room in Durham. Thurstan and Archdeacon Ranulf sat listening, sipping mulled wine as I told them what Aimeric and I had learnt in Cumbria.

"I am an old fool," said Thurstan ruefully. "Two years ago, I should have advised Stephen to throw the Scots back over the border, whatever the cost. I should have seen what would come of leaving it all to fester beneath unkeepable promises. Stephen has the Norman gift for war, but so little trust and wisdom. I misjudged him."

"You were working for peace," protested Archdeacon Ranulf. "You did what was best, at that moment, for Northumbria."

Thurstan smiled doubtfully. "Shall I tell you what the Sacred Blade has come to mean to me?" he asked. "I see it as a symbol of all the holiness and power of the past of this land; the power I felt when I first came here; the power I have spent my life trying to grasp and somehow . . ."

Frowning, he gazed over our heads, as if he were trying to see through the walls and over the rooftops to the great Norman cathedral that stood in the place of Saint Cuthbert's minster.

"Unless we can touch the past," he said, "hold its embers in our hands and make our lives the breath to kindle a new fire, we will never be more than intruders. To hold a land by conquest is nothing. Men are judged not by their conquests, but what they make of them."

"My lord," I said, "you have done more than anyone to give Northumbria back its ancient place in Christendom."

The archbishop shook his head. "I have covered it with a cloak of civilisation," he said. "I have tried to make it disappear. Even now, after so long, I am afraid of it."

Yet Thurstan was a driven man, or he could never have endured the days that followed.

We rode north, crossing the Tyne at Corbridge, and on through Northumberland by a road that led straight up onto the border hills, in an arrow-line for Scotland. The weather was cruel, but day after day, the old man clung to his saddle, almost angry when the night held him back.

In the season of Advent, we came down onto the plain of Lothian, through winter-bare forests to Rocksburgh.

King David was gracious as ever, and when the

torches were lit in the tapestried hall, we were ushered to the high table. Prince Henry and FitzDuncan were nowhere to be seen; nor, to my disappointment, were Robert and Drustan.

Supper began badly, with a quarrel over the Church. It appeared there were now two popes, each of them claiming to be the ruler of Christendom. David believed in one, Thurstan in the other, and however deftly Thurstan argued, the king countered with a passionate faith that seemed to come straight from Saint Margaret.

"I hear Stephen supports Innocent," said David gaily. "A false pope for a false king?"

Thurstan took the bait.

"My son," he said imploringly, "whatever Stephen's failings, you must not break the peace."

David was unmoved.

"So you think it is not enough," he asked, "to have given Stephen two years, and had nothing but insults and broken pledges in return? Northumbria belongs to me and mine. It can wait no longer."

"Northumbria belongs to God," protested Thurstan. "When kings go to war, lesser men seize their chance to do whatever they wish, and more often than not it is evil. You cannot love Christ and plunge his people into misery. It is one or the other."

"The Conqueror came to England waving a banner blessed by the Church," replied David, with grievance in his voice. "Was it on the love of Christ's people that the Normans built their rule in the north? God has given me my power. Surely you can see that with the power comes the duty?"

"What you are calling duty, I call greed and folly," said Thurstan.

"See it, then," said David, "as trial by combat. God will decide which of us belongs in Northumbria."

Only Aimeric and I could know how deep that thrust must have gone. Thurstan sagged, but for a Norman like him there was only one reply to make.

"Break the peace, and I will fight you," he warned. "I will fight you with all my power."

"I have no doubt," said David mildly, "that you will do whatever you believe is right. So must I."

He beckoned for more wine, and broke into a smile. "I hear there is a new king in France," he remarked. "Is it true that he has married Eleanor, the heiress of Aquitaine?"

Thurstan was floored. There was nothing else he could say. He could hardly ask David when he planned to make his attack.

When the hall began to empty, I spied Robert and Drustan at the far end. I hurried over, but when I stood before them, Drustan gave me a thin smile, while Robert sprang to his feet. "Outside," he ordered.

In the bailey, he pushed me against a wall. "Tell me what you know of the Sacred Blade," he demanded.

"It is nothing but a legend in a song," I countered, but he had caught me unprepared, and the alarm showed in my face.

"Do not lie to me, Simon," said Robert. "FitzDuncan told us all about you and your search."

"Then let me tell you about William FitzDuncan," I said. "Do you know . . ."

"He told us," interrupted Robert, "that one of his servants robbed you of some riddle or something in Morpeth. If you remember, I was there, and it so happens my dreams were hellish that night. I remember a girl emptying our wallets and bags, while I lay under a spell, unable even to speak; but when I woke, our bags were there and packed, and you and Aimless were acting as though all were as it should be. It was only when FitzDuncan told his tale that I realised the girl in my dream was the same little witch who was clinging to you when you rode out of Caerluel. So do not tell me there is nothing in all this. Just give me the truth."

"I cannot tell you, Robert," I said sadly. "Do not ask me."

His face took on a look of disgust. "I trusted you," he said. "You were my truest friend. I told you all that was in my heart, and now I find you told me nothing of yours."

"I was forbidden . . ."

"Forbidden," he repeated, nodding intently. "Who was it? Walter, I suppose. I do not think I wish to know any more."

He turned to go, then some unspoken thought made his anger sputter back into flame, and he jabbed a finger at my neck. "Next time we meet," he said, "it will be as enemies. It can never again be as friends."

When Aimeric found me later, I was sitting on the ground with my face in my hands.

Everything was going under, splintering like the White Ship on the rocks of the Normandy coast.

We left at daybreak, through the empty streets of the burgh to the sound of the bells of the Abbey of Kelsow. Ice rimmed the banks of the river. We were the first through the gates, the first to pay the ferryman.

Thurstan took the road that followed the Tweed to Carham, and where the road turned south before the gates of the castle, he beckoned me to his side.

"Take Jordan my greeting," he said, "and tell him to hold fast. Tell him he is the shield of Northumbria."

When he pulled off his sheepskin glove to make the sign of blessing, I saw that his fingers had already gone white with cold. The sapphire on his ring was as blue as the winter sky.

Aimeric and I joked our way quickly through the parting. I drew Loki off the track and waited until the cavalcade had gone by, then I turned towards the castle on the border.

PART THREE

The Year of the Blade
*December **1137**–December **1138***

17. *A SONG OF DEFIANCE*

J ORDAN led me proudly round our stronghold. It was over a year since I had left him there, when I rode south with Walter, and he had been busy.

Carham had been transformed. Above the gateway, Jordan had built a wooden tower with a sloping roof, and the walkway around the palisade was now covered for most of its length. Outside, the ditch had been deepened and, inside, the bailey was crowded with new buildings: a gabled hall with living-quarters, stables and a smithy, and enough store-huts to make a squirrel die of jealousy. One of them held nothing but arrows, bundle after bundle of them.

To do all this, he had needed men, and he had gathered a garrison of almost a hundred. Drawn by his name, they had come from all over the north. There was a veteran knight, Landric de Rennes; restless younger sons, like Arnoul and Hemming, my own age and my friends at once, if only because I was the son of their lord; then all manner of misfits and outcasts, like Herfast the Gambler, whose father had served Robert de Mowbray, and like my grandfather lost all that he owned.

The kitchens and stables were run by folk from the villages around the manor, who had seized the chance to leave the fields for the life of a Norman household.

There were so many people that the welcome over-powered me. My mind was still in the pit of Caerluel, and at first I could hardly talk. It took the twelve days of Yule to break me open.

Orm never thanked me in words for riding to Longth-waite, but each day, whatever the weather, he took me out into the bailey and battered away at me until he had knocked some muscle back into my arms. Once I was strong enough, he taught me to use a shield.

Then a messenger came, from Ranulf de Merlay, to ask courteously if I would care to ride to Morpeth and pay him a visit.

"Best go and see what he wants," said Jordan. "We need the goodwill of our neighbours."

"Why should he ask for me?" I said. "Remember what happened last time I was in Morpeth. I could be riding into an ambush."

"Then take an escort," said Jordan. "After all, you are the son of one of the lords of the border."

In full armour, with Orm and Arnoul and Hemming at my side, I rode into the castle of Morpeth.

Ranulf de Merlay came out into the bailey to greet us, and as soon as I saw him I knew his summons was true. He welcomed me as if my friendship were important to him, and though he blustered with good cheer, he looked a worried man.

"Do you remember the advice you gave me?" he asked. "I called you here to see me take it."

Kneeling in the chapel, hidden in their hoods and deep in prayer, were thirteen white monks.

"I wish you to be a witness," said Ranulf, "to the

charter of foundation from which the Priory of Newminster will be born."

I told him I was honoured. The monks, it turned out, were not from Rievaulx but from the Abbey of Fountains, which also lay in Yorkshire, and had been founded on land given by Thurstan. Newminster would be their first daughter house.

Scratching my name, the way Aimeric had taught me, on the charter of foundation, I felt as if I were King Oswald, watching the birth of the Abbey of Lindisfarne.

The Sacred Blade still shone for me, even if Thurstan would say I were only helping him throw a cloak of civilisation over Northumbria.

The next morning, in driving sleet, the monks formed a procession and marched out chanting psalms to the place in the woods, a bend upstream of the castle, where their priory was to be built.

"Let's hope you've bought yourself a sacred shield," Orm remarked to Ranulf. "David is unlikely to harm a place which has an abbey."

Ranulf looked uneasy. "Have you heard the news from the south?" he asked. "King Stephen has raised an army and is laying siege to Bedford. Miles de Beauchamp holds it against him. It is an evil world where kings go to war in the holy season of Christmas."

"Oh, indeed it is," agreed Orm. "I don't suppose you happen to know if word of this has reached David?"

Five days later, the Scots crossed the border.

Rumour of their gathering came ahead of them, and brought the folk of Carham running to the castle. They brought their livestock and their women and children, turning the bailey into a market-town. Watching from the keep, I found it comforting. This was how it should be, with the castle as the stronghold of the people of the land, and the knights as their guardians.

Jordan knew it. He made all welcome, and put us to work. I built a row of pens for the animals, while Orm gathered for practice all the villagers who looked good to draw a bow.

Then we closed the gates, and by daybreak, the Scots were knocking on them.

They were everywhere. Their numbers ran to thousands. They came pouring across the ford from the plain of Lothian, swarming down the south bank of the Tweed from Rocksburgh, in columns so wide they spilled off the road and trampled the fields.

Here and there, banners flew and armour shone, but mostly they were rabble, the sons of the wild hordes of Malcolm Canmore, mounted on garrons that made Loki look thoroughbred.

They swarmed towards Carham, halting just outside the range of our bows to jeer and stare and threaten. At first, we could make out no order to the host, but then we saw that on the western tip of our land, where an old church stood on a knoll above the beck that flowed into the Tweed to make the angle of the border, lordly figures were gathering.

Pushing forward through the host came a herald, flanked on either side by standard-bearers with banners held aloft.

"By the Holy Spear of Golgotha!" burst out Jordan. "Have you seen what they're waving?"

One of the banners I knew, the blue boar of the house of Canmore I had seen flying above Rocksburgh. The other was crimson, and as it furled in the wind I saw that emblazoned on it was a long, golden dragon.

"The royal banner of Wessex," Jordan told us. "No one has flown it since Edgar the Aetheling gave up the fight and went into exile."

Whatever its power, I said to myself, it was not the Sacred Blade. The royal banner of Wessex had been flown by too many losers. Orm was grinning.

"I wonder how David got hold of it," he said. "Saint Margaret must have hidden it in her bed-linen."

The herald stopped well short of the ramparts, and raised a hand in greeting. "Jordan de Falaise, open your gates in the name of Henry, earl of Northumbria, and of Matilda, the true queen of England."

Jordan cupped his hands to his mouth. "Go to hell," he bellowed.

"Tactful as ever," remarked Orm.

The herald bowed and rode back through the Scottish host, who answered us with a braying of horns and a thumping of cattle-hide drums, as if we had given them just what they wanted.

Nothing happened for a while, then with a swirl of movement, half the Scottish host took to the road that led downstream, towards the fortress of Norham. Those who remained, and there were thousands of them, were dismounting and leading their horses back to a hedged field, turning them loose to graze. As they massed again, on foot, on the sward before our gates, they gathered in purposeful groups, each with a long wooden ladder.

Jordan quirked an eyebrow at me. "Aimeric's song?" he suggested.

We filled our lungs. I had taught the song to the garrison over Yule, and now we roared it out at the top of our voices.

"Fight the skies
  when ravens fly,
Fight the wolves
  that run through the trees.
Hold the bridge,
  the rainbow, the ridge,
Strong in the wind
  that blows in from Cuthbert's sea.
Fight the mind
  that thinks only lies,
Fight the eyes
  that follow the blind.
Hold the heart
  that laughs at the dark,
Strong in the wind
  that blows in from Cuthbert's sea."

We were still singing when the Scots charged the ditch, and our first arrows went hissing down among them.

"Go to your posts," Jordan told us, and the walkways shook with men running along them in full armour.

My post was with Orm and the guard of the north wall, overlooking the Tweed. It was one of the few lengths of rampart that had not been roofed, which made it certain to be attacked; but it was tall, and there was only a narrow strip of land between the ditch and the Tweed, which meant that any Scottish archers who tried to ply their craft would find themselves forced to stand well within the range of our own.

Out of sight to our left, we heard the first wave of the attack strike the gates. Then men came running round onto the sward beneath our rampart.

"Good," said Orm, "by their clothes they look to be

from Galloway." He kissed the blade of his axe.

From the moment they scrambled down into the loose earth of the ditch, they were at the mercy of our arrows and all we had gathered to drop on them. We crippled a good few before they even got their ladders against the palisades. The top of one lodged against the rampart a few yards from me. I tried to push it away, but it was held in place by the weight of the men climbing it; so I drew my sword, leaned out, and split the skull of the first man who reached me.

I had only to think of the blackened villages and corpses in the Vale of Eden, and of Thord Hoskuldsson, cut down by his father's hall in Longthwaite; then I was grateful for the heavy blade in my hand, which God had given me to use to avenge them.

The Scots made three assaults on our wall, but none of the attackers who made the rampart got any further. By sunset, the ditch was littered with dead. I had killed five men, and come close to death only twice.

Exultant, we gathered in the hall and ate like hogs to prove we were still alive. We had lost nine of the garrison, and one of the villagers. Our wounded were stretched out in the granary.

"Tomorrow," Jordan told us, "I want every wagon we have set against the gates. They are bound to try and batter their way in now they know what it costs trying to come over the walls."

"Winter has its uses," remarked Landric. "The ground will be too muddy for them to get all their weight behind a ram."

We were sitting there in our armour. As the hall grew hotter, I asked Orm to help me out of my mail-shirt.

"No, leave it on," Jordan told me. "You will be keeping the first watch."

It was a cold vigil, but the land was jewelled with the cooking-fires of the Scots, and the Tweed was a ribbon of mirrored moonlight. I gazed downstream, wondering how the day had gone at Norham.

Come midnight, when Orm took over, I was still too shaken to sleep, so I went in search of Jordan. I found him in the upper chamber of the keep, which he had made his eyrie, and he poured me a cup of wine.

"So now you know battle," he said. "What did you make of it?"

There was more than I could straighten out into words, but I told him how when the fighting began, my fear had vanished and I had felt as if nothing could harm me.

"Yes," he said, "but that was only grey fear and red courage."

"What do you mean?" I asked. "They were real enough to me."

"Grey fear," he explained, "is my name for the fear of the night before, when the demons of suggestion howl in the mind. When the test itself comes, there is no time to listen to them. That is when you found your red courage, your battle-fury. It shows you are a born fighter – and it is strong while it lasts – but it cannot endure. White courage is what you need when you face a test unarmed by fury."

"So what is worse than grey fear?" I asked.

"There is black fear," said Jordan, "the fear that grips you when all goes utterly wrong, and you cannot think fast enough. It is the ultimate test, for if you let it overwhelm you, you are as good as dead."

In my mind's eye, I saw a beard the colour of fox fur. "I know it," I said. "I get it every time I set eyes on Ruari MacGillemor."

Jordan laughed. "Yes, it can take human form."

His voice was rueful with experience, and made me think of all the wars and battles he had known.

"It is no use," I said. "I cannot live my whole life the way you have lived yours."

Jordan gave a grunt, and rubbed his chin, rasping the bristles. "I keep forgetting," he said. "For you there will always be a choice." He was disappointed. Without meaning to, I had hurt him in the very moment he felt close to me.

"Tell me, then," I said, "how do you bear it?"

"You tell yourself that each fight is bound to be the last, and that when it is over, you will never again need to hold a weapon."

"And each time, you believe it?"

Jordan grinned. "I never said you had to believe it."

All the next day we were under attack. There was hard battle at the gates and one maddened assault on the north wall, but when it was over, Carham was still ours.

At daybreak we were back on the ramparts, aching but ready, and what I saw seemed too good to be true. The Scottish host was striking camp and swarming southwards, towards the Till valley and the heart of Northumberland. Behind them, on the knoll of the old church, they left a force of men who were throwing up turf bothies and settling themselves in.

"Damn them!" said Jordan. "How many would you say are left?"

Orm narrowed his eyes. "Two, perhaps three hundred, and with a banner, so one of David's knights must be holding the reins."

"Damn them!" repeated Jordan. "Too few to take us by storm, but enough to cut us to pieces if we set a foot outside."

"Why is it so bad?" I asked. "Surely it means the attack has failed?"

"It means the Scots are loose," he explained. "Our task was to hold them here, to force them to lay siege to us. If their army were smaller, they would have had no choice, but David has men to spare. This way, he can keep us penned, leave us to starve, and come back when we are weak and ripe for the picking. In the meantime, we are powerless."

When I saw what he meant, I felt as sickened. Palls of smoke began to rise from the lands to the south, as the Scots burned every village they came to. There was nothing we could do but stand there in our armour and watch the spread of the Waste Land.

"What now?" I asked.

"We wait," said Jordan, "and keep our tempers and our appetites low."

The weeks that followed were a strange captivity. At night, it rained arrows, when the Scots crept up and sent their volleys high over the palisades. They killed a pig or two, and it meant that we were always tripping over, for we hurried between buildings with our eyes on the sky.

In the hall, life was as it must have been in the days of the kings of the Sacred Blade, with the lord and all his folk gathered together under the same roof, warding off the winter. A comradeship bound Norman and villager, and we mixed at the tables, sharing our songs and tales. For all that, the older villagers kept their reserve. There had been other lords of Carham. Jordan had no lady, and I was his only son. They saw no reason to open their hearts to us when we might so soon be swept away. We were their shelter from the storm, but that was all.

When I walked into the hall, I was what I had wanted for so long to be. Folk made way for me, listened to me, watched me. Jordan told me to be worthy of it, and I walked like a strung bow, trying to speak only with courtesy. There was a girl I often caught looking at me, and when I gathered my courage and spoke to her, she blushed, and we could find nothing to say. My own silence came from a stab of guilt, not that I was her lord, and could have her for the asking, but from suddenly feeling unfaithful.

For it was Catriona I longed for. She was always in my mind. I would have given it all away to be back in her arms, even if it meant throwing myself back into the pit of Caerluel. One night when the wind was howling, I told Jordan all about her. I was expecting him to roar with laughter and clap me on the back, but when I had finished my tale, and sat staring at my hands, he let a moment go by, then shook his head.

"And how do you feel now," he asked, "about leaving her in Longthwaite?"

"Witless," I said. "It is the biggest mistake I have ever made – but I made it. I know I deserve no pity."

"Well, I pity you," said Jordan. "I once made the same mistake myself."

At last, at Candlemas, the Scots returned. They came swarming out of the Till valley, their host swollen with cattle and horses and wagons of plunder. But they had not come for us. They poured past, over the border, and by nightfall, our besiegers had struck their camp and followed.

In the morning, Jordan gave the order to open the gates.

18. THE PLAGUE OF LOCUSTS

LESS than a week later, King Stephen and his chivalry came riding out of the valley of the Till.

He bid his army halt on the sward before our gates, and with his captains came riding into the bailey. Several barons were with him, but not Walter. Jordan knelt and held the king's stirrup for him to dismount.

They were soon side by side at the high table, and I was standing by the king's shoulder with a pitcher of wine. In the cellars below, I could hear our steward arguing with the cooks as they tried to find the wherewithal for a feast.

"This is my first journey to the northern edge of the realm," remarked Stephen. "I hear the hawking along the Tweed is excellent."

"Is that what brings you, my lord?" Jordan asked him.

"It may keep me," he replied, "but I have come to strike David such a blow that he will never harm my kingdom again."

"I hope he rises to the challenge," said Jordan. "He may have his father's knack for making himself scarce whenever we go hunting for him."

"Then he will suffer the shame of seeing his citadels

burn," said Stephen. "Eustace FitzJohn has advised me to take Rocksburgh."

Jordan's eyebrows went up like startled herons. "That would be bold," he said warily. "Rocksburgh has water on two of its three sides, and the other side is built for siege. I will be interested to hear my lord FitzJohn explain how it might be taken, and in winter. Is he here?"

"He is gathering his forces," replied Stephen.

Jordan and Orm exchanged glances.

Just then, I caught sight of Roger de Mowbray among the crowd of knights who were pushing their way into the hall. As soon as I could, I went over to greet him.

He unbuckled his wallet, and held out a fold of parchment sealed with wax.

"A letter for you."

"From Thurstan?"

"No," he said, "from Adele. You should be able to find one of the clerks of the king's chancery to read it to you."

"So how goes it with Adele?" I asked. "Are you to be married?"

Roger looked embarrassed. "First," he said, "a choir of angels would have to come and carry my mother off to heaven, and I can see no sign of that. Lately, I have been spending less time at Elmeslac."

So Adele would be suffering days of embroidery with the lady Albrea and her daughters. My heart went out to her.

"Tell me," I said, "how far did David strike?"

"He reached the valley of the Tyne," said Roger. "We saw it on our way north. The land around Hexham is a wilderness. It is not how I thought David would wage war."

It was well after dusk before we had found all the high-born among our guests a dry place to sleep, and I was free to go in search of the clerk. He was a thin man with a gurgling cough, who looked as if he were suffering the hardships of campaign in the hope of rewards to come. Aimeric had told me that the king's chancery had been Thurstan's stepping-stone to the archbishopric of York. For all I knew, this clerk might one day follow him.

While I held a butter-lamp, he read out the letter:

"From Adele Espec to Simon de Falaise, warmest greet-ings. Know that however wide the land between us, you are close in my thoughts. My father speaks often of Jordan, and our fear for your safety in these troubles is only made bearable by our trust in your strength. There are two new gerfalcons and a goshawk in the mews, awaiting your return as do I. Fare well then in the hope of your sister Adele, by the pen of Godfrey, scribe to the priory of Kirkham, in the octave of Candlemas in the year of our Lord's incarnation eleven hundred and thirty-eight."

For a moment I was back in Elmeslac, sharing a morning's ride with Adele of the honey-coloured eyes.

I went to tell Jordan of the letter, and found him with Landric and Orm in the upper chamber of the keep. They were talking of Stephen and mirthfully incredulous.

"He would do it!" said Jordan. "He would ride up to Rocksburgh without a glance over his shoulder!"

"Is there no chance of bringing the Scots to battle," asked Landric, "somewhere out in the open, where we could make a good charge?"

"There may well be," said Jordan, "once they hear Stephen has only two thousand men. Think about it. We would be massacred."

"Why did he bring so few?" asked Landric.

"He left the body of his army laying siege to Bedford, and rode north trusting the barons here would rally to him. They seem to have been generous with bad advice, but little else."

Orm looked up grimly from a piece of wood he was carving. "If all Stephen wants is to strike at David," he said, "he may be willing to settle for the blow that is easiest to strike. Tell him to cross the river and spread the Waste Land through Lothian."

Jordan frowned. "Burn villages, you mean? Stephen will think you insult his knighthood."

"Tell him to do it in a knightly way," said Orm. "He can burn the villages, but spare the people. Only, keep him near the Tweed, so that when David strikes, we can pull out fast."

He tossed his carving into Jordan's lap, and Jordan laughed and showed it to me. It was the likeness of a large grasshopper.

"They call it a locust," he explained. "We heard of them in the Holy Land. They move in swarms, and they can strip a land of all its goodness in less than a day." He grinned at Orm. "I agree. Whatever we do, we must get Stephen away from Carham. We cannot feed him."

At first, the king was cool to the proposal, but we whispered it among the army, and they clamoured for it. By nightfall, the king had announced it as his wish. It was a popular decision, and Stephen, as we were learning, wanted above all else to be popular.

With banners flying, we rode downstream to Norham, the castle held by knights of the bishop of Durham, who like us had held the Scots at bay and were recovering from the past few weeks. At the ford the castle had been built to guard, we crossed the Tweed and brought the Waste Land to Lothian.

In the first village we struck, the men put up a fight, and there were killings. In the second, everyone had fled. In the third, an old crone had to be dragged from her hearth and left lying in the mud, screeching curses at us as all she owned went up in flames: and she cursed us in English, for Lothian had once been part of the kingdom of Northumbria.

I could stand back, but I could not close my eyes. I saw honest folk thrown out into the winter, and I saw that not all King Stephen's army were knights.

Within a week, we had destroyed half the Merse, as they called the plain that stretched from the Tweed to Lammermoor; and we had burned the town of Duns, while King David's knights watched powerlessly from their castle. Orm had been right: we were a plague of locusts. Wherever we went, we devoured the land, and whenever we moved on, we left nothing behind.

Of King David there was no sign. From Rocksburgh he should have been able to see the smoke. In my guilt at what we were doing, I could almost feel him watching me, and I was not the only one. The talk around our evening fires was all of when and where David would strike. A rumour spread that he was gathering an army so huge that when it rode out, it would sweep us into the sea.

Jordan went to the king's tent and offered to ride westwards to guard our flanks.

"Do as you wish," said Stephen gaily. "I have the patience to wait. There is nothing I want more than battle. If David has the courage, he knows where to find me, but I shall not stoop to searching for him myself."

"Very wise, my lord," replied Jordan.

Two mornings later, Orm and I were with him on a

hill which gave us a distant view of the roofs of Kelsow Abbey, though Rocksburgh and its castle were hidden by forest and the lie of the land.

All the villages we could see were deserted. Everyone had fled, so it was with interest that we caught sight of a lone figure riding towards us on a palfrey. He wore the black cassock of a Benedictine monk.

"Aimeric!" I cried.

We galloped down to greet him, only to find it was a monk in his middle years, with a small brown dog perched between his lap and the pommel of his saddle.

"A good day to you, brother," said Jordan. "Where are you travelling?"

"Coldingham," he replied.

"Then let me advise you against it," said Jordan. "The Merse is in flames. Turn back to Rocksburgh, where you will be safe."

The monk shook his head. "With all due respect, my lord," he said, "I prefer to place my trust in God and the mercy of King Stephen. I know your designs for Rocksourgh, and I would sooner not be there when the trap is sprung."

Jordan leaned forward and took hold of the monk's reins. "What trap?" he asked. "Tell me."

The monk was appalled. He had taken us for knights in the service of King David.

We calmed him down, then we made him talk.

"Rocksburgh lies empty," he told us. "A few burgesses remain, but King David and his chivalry are deep in Ettrick Forest. When King Stephen attacks, he will find the gates almost undefended, and once he is inside, the Scots will pour out of the forest and have him like a pig in a pit."

"David seems to have all his father's cunning," said

Jordan admiringly. "I wonder what makes him so sure that Rocksburgh is where Stephen will strike?"

The monk could only shrug. "I cannot say," he replied, "but the burgesses have been expecting him every day this past week."

We let the monk ride on his way. He would be as safe on the road as anywhere else.

"What I would like to know," said Jordan, "is who told David what Stephen had in mind."

"Look at it another way," suggested Orm. "Let's wonder who told FitzJohn to advise Stephen to attack Rocksburgh." He looked at me. "Do you remember who we saw sitting beside him in Alnwick?"

A month earlier, on our ride to Morpeth, we had broken the journey at FitzJohn's castle. I only had to shake my memory to see again the crowded hall, and the faces at the high table.

"Hugh de Morville!" I said.

"That's right," said Orm. "FitzJohn's guest of honour was none other than the lord constable of Scotland. I suppose you'll say they were just discussing their favourite stories from the Scriptures?"

"This is beginning to stink," said Jordan.

"I have a feeling," said Orm, "that it would be wise to get Stephen back over the Tweed before David gets tired of waiting."

When we returned to the unlucky village Stephen had chosen as his camp for the night, Jordan spent the whole evening in the king's tent, alone with Stephen and his captain-in-chief, William of Ypres. He came out looking weary.

"At least I left them arguing," he told us, and went straight to sleep.

At daybreak, William of Ypres made his rounds of the army. Our lord the king, he announced, had shown the Scots the power of his retribution; but now that he saw King David was too cowardly to meet him in battle, he had decided to return to England.

We were in Norham in time for dinner.

At Norham, the king ordered a feast in honour of our victory, yet when the food reached the tables, we almost had to fight over it. The constable explained that the land around us was now so bare he had found it difficult to get anything at all.

King Stephen took it courteously. He ate the modest meal with relish, and had a purse of silver given to the cooks. We were so glad to be back in a warm hall that no one gave a thought to all the folk whose homes we had burned. I could tell the weight of the fear we had been carrying inside ourselves by the loudness of our laughter as it went up with the hearth-smoke to hang among the rafters. Faces shone as if we were purified by ordeal. The king was in high spirits, and with his golden beard glinting in the torchlight, he looked the perfect knight.

"The skies are clear, my lord," said Jordan. "Tomorrow will be a fine day for hawking."

"Tomorrow, I myself will be the hawk," replied the king. "William will take half the army to Alnwick. We will take another road, for I trust you will ride with me some of the way?" He looked meaningfully at Jordan, who seemed mightily amused.

From Norham, the king led us eastwards, around the foot of the outlying hills to the coast, to the castle of Bamburgh on its rock above the sea.

In the crush as we dismounted in the bailey, I kept by

Jordan and we shouldered our way to Stephen's side. We reached him as from the doorway of the hall stepped the constable of Bamburgh and lord of Alnwick, Eustace FitzJohn.

"My lord," he cried joyfully. "I am glad to see you safely returned."

I looked hard at FitzJohn. The skin of his face made all the right wrinkles of welcome, but his eyes were as dull as those of a fish three days out of the water.

When FitzJohn led us into his hall, Jordan contrived to be only two places from the king in the seating at the high table. I chose to stand by my father's shoulder, as any well-bred son might be expected to do.

Servants came with cheese, ale, and cold venison.

"The glory of your deeds has run ahead of you," FitzJohn told the king.

"I had hoped you would come and share in them," replied Stephen.

FitzJohn professed surprise. "Surely my lord had no need of me? I judged it best to guard the border behind you, as is my duty."

"A duty close to my heart," agreed Stephen, with one of his charming smiles. "Now I have seen this northern rim of my kingdom, I am able to judge better what I hear of it; and I fear all is not how I would wish."

"A fresh eye often sees further than the old," agreed FitzJohn. "Perhaps my lord wishes to advise us on our defence?"

Stephen's smile was undiminished. "I see a pattern of castles," he said, "which together should halt an invader, yet last month, they failed. I can see how the land was overrun, but I wonder at the speed of it."

FitzJohn listened impassively.

"The Scots were halted for two days by the knights of Carham and Norham," continued Stephen, "yet two days later, they reached Morpeth. It would seem they rode straight past your castles of Alnwick and Bamburgh. How can they have believed that to be safe?"

"They laid us under siege," replied FitzJohn. "Small wonder if they took one look at our strength and let the body of their pack run on to easier prey."

"Yet you of all my barons had the strength to attack them," Stephen reminded him. "You had two days' warning of their coming. I would not say you made the most of your chances."

"My lord, you did not see the size of their host," protested FitzJohn. "Besides, I was caught in Alnwick, and half my knights were here."

Stephen's smile reached its fullest flowering. "As I thought," he said, "you were overstretched. It is easy for a distant king to ask too much of his barons. Now I see that for the good of the kingdom, I must command you to allow me to ease your burden."

FitzJohn ran his tongue along his lips, as though his mouth were going dry. Everyone in the hall was now alert to what was happening.

"I relieve you of the duties of constable of Bamburgh," concluded Stephen. "I will leave men for a new garrison, under a knight untroubled by the cares of a barony." He paused, to let his words sink in, and to savour his power. "Let it be done by sunset," he added. "You and your followers will ride on with me to Alnwick, where William of Ypres awaits us for supper."

"As my lord wills," said FitzJohn, colouring with silent fury.

Stephen let his eyes rove over the men who had ridden

with him to Bamburgh. Beside me, Roger de Mowbray drew himself up to his full height. Jordan seemed to be holding his breath. The king's eyes went back and forth, then came to rest on a landless son of one of the great southern families.

"Joscelin de Warenne," he asked, "will you do me homage for my castle of Bamburgh?"

The young knight almost cut himself in two with his sword in his haste to go down on one knee, and the whole hall was witness to his oath and what had been done.

"Come, my lord," said Stephen to FitzJohn. "We must be on our way."

FitzJohn rose obediently to his feet, his followers scattering to gather their belongings.

Out in the bailey, King Stephen swept through the crush and swung up into his saddle in excellent humour; but I could hear the mutterings of his knights, as they tried to guess the reason for what had happened.

None of them knew, as we did, the evidence of FitzJohn's treachery. To them it looked a wilful breaking of the trust that bound a man to his lord and a lord to his man. It was not the way a king like David would act. I knew then that it was cunning gone wrong, and that when the dust settled, FitzJohn would walk out of it looking the one who had been betrayed.

When the host was ready to leave, the king thanked Jordan for his company and counsel, and declared that if ever David crossed the border again, he would be back at once.

We climbed to the ramparts and watched, as with a fanfare of trumpets, King Stephen rode south to face whatever his kingdom found next to jolt his troubled crown. There was an iced wind keening in from the sea. With my hands over my ears, I gazed north over the waves to the Isle of Lindisfarne and my thoughts went to the Sacred Blade.

Orm nudged us. "Look down there."

Below us in the bailey, Joscelin de Warenne was walking round his castle like a girl with a new gown.

Jordan slapped his gloves against the parapet. "Let's go home," he said.

19. DAVID'S FLOOD

T HROUGH the holy season of Lent and the Easter that followed, there was peace, for David was a Christian king; but when Easter was past, he loosed his demons.

One morning we woke to see a host of Scots gathered by the old church that faced the gates. They were not there to attack us, but to take us by surprise: to keep the villagers from trying to reach the safety of the castle, and to trap us inside, with only the garrison to man the walls, and only the food we already had in store.

Later, we saw palls of smoke rising over the eastern rim of the Northumbrian hills.

"So David is over the border," said Jordan, "only this time he has taken the coast road, and we have not even been able to slow him."

So began the second siege of Carham.

There was nothing to do but keep our heads down when the arrows flew and try to keep ourselves in training on a diet fit for mice. Day followed day with a repetition that dulled the wits: the same hunger, the same watch, the same faces each evening in the hall. Outside, the land we were forbidden was breaking into spring.

The Scots had the run of it. They came and went untroubled by all the roads we could see; from the Till valley towards Rocksburgh, from Rocksburgh to Norham and back again.

In the fifth week of the siege, a baggage-train came rolling through the Merse to ford the Tweed. The wagons were so full they each had six yoked oxen to pull them, and as they lumbered up the slope and past our gates, we watched with watering mouths. With a slowness that made our stomachs howl, they trundled by, and away along the road to Norham.

"Just look at them," said Jordan. "That will be food from the unravaged plain beyond Lammermoor."

"If they do it again," said Orm, "I say we should charge a toll."

It just so happened that another came the very next day.

By the time the first wagon splashed into the Tweed, forty of us were armed and ready in the bailey, our horses prancing all over the place, snorting as they caught the smell of our fear. The rest of the garrison were on the ramparts, their bows strung, their quivers full.

Jordan gathered the younger of us into groups of three.

"Stay together," he told us. "Pick a wagon, and ride for it. Most have a man leading the oxen and one or two perched on the load. Frighten them off, then get your wagon through the gates. The rest of us will take the Scottish camp our greeting, then make our way back as soon as we see you have the wagons."

The gates were pulled open. Through their archway I saw a sward of green turf, the baggage-train spread over it like dishes on a table, and beyond, twelve bowshots away, the old church and the huddle of bothies that marked the Scottish camp.

"Saint Cuthbert's Land!" cried Jordan, giving spur to his destrier. Orm yelled a battle-cry that made no mention of the saints, and we poured out of Carham like the wolves of Ragnarok.

There were now ten wagons on the English bank, and the sight of us set their drivers alight with panic. Some tried to hurry their beasts forward; others leapt from their loads and ran.

With Arnoul and Hemming, I made towards a wagon that had just pulled clear of the Tweed. Ours would be the glory of taking the prize that lay furthest from the gates. One of the drivers stood up and raised a spear, then thought better of it and flung himself into the river after his companions.

Arnoul and I grabbed the leading oxen by their yoke, and dragged them up the bank towards the castle while Hemming whacked at their flanks with the flat of his sword. Away to our right, I heard the tumult as Jordan and his companions struck the Scottish camp.

Ours was the last of seven wagons to be dragged into the bailey. Turning, I saw Jordan and his band riding back. As they galloped in, the archers on the ramparts loosed their shafts into the handful of pursuers; then the gates were slammed and barred, and we were riding in circles around the wagons, shouting and throwing our helmets at each other.

Jordan and Orm were unhurt, but three of their band had been brought down, among them Herfast the Gambler, who owed money to half the garrison. Landric had returned, but he was swaying in a blood-covered saddle, his hand pressed over the gash where a weapon had sliced through his hauberk of mail as if it were linen.

It took us till evening to unload the wagons. One was

laden with flour, two with bacon, another with arrows. There was fresh cheese, malt ale, and even wine from Anjou; and if all that were not enough, we were now the hungry owners of forty-two oxen. By Orm's reckoning, it was food enough to last us until Michaelmas.

Two days later, Landric de Rennes died. We buried him in unhallowed ground, at the foot of the motte, where we had buried all who died in the first siege. We had no priest, so there was no one to chant a blessing as his soul flew free.

Midsummer came, but no sign of King Stephen. We held Carham, and Carham held us prisoner, and the Scots sent no more baggage-trains over our ford.

Then, one morning in the thirteenth week of the siege, a knight came riding towards our gates holding the white wand of a herald.

"Jordan de Falaise," he called. "King David offers you a meeting."

"Where would it be?" shouted Jordan.

"Where I stand now," replied the herald, "three bowshots from the gates. You may ride out unarmed, with a companion, and you will have the safe-conduct of the king."

"Tell him I come at once."

As the herald turned back with the reply, Jordan beckoned to me, and we made for the stairway.

"Wait a moment," said Orm. "What makes you believe David is out there? Why should he risk himself to talk to the likes of you?"

"I have a name for honour and so has he," answered Jordan. "I'll take that chance."

"Just remember what happened to Robert de Mowbray," warned Orm; then his face brightened. "Are you going to go looking like that?"

Jordan was outlandishly dressed, in a silk gown and enamelled belt he had bought in Constantinople. It certainly made him a striking figure as we rode out of the gates.

Two men rode towards us from the Scottish camp, the king and Hugh de Morville, and they were unarmed. David looked fit and lean after a spring on campaign. There were a few more grey hairs in his pointed beard, but his eyes were gentle as ever, and he greeted us warmly.

"You have held your castle well," he said, "while all around you have fallen."

"All?" asked Jordan.

"All save Carham and Bamburgh," replied David, watching our faces. "Norham is mine, and my banner flies at Alnwick and Newcastle."

He was telling us he was now lord of Northumberland. If the border were now the Tyne, we were a long way from help.

"In my castle," said Jordan, "I stand on a rock and watch the tides sweep in and out."

"Then witness the flood," David told him. "Let me tell you what is happening in England. The barons have risen to take back the crown. So waste no more of yourselves on Stephen de Blois. He will not be coming north. When he flees, it will be to France."

Jordan contrived a smile. "Are you suggesting I should ride to his help?" he asked.

"If I did, I would be giving you bad advice," answered David. He looked us up and down. "I see no reason why good knights should die for a usurper. Surrender your castle and you and your men may leave with all your belongings."

"I hold Carham for Walter Espec," said Jordan. "You

know him as well as I, my lord. Do you think he would wish me to yield?"

"Would he wish you to die to no purpose?" countered David.

The gentleness went from his eyes, and his face took on a look that made me think I was seeing Malcolm Canmore.

"I am riding south to take the rest of Northumbria," he said. "When it is done, I will throw my strength at Carham, and you will be judged as rebels. Mark my words, the offer I make today is the last you will receive."

Jordan breathed heavily. "Then you mark mine, David FitzMalcolm," he replied. "We are knights of the Sacred Blade. As long as we hold, you cannot call yourself master of Northumberland, let alone of Northumbria."

"As you wish," said David mildly. "I have said all I came to say."

With a last glance at the castle, he turned and rode towards the Scottish camp, Hugh de Morville at his side. We cantered back into the bailey, and the gates closed behind us.

"Well?" asked Orm.

"Why talk about it?" said Jordan. "You will only be angry.'

It was high summer, the land rustling and green, the season when once I had ridden the trails of Ettrick Forest with Robert and Drustan. Clouds of midges writhed like lost souls on the surface of the Tweed.

It grew hard to sleep evenly at night, and harder to be wakeful in the days. People were saying strange things they had found in the back of their minds.

I was haunted by the Sacred Blade, and a belief it would always be hidden to us. It belonged to the high and holy past, not our own age of castles and greed and betrayal.

If it came again, it would surely be to sweep us away, all of us, Normans and Scots.

Or so I thought, until Saint Cuthbert spoke to me.

It was a blindingly bright afternoon. I was on watch. Out of discipline, we still wore armour to man the ramparts, and my coat of mail was hot to the touch. I was squinting at the old church and the Scottish camp, when a voice spoke the last of the riddles.

> *"Endless madness known as man,*
> *Dig my grave to slake your thirst*
> *Where a night they let me lie.*
> *If in love you lift the stone*
> *Night and fear are both outgrown."*

It was an old, rusty, English voice: Saint Cuthbert, angry at being dragged once again from his hermitage by the troubles of earthly kingdoms.

"Dig my grave," he was saying, *"where a night they let me lie."*

So the Sacred Blade must be buried in one of the places where the saint's body had rested on the flight from Lindisfarne. All we had to do was search them.

When I told Jordan and Orm, they went helpless with laughter.

"Hop on your horse," suggested Orm. "Trot down to York and tell Thurstan."

"Ah, well," said Jordan, "I always wanted to have a secret to take to my grave."

By then, we were all making jokes about our graves. It was so long since David marched south that it could hardly be much longer before the fate of Northumbria was settled, one way or the other. Whatever happened, we would be the last to know.

Just as I had accepted that Carham would be the last

place in my life, Catriona came knocking.

It was at night, in the nineteenth week of the siege. I was in the upper chamber of the keep with Jordan and Orm, when Hemming came racing up the stairs.

"There is a girl outside the gate," he said, a smirk spreading over his face. "She is asking for Simon."

I ran along the ramparts, and looking out saw a smudge of darker shadow against the palisade.

"Simon?"

"Catriona? Are you alone?"

"No, I have William FitzDuncan and a thousand men hidden under my cloak. Stop asking questions and open the gates."

We let her in and I caught her in a hug.

"You must forgive our manners," I told her. "We have so few guests. Come and meet my father."

I led her towards the keep, holding her close. "Why did you leave the Lake Fells?" I asked.

"I grew tired of waiting for you," she said reproach-fully. "At first I hated you, but then I remembered how in Caerluel, you left it to me to cross the floor even though your thoughts were glowing like candles in the dark."

"You are the candle in my darkness," I told her.

"And from what Sigrid tells me," said Catriona, "I am not the only one to whom you say such things."

"No," I admitted, "and all I said to Sigrid I meant as deeply as all I say to you. And there is another, whose name is Adele, who I love like a sister. I cannot help it: it is the witchcraft of love. But for no one have I ever had the longing I have for you."

Catriona laughed and we walked in silence until we came to the steps that climbed the motte.

"So how goes it with Sigrid?" I asked.

"Longthwaite is peaceful, Hoskuld has built a new hall, and Sigrid is with child. They are good folk. I felt I should leave before I started to make mischief."

"But how did you reach our gates?" I asked.

"Never ask a thief her secrets," retorted Catriona, "but I can tell you that no Scots will come creeping to your ramparts tonight. When I left them, they were passing round a skin of fresh barley beer."

We climbed the stairway to the upper chamber, where Jordan and Orm rose curiously to greet her.

As Catriona stepped into the torchlight, I caught my breath in surprise. She was still birdlike, her blue eyes darting from face to face, but no longer the bundle of rags I had found in the pit of Caerluel. Her hair was a chestnut mane; some hung loose, some in plaits. Her shawl had the bold-coloured patterns of Cumbrian weave and was pinned with a ring-brooch of burnished bronze.

Perched on a stool, she told us all she had learnt in her wanderings through Northumbria. She spoke with the precision of FitzDuncan's trained spy, and our eyes widened as much at the teller as at the tale.

"FitzDuncan has run wild in Cumbria," she said. "Appleby and Brough are under siege, and he has ridden down through Furness, routing the Normans who came against him.

"King David has crossed the Tyne, and the men of Galloway are with him. By now, he will be laying siege to Durham, but even if it endures, he will press on to the Tees. The design is for FitzDuncan to come over Stainmoor and join him, and once together, they will ride to take York."

"By God, they know what they are doing," murmured Jordan. "Any word of the size of the army gathering in Yorkshire to face them?"

"Only Scottish laughter because there is none," said Catriona. "Rumour goes that none of the barons will fight for Stephen, and the people will not fight without their lords."

Orm gave a long groan. "Well, my lass," he said, "you have just stolen the last scraps of hope I had left."

Catriona responded with a thin-lipped smile. "King David will prevail," she agreed, "and before long, there will be men from Galloway with time on their hands and old scores to settle. They will come hunting you. That is why I came. I want to take Simon away before he is killed."

We stared at her, and she looked at me intently.

"If you wish," she said, "I can take you safely through Northumberland. I know the quiet roads. I can lead you to the Priory of Tynemouth."

"What are you suggesting," asked Jordan, "that Simon become a monk?"

"King David has declared it a place of sanctuary," said Catriona. "Anyone who takes refuge there is safe, and you might easily, at Tynemouth, find a boat to take you further down the coast."

I had only to look at her to know how much I wanted to live.

Jordan rose, took me by the shoulder and guided me to the stair-ladder leading up onto the roof. Behind us, Orm began to ask Catriona about Hoskuld and his kin.

We stood listening and Jordan laid a hand on my shoulder. "You do know this could be a snare?" he asked. "She may have gone back to FitzDuncan."

"No," I said, "I trust her."

He considered a moment. "Then you must take this chance, and go and tell Thurstan how to find the Sacred Blade. If he could brandish it now, it would wake Northumbria. We may have been fools even to think we could unearth it for less. Did not Ulrica say that it would only come again in the hour of need?"

He looked at me thoughtfully. "Have you ever met the lady Gundreda de Mowbray?"

"Once, in Thirsk."

"How did she strike you?"

I thought of the wizened but wilful lady who had forbidden her son to marry Adele. "She struck me as having a heart of flint."

"Well," said Jordan, "she was not always so. She was only a girl when she married Robert de Mowbray and he found himself at war with William Rufus. When the king's men were laying siege to Bamburgh, they had almost lost hope of ever taking it, when Earl Robert was lured out and snared. Next day, they marched him to the gates, shouting that unless the castle yielded, they would tear out his eyes. It was more than the lady Gundreda could bear. She gave the order to yield, even though she knew it meant the end of the house of Mowbray in Northumberland."

"Why are you telling me this?"

"Because if the same thing were to happen to you, I wonder what my answer would be." He looked at me bleakly. "Make me one promise. If you reach York too late, accept it. Go home to your mother. Forget all this ever happened."

That was an easy promise to make. I was beginning to go rotten with fear. Carham had been a prison, but beyond its walls lay a world howling with the likes of Ruari MacGillemor.

"What if I never see you again?" I asked.

Jordan only laughed. "No great loss," he said. "Ever since I came to claim you, I have done nothing but lead you into trouble. It would be altogether selfish to expect you to die with me, though it may be as greedy to want you to live on. It has not been bad, these last few years, having a son."

"I will always be glad you came home," I told him, and let him read the rest in my face.

"So will I," he said.

He turned away, and looked out over Northumberland.

"Waste no tears on me, Simon. I may have done no good, but I have come the full circle. This is where I was born, and the land where I have always hoped to – to make my stand. Go now. I will watch from here."

In the chamber below, Catriona was waiting. While Orm went to fill us a bag of food, I changed into my roughest clothes. We would be travelling on foot. I fastened my sword-belt under one arm and over a shoulder, so the sword hung on my back, out of the way.

Orm hugged us both, then he hurried us through the bailey and unbarred the gates, muttering oaths for good luck as he stood back and we slipped past him and out into the night.

20. LAST SANCTUARIES

B Y dawn we were on the hills between the Till valley and the coast. All night we had been flitting along hedgerows from copse to copse, until the ground grew rough and we climbed into the wind from Saint Cuthbert's sea.

We came to a cave on a wooded hillside, hid there all day, then at nightfall set out again. By daybreak we were in sight of the castle of Alnwick, but well hidden, in a clump of tall trees that grew on the ring of an old earthwork.

"Since Caerluel," I told Catriona, "you seem to have lost your fear of the dark."

"When I was small," she said, "I used to think the darkness hours were the time of wolves and demons. Now I only feel safe when the rest of the world is asleep."

We lay back, looking up at the light shafting through the trees. I remembered the high windows of the cathedral of Durham. "When do you think FitzDuncan will strike at David?" I asked.

"Not while he is winning," said Catriona. "They will wait until he has taken Northumbria. In York, David will be a long way from home, and when his barons go off to pace out their new lands, FitzDuncan and MacGillemor will stay by his side. Soon they will be his escort whenever he rides out. Perhaps he will have a hunting accident, like William Rufus."

"How can you see it all so clearly?"

"Call it a curse," she said. "I have always been able to see too far."

That night, we crossed the lands of Eustace FitzJohn, and in the morning stopped only to rest our feet and eat the last of our food before pressing on. We were on edge until we reached the Wansbeck, whose wooded valley we had only to follow downstream to come to the Priory of Newminster.

We found a cluster of buildings, and some looked to have been burned and rebuilt, but to reach them we had to weave our way through a maze of bothies and shelters that had been thrown up between the trees. Living in them were whole families, crouching in poverty over the few things they had been able to save from their homes.

At first I was overcome with shame: these were the folk of the land, and their knights had failed them. But after the shame came a curious sense of purpose, for in their misery, these folk had turned for help to the white monks, to part of that cloak of civilisation that Thurstan had thrown over Northumbria.

The first priory building we came to was the infirmary, and as I stepped inside, I came face to face with Robert de Brus.

He was sitting at a table, his hand held out to a monk who was bent over it, cleaning a shallow wound on the knuckle of his wrist. At the sight of me, Robert jerked to his feet and reached for his sword.

"My lord!" protested the monk.

"For God's sake, Robert," I said wearily. "Do you honestly think I have come here to kill you?"

Robert gave a grunt and sat down, thrusting his hand

back towards the monk and glaring at me.

He was much as I remembered him; the same cropped black hair, the same strong-lined Norman face with a scar on his chin that came from falling off a horse as a boy; only now there was a new bitterness in his eyes, as if he no longer made any effort to hide his hatreds.

"So why are you here?" he asked, "not that I will believe anything you tell me."

"I happen to be one of the founders of this priory," I replied. "As I was passing, I felt an urge to know if King David had burned it down. Why are you here? Have you grown sick of the murdering cowards you ride with and turned to God?"

"I am here gathering knights for King David," he retorted. "Ranulf de Merlay has done homage to Prince Henry for Morpeth. We are helping him gather his strength."

"Poor Ranulf," I said. "So you are the escort to force him to ride to war? I am glad to hear that David has won the hearts and minds of the people."

The monk had finished dressing Robert's wound, and with his eyes still fixed on me, Robert stood up and flipped a coin from his wallet onto the table.

"You will come with me," he said. "Eustace FitzJohn is in Morpeth and I know he will be pleased to have you with us."

"Stop acting like a half-breed from Galloway," I told him. "It does not become you."

"Shall I say it again, more slowly?" he asked.

"My lord!" protested the monk. "This is a place of sanctuary. Threats are not made here."

Robert shrugged. "We will come for you in the morning," he told me. "Run if you like. We enjoy our hunting."

He walked out, threw himself on his horse, and spurred it carelessly through the bothies. I turned to see where Catriona had been hiding.

"Did you hear that?" I asked her.

"Is he the friend who saved you from Caerluel?" she asked in bewilderment.

"That was last year."

The monk came over to us, drying his hands on a cloth. "Is it sanctuary you have come for?" he asked.

"Not here," I said. "We are travelling to Tyne-mouth."

"That would be fraught with danger," he warned us. "The land around Newcastle is infested with Scots. If you are hunted, you would soon be at bay."

"In that case," I said, "I ask sanctuary."

Spent and subdued, Catriona and I joined a line of people waiting for a monk to ladle lentil stew into their bowls.

"I cannot stay here now," I said. "Eustace FitzJohn will think breaking sanctuary a small price to pay for the pleasure of marching me up and down before the gates of Carham."

"Have you any money?" asked Catriona.

I turned so she could open my wallet, and she took a few farthings.

"Trust a thief," she said. "I know an old ruse."

While the monks were singing Vespers, she went among the bothies and returned with two tattered and colourless cloaks, a pair of wooden bowls, and a pot of ashes.

"What we need now," she said, "is fish-glue."

She ran a finger along the fresh timber of one of the priory buildings, and held out a fingertip dripping with what looked like clear honey.

"Or pine resin," she said triumphantly.

She smeared it onto my face, in patches, and on top of it dabbed the ashes. I felt as if my skin were being covered by a crust of scabs.

"Is this witchcraft?" I asked balefully.

"Of a kind," said Catriona. "I am changing you into a leper."

When she had transformed me from plain to repulsive, she went to work on my hands; then stood still while I used the same sorcery to ruin her beauty. By nightfall, we looked like creatures of disease.

We slipped away from the priory and took a track running south.

"Are you sure we will be safe at Tynemouth?" I asked.

"David himself named it a place of sanctuary," said Catriona. "His father was buried there, and even the Scots will not break a sanctuary named by their king. Why are you laughing?"

"Because the only safe places in Northumberland are now the places under David's protection."

The night went by too fast, and at daybreak we had to slow our pace, look afflicted, and hobble. Catriona walked bent, her shoulders hunched, shuffling like the crone she would one day become. I dragged my right foot, as though I were lame, one hand on the strap of the shoulder-bag that hid the shape of the sword beneath my tattered cloak, my begging-bowl in the other.

The roads filled with horsemen and wagons. Whenever they passed we took to the edge, croaking out the lepers' cry – "Unclean! Unclean!" – and thrusting out our bowls for alms. I kept my eyes on the ground, but I could sense folk looking at me with horror and curiosity.

As the day grew hotter, the air became full of tiny flies, that stuck to the resin of our sores.

Then we heard a large group of horsemen at our backs, coming up with a jingle of harness and mail. We were among fields, with nowhere to hide. I covered my face with a leprous hand, crouched, wailed, and held out my bowl. They passed in a cloud of dust, perhaps a hundred of them, with a drumming of hooves that made the earth shake. Then they were gone, vanishing with a swish of tails down the road to Newcastle.

Within a mile, we reached a track leading eastwards to Tynemouth and the sea.

The priory stood on a headland walled on three sides by cliffs, a place so perfect it must have been a stronghold long before it was given to God. The only sounds were the breaking of the waves and the cries of the circling gulls.

I made for the gates, and Catriona tugged at my sleeve. "Perhaps you should wash," she suggested.

We ran down onto the beach below the priory, where I pulled off my shoes, most of my clothes, and splashed out to wash in the sea. The resin would take days to scrub away, but I came out with lips no longer tasting of ash, but of salt and sunlight.

"And yourself?" I asked Catriona.

"I will keep my guise for a few more miles," she said. "This is where we part."

"No," I protested. "You cannot leave me now."

"Why not?" she asked mischievously. "You left me in Cumbria. This way, I pay you back coin for coin."

"Never leave me," I begged. "Never."

She looked me hard in the eyes, and her smile curled. "I cannot see it," she said. "I cannot see myself beside you at a Norman high table, and I cannot see you beside me over a crofter's hearth in the wilds."

"What do you see?" I asked.

She faltered. "I cannot see what will become of you."

I wondered what she could see but would not say. She was staring into me, and all the promises I wanted to make died on my lips. Catriona knew me better than anyone. No promise I could make would impress her. She knew I had nothing to give but a troubled mind and a hungry heart.

If only I had kept my word, and gone to her in Longthwaite – if only I had not hurried back to York to take the hermit's riddle to Thurstan – our roads would still be the same. The Sacred Blade had cost me Catriona, just as it had cost me Robert. It had turned MacGillemor into a killer, and turned me into a betrayer, and a fool.

"It is true," I said, forcing a smile, "that you will be safer without me. Wherever you go, you will be safe, with those wits of yours."

"Our paths may cross," she said.

"If ever," I began, but Catriona threw out her arms and gave me an embrace to remember till the day I died. Then she slipped from my grasp, and turned, and a moment later all I could see was a leper, hurrying inland.

Alone, I walked through the arched gateway of Tynemouth Priory.

It was like entering a city. The wide court was crowded with the shanties and awnings of a hundred makeshift households. Goats were browsing a strip of turf left clear to form a street, at the far end of which rose a Norman church of golden stone, and a neat quadrangle of priory buildings.

The guest-master was a busy man, but he listened to me, and just before supper I was granted a moment with the prior in the outer parlour. I began to tell him how I needed his help to reach York, but he held up his hand.

"I must tell you, my son," he said, "that King David has granted us protection in the trust we will give no help to his enemies."

He was pointing at the sword-hilt sticking out over my shoulder.

"I travel in the service of Archbishop Thurstan," I assured him.

The prior tucked his hands into his sleeves, looking at me thoughtfully. "I hear Saint Cuthbert's Land is over-run," he said, "and Durham under siege. If, and may God forbid, you have anything to fear from King David, I would advise you to be down in the haven below the south cliff at sunrise. That is when our fishing boats set out, and one of the captains is a man named Ernost Spraybeard, who thinks nothing of sailing as far as the mouth of the Tees."

He had turned back into the cloister before I could thank him.

To the sweep of the fishermen's oars, their long, high-prowed boat cut out over the incoming tide. Aft of the mast, where the boat was widest, I crouched among the nets, trying not to think of the White Ship.

Ernost Spraybeard had shown no surprise when I appeared on the shore: he had been expecting me. Now, as the boat left the Tyne and the sail filled with wind, he swung on the steering-oar and the prow turned southwards.

Once I had got used to the buffeting of the waves, I was enchanted. The coast of Saint Cuthbert's Land unfurled like a tapestry. We passed Wearmouth, where the river that had curled beneath the citadel of Durham flowed out into the sea. There were fishing villages and church towers, from

Seaham to Hartness.

Through the haze I saw hills with a pattern I knew; the pointed summit of Odinshill and the giant's bench of the Wainstones. We had been following a coast no more than a tumble of earth, but in the distance it rose in soaring walls that overhung the sea. I had always wondered why the Vikings had named it Cleveland, the land of cliffs, and now I knew. They had named it from the sea.

Furling the sail, the fishermen returned to their oars to take the boat in among the marsh inlets that marked the mouth of the Tees. Seals were lolling on the mudbanks. I made my way to Ernost's side as we came in sight of the Priory of Middleburgh.

Ernost raised a hand to shield his eyes. "You are in for a troubled landfall," he said. "There are five or six armed men by the gates."

"As long as the priory is not burning," I replied, "they must be English."

"How very trusting," he remarked. "We will not beach. Come the shallows, you can jump out and wade."

In the mouth of the inlet, he called for the oars to be raised. The boat moved on of its own glide, through water that grew clearer until I could see the mud below.

"Thank the prior for his advice," I shouted, and sprang from the prow to flounder thigh-deep and splashing, while the boat slid by and the oars were dipped again to turn it back towards the sea.

The men-at-arms came down to the shore to meet me. They were sergeants, with mail-coifs and hauberks of boiled leather, and they wanted to know my name.

"Simon de Falaise," I said, without thinking. "Simon Aldredson," I added, "from the village of Leatham."

They looked at me doubtfully, but I could tell they

were impressed by my sword.

"I serve Archbishop Thurstan," I told them, "so if you care for your souls, you can find me a horse."

But not even the monks would lend me a horse. Swaying, as though still on the waves, I set off along the causewayed road through the marshes.

The land was harvest ripe. On the road to Gisburgh I fell in with a crowd of folk fleeing from the Tees to the hills. Children and the old were perched on wagons piled high with everything from washing-tubs to baskets of chickens. Dogs with hanging tongues loped beside the wheels, and geese snapped at my ankles.

Leatham, though, was off their road. I climbed the bank behind the mill and stood looking at the village. It was smaller than I remembered it. With its humped church and huddle of houses, it was a square of no importance in the chess-game of kingdoms, though I knew better now than to hope that would save it from burning.

Aldred was bent over the trough in our yard, washing off field-sweat. At the sight of me, he bellowed my name, and everyone came running.

We set up a table beneath the chestnut tree, and neighbours joined us. Over a gooseberry pie and jugs of sweet cider, we sat in the dusk with butter-lamps alight to draw the moths.

"Is there any word of King Stephen?" I asked Aldred.

"Only rumours," he replied. "He is said to be laying siege to Bristol, or Shrewsbury, wherever they are."

"Far away," I said. "It means he will not be coming north."

"We guessed that," said Aldred, "when Thurstan sent out his call for holy war."

"Holy war?"

"Holy war," repeated Aldred. "He is calling us to fight for the saints against the forces of darkness – to fight for Christendom against the burners of churches and the killers of children. We are to gather at Thirsk, in four days' time."

"Will you go?" I asked.

"The way Father Matthew put it," replied Aldred with a grin, "we have no choice. Either we answer the call and fight, or we burn in our homes and then in hell. So we fight. The twins will stay here, but all the men in the village will be going. I suppose we will be marching behind de Brus."

I wondered. If Thurstan had made this call to the people through their priests, it could only be because he had lost all faith in their lords.

It might even be because he had learnt that David had the Sacred Blade, and was about to make a summons of his own.

When at last I fell asleep, it was to sink so deeply that I missed the sunrise. One of the twins shook me awake.

"Simon! Robert de Brus is in the village. He is on his way here!"

I lurched to my feet so fast I cracked my head on a rafter. "Where is Aldred?" I asked.

"In the fields," said Mother.

"Stay in the house," I told them, and buckled on my sword-belt. I could hear horses. They were almost in the yard.

My thoughts were fast and bitter. So Robert had come hunting, driven by the hatred that had been his disease for so long. I would not give him the satisfaction of seeing me try to escape through the pig-pen. If he wanted my head, he could fight me for it.

My sword-hilt was still sticky with pine resin. I wondered where Catriona had turned when she left me at the gates of Tynemouth.

I stepped outside and blinked, for the armoured rider at the head of the pack was Robert de Brus the father, not the son. He raised a hand in greeting.

It was two and a half years since I had last seen the lord of Cleveland, Hartness, and Annandale; and now, with his stocky chest and grey beard, he reminded me of King David: King David without the gentleness in the eyes.

"Simon de Falaise?" he asked.

With all due courtesy, I bowed. "At your service, my lord."

"My men told me you were home," he said. "I travel to York to join Thurstan. I thought you might care to ride with me."

21. GAMES FOR THE PIECES

D E Brus had me ride at his side, and it was not out of kindness. He wanted to learn all I knew about where the pieces stood on the chess-board.

"So Eustace FitzJohn rides with David?" he asked.

"By his own choice," I said. "Other lords, like Ranulf de Merlay, have been forced to give David their homage."

"But Robert my son is with David?"

"By his own choice."

De Brus looked at me keenly. "Would you say that Robert's loyalty to David is unbreakable?" he asked.

I took a long breath. "Robert is full of hatred," I said. "If someone could quench it, there is no telling how he might be."

"I see you know him well," said de Brus. He gave a smile that looked uncannily like pride, as if Robert were exactly what he wanted him to be.

As we passed Stokesley, I expected us to keep to the edge of the hills, but de Brus turned north, to Castle Leven, where Pagan FitzWalter hurried out to hold the stirrup of his lord. FitzWalter only smiled when I was named to him, and as we took our places at his high table, where Jordan had once begged him to spare Ulrica, I began to overhear whispers, and caught people glancing at me. The tale was out that Jordan de Falaise still held Carham, and it seemed to be making them think.

I found myself sitting beside a young man not much older than Robert, and with Robert's face. There the likeness ended, for Adam de Brus was fair, and the first thing he gave me was an open and untroubled smile.

"I have met your father," he told me. "Three years ago, he stayed with us at Skelton, he and his Viking friend. I was sad when it ended in a quarrel."

"Jordan bears no grudge," I assured him.

"That is good to hear," said Adam. "Old quarrels are meaningless now."

We ate fast, so there was no time for chatter, but when the cavalcade set out again, we rode together.

"Was it Thurstan's call," I asked, "that made up your father's mind?"

"Has he made up his mind?" asked Adam in surprise. "All he has told me is that we are riding to York to see who is there and what they are saying."

Prickling with anger, I had to fight to keep myself smiling.

"Surely," I said, "your father could never now fight for King David, not after all he has done?"

"It is a harder choice for him than you may think," said Adam defensively. "Remember that he holds Annandale from King David, and Cleveland and Hartness from whoever is king of England. All the signs are that Stephen will not be king much longer, so why fight for him against the man who may soon be, if not king, at least the king-maker?"

"And will you follow your father wherever he chooses to fight?" I asked.

"I can hardly rebel," said Adam, with a smile. "It is my inheritance he is working to protect."

If de Brus chose to fight with David, I was left reflecting, he could order Aldred and the villagers of Cleveland to do the same, forcing them to choose between their priests and their lord.

The dust and heat were like Jordan's tales of Syria. It had been a dry summer. By the time the pointed roofs of York minster rose in the distance, all I could think of was my thirst. Only as we rode into the city and I glimpsed a girl I thought for a moment was Catriona, did I remember it was my goal. I counted the nights back to Carham, and found I had made the journey in just seven days.

It was supper-time, and most of the folk we saw in the streets were hurrying home. Much had been rebuilt since the fire, with here and there a flourish of carpentry Orm would have enjoyed, but some of the richer houses were shuttered. Several of the merchants seemed to have loaded their boats and slipped downstream.

We rode straight to the eastern castle, where the bailey was thronged with men and horses, and half a head above the rest of the crowd stood Walter Espec.

"What in the world brings you here?" he asked de Brus, with mock surprise betrayed by a wide grin.

De Brus looked around, and gave a dry chuckle.

"I thought I would come and find out your plans," he said off-handedly, "then ride and warn David."

When Walter caught sight of me, he hugged me like a son, and he kept hold of my arm until I had told him all there was to tell of Carham. He roared with laughter, calling out the choicest morsels to those within hearing even before I had finished. By nightfall, the tale of how King David had lost a baggage-train would be all over York.

Walter led me round to be the living witness as he repeated the tale to his friends. I met William d'Aumale, Ilbert de Lacy, and William de Percy: names I knew, the great lords of Yorkshire. As soon as I could, I slipped away and out of the castle.

I was crossing the market-place when in one of the taverns, someone struck a lute, and broke into song.

> *"Durham still clings to God,*
> *Caerluel is full of Scots;*
> *men of war say it's time to ride,*
> *men of peace say the river's dry,*
> *while the girls and the scholars*
> *say it's time to hi-ide ..."*

Aimeric was as dark and crowlike as ever.

"Don't tell me," he said, slipping the lute back into its bag; "Carham was too dull, so you have come here looking for trouble."

It was so good to see him.

"Take me to Thurstan," I said.

"Not tonight," said Aimeric. "He has a gaggle of barons sharing his supper-table, and I doubt he will have the strength for anyone else." He peered into my face. "Simon, you look weary."

He bought a jug of wine at the tavern, then took me by the arm and led me down a street towards the Jewish quarter by the river.

"These days, I have a room of my own," he said, "in a house belonging to one of the canons. This is the part of the city that was too damp to catch fire."

"Is Thurstan strong?" I asked

"In body or in spirit?" asked Aimeric. "In body, he is suffering enough to allow us to carry him round in a litter."

"What made him call for holy war?"

Aimeric's eyes took on a certain merriment. "I do not think he was guided by a signal in the heavens," he said. "I think it was the only way he could find of getting the great lords here so he could set about filling their hearts with the courage to ride out and face David. From what I have seen of them, if he can do it, he is a greater wizard than Merlin."

We came to a doorway, and Aimeric reached for a key that hung at his belt. "They talk," he went on, "of King Arthur's last battle, which I take to mean they believe the end is near for the Norman kingdom of England."

I looked past him, to the wide river flowing by the end of the alley in a rippling reflection of the sunset sky. "The Northumbria of the holy kings ended in fire," I said. "So did the Viking land that came after. These things happen."

"Take care," warned Aimeric. "You are beginning to talk like a scholar."

He led me up a wooden stairway to a loft. By the window in the gable-end stood a writing-desk, and beside it a cedarwood chest piled with manuscripts. A truckle-bed and a cross-legged stool were the only other furnishings. I pulled off my shoes and stretched out on the bed, while Aimeric found a tinder-box and lit a tall yellow candle.

"I have been teaching in the cathedral school," he said, "just grammar and rhetoric, but in time perhaps a little philosophy. Have you ever heard of Peter Abelard? Or Bernard Sylvestris?"

"Are they from Galloway?"

"No. They used to give lectures in Paris and Chartres." He lifted a cloth to reveal a pewter plate with a pasty and half a cheese. "This will be almost as nourishing as their teaching."

With the food and then the wine, I began to revive. I

told Aimeric of the siege of Carham, and how when the Scots charged, we sang his song. I told him how I had heard Saint Cuthbert's voice.

Aimeric listened wide-eyed, then covered his face with his hands.

"We should have guessed," he said. "We should have guessed two years ago."

"Well, now we know," I said. "You said there was a list . . ."

"Oh yes, there is a list," said Aimeric, "a litany of the forty-five churches where Saint Cuthbert's body rested between Lindisfarne and Durham. I have a copy, but it can hardly help us now."

"Yes it can," I said. "We have only to . . ."

"No," he said, with a certainty that silenced me. "Every single one of those churches lies on land the Scots have over-run. David may never know it, but he is already lord of wherever it is the Sacred Blade lies hidden."

I was woken by Aimeric kicking open the door. He came in and heeled it shut behind him, in one hand a fresh loaf, in the other a hunk of ham.

Sunlight was streaming through the shutters. I could hear voices in the street, and smell the tanneries by the river.

"You have just missed a rare piece of sorcery," he told me. "Thurstan summoned the barons to Mass, and went straight for their souls. He told them to fast for three days, and each make his confession, all so they may be purified for the trial by ordeal that is to come. He was like Joshua. He told them they will march out behind his own cross, and set in it will be the consecrated host. Their banner will be the banner of Saint Peter, the rock on which the demons of hell break like spray." Aimeric sighed with pleasure. "He is putting the fear of hell into them," he said happily, "and by the time he has finished, it will be stronger than their fear of David."

He passed me the loaf, and I hesitated. "Should I be fasting?" I asked.

"No need," Aimeric assured me. "I doubt you have as many sins to be cleansed as our good Norman lords."

We spent the rest of the day in the tavern.

On the second day of the barons' fast, Bernard de Balliol rode in from the south at the head of a force of several hundred knights.

He had come from King Stephen, who was now besieging Gloucester, and he came with a breeze of purpose; for de Balliol was lord of Upper Teesdale, which lay straight in the path of the Scots. Better even than his coming was the rumour of the crowds he had seen on the road. Whole villages were on the march behind the crosses of their parish priests. Thurstan's call was being answered. The gathering at Thirsk had begun.

That evening, Adam de Brus came to bring me a summons from Walter Espec. He found me in the tavern, and I could tell he had been fasting by the way he shivered at the smell of the cooking.

Walter was in the keep of the eastern castle, sitting at a bare table with several other lords, none of whom gave the appearance of feeling purified.

"De Brus and de Balliol are riding to seek out David," he told me. "Once he hears of the army Thurstan has gathered, he may think better of carnage, and come to a settlement. De Brus is asking that you ride with him."

"Why, my lord?" I asked de Brus.

"You are close to Robert," he said. "You may be able to make him see sense."

"Even if I could," I said, "I would still refuse to go."

They looked surprised, as if they had never expected cowardice from the son of Jordan de Falaise.

"While my father holds Carham," I explained, "I am a danger to him. He told me the story of Robert de Mowbray at the gates of Bamburgh. The one thing he fears is that the Scots will catch me to brandish in front of Carham."

I wanted to say more, but it seemed better to keep to myself my suspicion that when de Brus reached David's side, he would stay there.

Walter looked at me thoughtfully. "Simon is like a son to me," he told de Brus. "I will keep Adam here in York, so that if David or any of his barons try to take Simon, you can tell them that your own son is hostage for his safe return. How does that seem to you?"

"Clever," said de Brus. "I see we trust each other."

We did not even have to cross the Tees. King David was in Yarm.

We rode in late the next afternoon, covered in sweat and dust, to find David holding court in a merchant's hall by the river. On the far bank, palls of smoke were rising into the windless sky as the men of Galloway freed Saint Cuthbert's Land from the Normans.

David greeted de Brus and de Balliol with open joy.

"Now we are complete," he declared. "I knew you would come."

He made a gesture of welcome that seemed to be drawing them into the group of men gathered round him. They were a powerful assembly. Scattered around the hall were Prince Henry, the earls of Scotland, Eustace FitzJohn and many Normans, with FitzDuncan standing carefully apart from a group at whose centre was the lord of Galloway. No one who saw those faces could fail to sense the power of David's purpose and its nearness to fulfilment. There had been nothing like this since the Great Rising, but those vanished companions were cheap wooden chess-men compared to the tall ivory figures that had gathered now to play for the land of Northumbria.

De Brus and de Balliol stood before them, facing men they had known and trusted all their lives. De Balliol was the first to find his voice.

"We have only come, my lord," he said, "to bring you warning. Thurstan has called for holy war. He has raised the whole of Yorkshire against you."

David's smile shrank, and his widening eyes were Saint Margaret's.

"Holy war?" he repeated softly.

"An army is gathering at Thirsk," said de Balliol, "under the banners of three saints. They believe they are fighting to save Christendom from the hands of your heathen."

De Brus nodded grimly. "Why in God's name," he asked the king, "did you swell your ranks with the filth from Galloway? You and I know they are the ones to blame for the burning, but the folk of Northumbria blame you. You could so easily have won our hearts, but instead you let demons loose on us, and threw the whole game away."

"Turn back, my lord," said de Balliol. "Turn back now. We will get Henry the earldom of Northumberland – I swear it – but you must turn back."

"Is this what you call loyalty?" cried the voice of William FitzDuncan.

He pushed his way forward, and behind him I saw Robert and Drustan. Robert was gazing disdainfully at his father, but he took the time to give me a glance heavy with loathing and contempt.

"How long will you suffer their promises and threats?" FitzDuncan asked the king. "We have been living on their hollow words for years. Tell them, my lord, that the day has come for reckoning."

"Are these your counsellors now?" de Brus asked David.

"Traitor!" sneered FitzDuncan.

"Am I, my lord?" de Brus asked the king. "How many years have we known each other? How many times have we fought side by side? I remember when we rode against the men of Moray, and the times we have stood together against Galloway. Have you ever known me give you anything but my heart?"

There might have been no one else in the hall, so intently were David and de Brus now locked in each other's stare. David let the anguish show in his face, until it looked as if Saint Margaret and Malcolm Canmore were fighting for his soul. It must have been his father who won, for his face slowly set into a mask of stone.

"Yes, we have always ridden together," he said. "Do you ride with me now?"

"No," said de Brus, and he shook as he said it. "I cannot burn my own and my neightbours' land. I cannot ride with the men of Galloway."

"I am your lord," said David gently. "I command you to ride with me."

De Brus stared at the ground for what seemed an eternity, and when he looked up, there were tears running down his cheeks. I was not the only one who gasped.

"Then I renounce my homage," he said. "The love and trust that bound us are broken."

"And I renounce mine," said Bernard de Balliol.

"You break my heart," David told them.

The hall had gone silent. None of us had ever seen the breaking of a loyalty so deep. I stole a glance at FitzDuncan, and saw the effort he was having to make not to smile.

"So the English gather at Thirsk," said David stiffly. "You have my safe-conduct to go and tell them we come."

Robert leapt forward. "My lord," he cried, "give me the lands that are held by my father. I will hold them loyally for you."

Frowning, David turned to him. "What are you asking?"

"Annandale, my lord," said Robert eagerly, "and Hartness is now yours to give. Grant them to me and to my sons after me, and our loyalty will be to Scotland, never to England."

David looked at de Brus, but de Brus was silent. His face showed nothing of his thoughts.

"They are yours," David told Robert.

As we left, Robert was swearing his oath of loyalty for the lands of Hartness and Annandale.

We galloped all the way to Castle Leven, where de Brus strode into the hall before FitzWalter had even been told of our arrival.

"Send your womenfolk to Skelton," he told him roughly, "then gather your men. We are riding to Thirsk."

Everyone scattered, the ladies to their chambers and the men to the stables and armoury. When the hall had emptied, de Brus sat down at the high table with a gesture for us to join him. He reached for a dish of roast duck and poured us ale.

"Eat now," he told me, "before the fear sets in."

"You always were a cunning one," de Balliol told him.

De Brus gave him a bleary smile. "I thought it all through beforehand," he replied. "I thank God I did, for I almost lost my wits when David began tearing my heart in two."

"What is all this?" I asked. "Are you saying that what happened in Yarm is what you wanted?"

"Indeed," said de Brus. "It gives me no pleasure to see my domain broken in two, but it is better than losing it all. Whatever happens now, I will have a son on the winning side."

"Then why," I asked angrily, "did you want me with you?"

"It has been a long day," replied de Brus, "and nothing could matter less to me than your peace of mind, but I will tell you if it will help you die happy."

"I would be grateful, my lord."

"My son Robert," he said, "is rash and thoughtless, which makes him unpredictable. For all I knew, when he saw me break loyalty with David, he might take it into his head that a son is bound by honour to fight beside his father, or some such nonsense. I brought him up to do the opposite, but you never can tell. The trick was to keep him from even thinking it. I guessed the sight of you by my side would keep his mind full of jealousy and greed, and I was right."

I stared at him. The riddles of the Sacred Blade were clear water compared to the minds of the lords of Northumbria. No wonder Robert had always been so tormented. His father had made sure it was his inheritance.

22. *THE BATTLE OF THE STANDARD*

A s we reached Thirsk, I thought the world had turned upside down. The sky was murky with clouds, but the land was a sky of stars. On the meadows by the castle burned a thousand cooking-fires.

The castle was crowded with knights. De Brus and de Balliol elbowed their way into the hall, towards the high table where I could see Walter and the lady Gundreda; but I took one breath of the heat and sweat, and chose to stay outside. Great hearths were glowing in the bailey, and everyone was making the most of what might be their last meal on earth.

Roger de Mowbray caught hold of my arm and spun me round. "I have been hearing all sorts of tales about you," he said. "Is it true you walked through Northumberland, straight under FitzJohn's nose?"

"That is only half of it," I told him. "I was guided by a sorceress, who turned me into a leper and made me sleep away the days in the places of the dead."

Roger guffawed. "Let me tell you something true," he suggested. "All day, our ranks have been growing. I believe we are going to win this battle."

"Have you by any chance," I asked him, "got a spare

shirt of mail?"

He looked at me with alarm. "We have emptied our armoury," he said. "I will see what I can find, but we march at any moment."

"Where?"

"As far north as we can go before sunrise."

He was back a moment later, holding a coat of old-fashioned ring-mail, richly lined with quilted leather and collared with silk.

"You are honoured," he told me. "This belonged to Robert de Mowbray. My mother keeps it for his sake, but when I told her you were the grandson of a knight who served him, she sent it with her blessing."

I pulled the shirt over my head, and Roger laced the thongs at the back of the neck. Earl Robert must have been my height, though with broader shoulders. The mail had a comforting weight, and shimmered like a dragon's scales in the torchlight.

"Jordan will be proud when he hears of this," I said, and caught the flicker of doubt on Roger's face.

"How long has Carham been under siege?" he asked.

"This will be the twentieth week."

"No matter," he said confidently. "Once we have won in battle, we will soon chase David back to the border. Have you a horse?"

"I have the use of one that belongs to de Brus."

"Then perhaps you had better ride with him. In the battle, though, you would be welcome among my knights."

Roger hurried away. I buckled my sword-belt over my shirt of mail, and went to make certain of my horse. I was leading him from the picket when I brushed against a palfrey I knew even before I saw the sandalled feet in the stirrups.

"Aimeric!" I cried. "What are you doing here?"

He gave a grimace that I took to be an attempt at a smile.

"When the crusade left York," he told me, "I could not stay behind. That is the trouble with holy war. Who can resist the temptation of having their sins forgiven?"

"There must be easier ways of going to heaven," I retorted.

"There can be very few that are quicker," he said balefully.

I swung myself up into the saddle. The trumpets were sounding and men running in all directions. Aimeric looked scared out of his wits.

"Stay out of this," I urged him. "You have never hurt a fly in your life."

"I had to come," he said. "I cannot kill, but I know something of healing. I can clean and stitch and bind a wound."

I reached for his hand. "We will always be good at different things, you and me," I said, "and together, we will always be stronger than alone."

Slowly, the army gathered itself and swarmed out of Thirsk onto the northern road. Less than a quarter of the host were Norman knights. The rest were the people of Northumbria.

Someone began to sing, an old English battle-song, and the singing spread unevenly along the line of the marching host. Here and there, the words had been forgotten, and the names had no meaning, but the singing itself had power.

"God, what a tune," said Aimeric.

"You should write new verses for it," I told him. "Tonight, I feel as if the two streams in my blood are at last flowing together. If we live, we will not be telling our children about the Conquest or the Great Rising or the Burning. We will tell them how the Normans and English came together to stand for Northumbria."

With so many of the host on foot, it took several hours just to reach Allerton. Not far beyond the town, Walter Espec ordered the trumpets to sound the halt. We were on a brow of open heath, with wide, shallow valleys on either side. Ahead of us, under the paling sky, stretched a forested plain at whose far edge lay the Tees and Saint Cuthbert's Land.

The singing had stopped. Men gathered in the groups of their village or their lord, and looked around. It was an open place. There were no palisades, and no ditches; even the trees were too scattered to give cover. If this was where we were to fight, we would have to stand fast.

Scouts were sent riding on towards the Tees, and the order went round to dismount and picket the horses behind the host. We would be fighting on foot.

Where men from Cleveland were gathering to de Brus, I saw Aldred, and took Aimeric to meet him. Adam de Brus waved and came walking towards me. At first I did not recognise him. All I saw was a metal head, with all but the eyes and chin hidden under a mail-coif and a helmet with a nose-guard.

"Do you think these are the right tactics?" he asked me. "Why are we all on foot when David has mounted knights to throw at us?"

"It's how it should be," said Aldred, "all in one shield ring."

De Brus overheard us. "It worked for King Henry at Tinchebrai," he said, "though not so well for Harold Godwinsson at Hastings. You might say it is a tactic we save for the great days, when a quarrel needs to be settled, one way or the other."

Once the horses were led away, we saw that a wagon had been pulled to the top of the light slope on which we were massed. On it, men were grappling with a pole, and as we watched, they swung it upright against the dawn sky.

It was a ship's mast. At its top was tied the cross of Archbishop Thurstan, and beneath, hanging from a spar tied crosswise, were the three bright banners of Saint Peter of York, Saint John of Beverley, and Saint Wilfrid of Ripon.

At the sight of it, a silence fell on the army, for the Standard had the shape of a cross, and the banners writhed in the breeze like the three who had been crucified on Golgotha, a thousand years before.

A man in holy robes was being helped up onto the wagon.

"Who is that?" asked Adam. "It's not Thurstan."

"Bishop Ralph of the Orkneys," said Aimeric, "one of the canons of York."

Bishop Ralph had a good voice. He told us how Thurstan was with us, keeping a vigil of prayer on the steps of his highest altar; then he gave us a long, harrowing litany of the crimes of the demons who by God's grace we must kill.

"Fight them for Christendom," he implored us, raising his hand in the sign of blessing. "We absolve you from all burden of sin, in the name of the Father, whose creatures they have foully and horribly destroyed; and of the Son, whose altars they have defiled; and of the Holy Spirit, whose elect they have killed like madmen."

Our scouts were already returning, which meant they had not had to go far to catch sight of the Scots.

We ourselves could still see nothing. As the daylight grew, the clouds trailed apart, and mist rose from the ground. Walter Espec pulled himself up onto the wagon, and stood looking out over the army.

"Not long to wait now," he said. He hooked his thumbs into his belt, then let a smile break through his thick black beard.

"Much has been said these past few days, and you must be sick of words. Mine will be the last, and I will not insult you by denying the truth. We are here to fight, and many of us will die. Most of you have never known battle, and you must be wishing you had never come. Well, take heart: so do I. If I had my way, I would be safe in bed, and the only battles I would fight would be with chess-men or dice, and the only great deeds in my life would be those of King Arthur and our ancestors. There is much that is good from the lips of storytellers, and bad when you have to live it yourself."

That drew some desperate laughter.

"Today, we face death," he said, "and believe me, it is nothing to what we face tomorrow, if today we fail. We know what the Scots will do to our wives, our children, and our churches. Better we die than live to see it."

To the north, we heard a braying of horns, and it was none too distant.

"Do you hear them, my friends?" asked Walter. "Shall we let them know where we stand?"

He was answered by the roar of twelve thousand voices; a sound as if the earth were tearing in two.

The mist was thinning and smoking away. To the east I could see the hills of Cleveland, their flanks blue in morning shadow. To north and west the plain stretched green, silver-hollowed with dew, the lines of field, forest and heath shaping the chess-board over which, with a glitter of armour, the Scots were riding towards us.

William d'Aumale and Bernard de Balliol ordered us into battle-line. We spread out, east and west of the Standard, a wall of men from one side of our low rise to the other. Men with shields or spears were gathered to the front, and behind them the archers. The rest of us made the third and deepest line. I found myself near its western end, with de Brus and the men of Cleveland. To our left was Roger de Mowbray. Behind us, where the land dipped, Aimeric had joined the older men, and women, who were setting up picket lines for the horses.

Then there was no more looking around, but only ahead.

So close that we could hear their taunts, the Scottish army came to a halt. Many were dismounting to fight on foot, but when the host had spread to match our line, it went on thickening and darkening. We were utterly outnumbered and we watched with the numbness of horror, like a hare frozen by the growing shadow of an eagle in swoop.

The centre of the Scottish line was a shapeless seething of ill-armoured figures. These were the scum that had crawled out from under every stone in Albany and Galloway, the vermin of greed who carried the plague of the Waste Land. Winging them on either side, all was order and chivalry. At the eastern end of the battle-line were David and the Scottish earls, under many banners, but chief among them the dragon banner of the lost kings of Wessex. At the western end were Prince Henry and a host of mounted knights. Among them I glimpsed Eustace FitzJohn; and somewhere among them, I guessed, would be Robert and Drustan.

"You see!" said Adam. "They are going to fight on horseback. They can cut through our shield-wall wherever they choose to strike!"

But it was not what came first.

Suddenly, without order, the centre of the Scottish line burst like a falling barrel into a horde of men running towards us howling the war-cries of Albany and Galloway. There were thousands of them, but they wore no armour, and at the first volley from our archers, they went down like barley in a hailstorm. Some picked themselves up, and ran on quilled with arrows, but our archers loosed another volley, at deadlier range, and the first to reach our shield-wall were so scattered and breathless that they were quickly cut down.

It was enough first blood to give us hope, and when the horde struck with its full weight, our shield-wall gave ground, but held, and fought with rage. Our archers bent their bows, and whenever the shield-wall buckled inwards, men hurried forward from the third line, and pushed it out again.

When the centre of the Scottish line emptied, the attack reached high tide. Scottish knights were riding with it, and they seemed to be trying to order it back, but the wild men would not listen. Those of us still only watching were now shouting ourselves hoarse, even de Brus and Walter Espec, for we knew that if we could break the men of Albany and Galloway, we could hold our ground against anyone.

It was then that Prince Henry sounded the trumpets and made his charge, and he rode not for the centre of the shield-wall, but for where we stood at its western end.

We braced ourselves, shoulder to shoulder. The archers did all they could, shooting at the horses, not the riders in armour; but when the charge struck, the weight of it swept us away. We were crushed backwards, knocked together and over. Something hit me like a boulder, and slammed me to the ground. I was rolling over when someone fell on top of me, crushing my face in the thistles.

The knights rode over us, trampling and hacking. I kept down until the air cleared of hooves, then looked up, to see the Scots wrenching their horses round to take the centre of our battle-line from the rear.

De Brus was back on his feet, and yelling at us to get after them. Away to the east, King David's knights were charging.

I joined Roger de Mowbray and a charge that took the Scottish knights in the flank. In turning, they had lost the force of their charge and their closeness of formation. Those of us with spears went for their horses; the rest of us took the knights once they were on the ground.

Everyone was now fighting to stay on their feet in a deafening whirlpool of slaughter. Some simply lost their wits and went down, but my head was cold and clear. With both hands on the hilt of my sword, I parried and hacked, the way Orm had taught me, and went for one man after another, hammering them into the ground. Nothing could touch me. With each man I killed, there was a moment when his strength began to ebb, and black fear widened his eyes. That was when he died, however long he still had to flail before I cut him down.

Face followed face, until I came to the one with cropped black hair, a square chin, and eyes that met mine with a glare of desire. Robert had lost his helmet and his shield. He shone with sweat, and the veins in his neck stood out so far they were like ivy growing up his throat. From the weight of his first blow, I knew that all he wanted was to take me with him to hell.

I took a step backwards, giving him room to swing wild and waste his strength on hatred. I fell back a little more, parrying his blows before they reached me, but only just, so he would think me tired. His lips set in a snarl; the sweat flew from the ends of his hair; and before he knew it, he was breathing out of time with the rhythm of his sword-work, and I had worked out how to kill him.

I braced my legs, and struck back hard. Caught off balance, he stumbled, and parried my next blow so narrowly that our knuckles smashed together. To keep him dazed, I swung blow after blow at him, measuring each one, until he was reeling backwards, parrying clumsily, the black fear in his eyes. He was in full retreat when he stumbled over a body and fell headlong.

Someone ran past me, and I saw Adam de Brus fling himself onto his brother, pinning him to the ground and wrenching the sword from his hand.

"God bless you, Simon," he said. "We have him alive."

When Robert struggled to rise, Adam gave him a fist in the face that knocked him senseless. I lowered my sword and stood still to catch my breath. De Brus came up and laid a hand on my shoulder.

"Well done," he said warmly. "I will not forget this."

"Robert be damned!" I protested. "Leave him and fight the Scots!"

"No need," said de Brus. "They are running. Prince Henry and those who could have just cut their way free."

Eustace FitzJohn galloped past, his sword-arm running with blood from a gash on his shoulder. Some of our knights were already running to the picket-lines to get their horses. The battle was breaking into a mess of ragged combats; and where I stood, there was no one left to fight.

I swayed on my feet, all my anger draining away as I caught sight of the faces on the ground. One of them was Drustan. He had already been stripped of his armour. He lay spread-eagled, eyes wide, torn for ever from the midsummer trails of the Ettrick Forest.

I was walking towards him when Aimeric bawled my name. Turning, I saw a horseman bearing down on me, his hair and beard the red of fox fur.

There was no time to raise my sword. I sprang sideways, but his spear-thrust took me high in my left leg, and the twist he gave the spear to pull it free threw me head over heels.

MacGillemor wrenched his horse round to come at me again and finish the job. I was too stunned even to think of rolling out of the way. I could see his eyes, and the fear in his face, and knew that for the past three years he had been as frightened of me as I had of him. We had haunted each other, and I had spent so many nights thinking of all the ways he might kill me that it was almost a relief to see how quick it was going to be.

Then Aldred was beside me, and his axe flew through the air to take MacGillemor in the chest with a force that threw him from the saddle.

As he hit the ground, Roger de Mowbray reached him. I cried out to take him alive, but Roger's sword was already set on its downward swing.

23. DREAMERS AND THE DREAMLESS ONES

O NE afternoon, I woke to see Walter Espec at the foot of my bed.

"I came to see Prior Waltheof," he said. "Father Lambert tells me you are a miracle."

"Did he say if he will ever let me leave?" I asked.

"He says it will be weeks before you can ride, and a year before you are strong."

After the battle, I had been one of the many loaded onto ox-carts and jolted down the dry, rutted roads to the douce valley of Kirkham Priory. It was a long way to be dragged, but one of the canons of Kirkham was Father Lambert, who had learnt the craft of healing from the heathen wizards of Cordoba.

He had saved my leg by stitching up the wound, then giving me draughts of unknowing to take me through the pain, and potions to nourish the blood I had left. I had seen enough in the infirmary of Kirkham to know it a miracle I was alive, and whole, and returning, but I was helpless as a baby, and still a bloodless white.

Walter had aged. A weariness showed in the hang of his cheeks and the stoop of his shoulders. He took a cross-legged stool and sat down beside me.

"How long has it been?" I asked.

"Tomorrow is Saint Matthew's Day," he said. "If Carham still holds, I make this the twenty-fifth week of the siege."

"Carham still holds," I assured him. "When I left, they had food to last them till Michaelmas."

"It will soon be Michaelmas," he said gently.

One by one, he put his fingertips together, until his hands had the shape of a sea-shell.

"Stephen dare not come north," he said, his eyes on his hands, "and David still holds Northumberland and Cumbria. We cannot find the strength to drive him out."

So the battle had done no more than save Yorkshire and Saint Cuthbert's Land. Northumbria was broken in two.

"Carham is the only castle in Northumberland still defiant," said Walter. "We would have heard if it had fallen."

"Will you send help, my lord?" I asked; but as I spoke, I remembered the length of Northumberland. Just to pass Newcastle would cost a battle.

"The pope has sent help," said Walter, talking as much to himself as to me. "There is only one pope now, so at least the Church is pulling itself together. Bishop Alberic of Ostia is in York. In a few days he leaves for Caerluel."

He sat frowning for a while, then shook himself and lumbered to his feet. "I must go," he said. "Thurstan expects me tonight. When you can leave, Simon, go to Elmeslac. Adele will care for you – and whatever the outcome of all this, I give you my word you will lack for nothing. You will have all Jordan wished for you, and more."

He looked at me intently, nodded, as if agreeing with

his own thoughts, then left.

I sank back into the trough I had moulded in my mattress of straw, into the days measured by the flap of the canons' tread, the bells and the stillness in between. I was too weak to move, and sometimes too angry to speak. Stephen had betrayed us all. Jordan and Orm were about to die for nothing, for Northumbria was broken, and Carham had already been surrendered to its fate.

I would not go to Elmeslac. I would keep my promise to Jordan, and go home.

A few days after Michaelmas, I crested the hill above Oswaldkirk, and looked out over the Forest of Pickering. The land was harvested, and turning to autumn. This at least had been spared the men of Galloway.

I was mounted on a docile hackney from the priory stables, but my legs could hardly grip. By the time I reached Elmeslac, I was lolling in the saddle and, despite my vow, I rode into the bailey.

The lady Albrea herself came to greet me, with Adele and all the maidens of the castle, and they could not have given me a warmer welcome.

"Do not look so surprised," the lady Albrea told me. "We have heard how you fought for the Standard. You have won yourself great honour."

They wanted to know if it were true that I had crossed Northumberland in the guise of a leper. I tried to keep to the truth, but by the end of supper I was growing to like the sound of my own voice. Chance had made me the hero Robert had longed to be, and I was bitter enough to wish he could have been there to choke on it.

I quickly began to wilt, and the lady Albrea gave the order for a chamber to be prepared for me close by the hall. I was led there, shakier on my legs than Thurstan, and when the others left, Adele stayed to light a lamp and then to talk.

It was almost two years since we had seen each other. She had bloomed into a wild, gaunt beauty, so strong I could not take my eyes from her. Her mind, though, was on anything but herself.

"Father is with Thurstan," she told me. "All their hopes are hung on the meeting at Caerluel."

"Alberic of Ostia has reached David?" I asked.

She nodded, and for a moment sat silent with her thoughts.

"It has been a cruel year," she said. "You can see the grief in Father's face. All his dreams have been broken."

"Dreams?" I repeated, curiously; for though I had always known Walter Espec was great-hearted, he had never struck me as a dreamer.

"He used to tell me," said Adele, "that when he first came to Northumbria, he vowed to bring it the guard against darkness it has not known since the days of King Arthur. That was his dream; but now he sees us falling back into war, while the barons betray their duty, and the land goes without law. While you were suffering at Carham, Father rode from castle to castle, begging the lords to defend the land. In the end, they fought because they had no choice, and they fought only to save their necks and their domains. Now the threat is past, none of them will lift a finger to win back the land that has been lost. It breaks Father's heart."

"The trial for Walter and Thurstan," I said, "has been to find themselves fighting a dream as strong as their own."

"What do you mean?" she asked.

"David's dream," I explained, "was to take North-umbria for Scotland. It was in the fate that came to him from his father that one day he would try. Well, now he has tried and failed and seen the cost. He will never try again. We have only to push him back."

"Do you believe that?" asked Adele. "Father says we are headed for anarchy and darkness. When he first came to Elmeslac, he grumbled at even having to build a palisade. Now he talks of building a keep, and ramparts of stone."

"Wherever we are headed," I said, "Northumbria was reborn at the Battle of the Standard. The barons were there to save their necks, but the rest of us were fighting for Thurstan and your father, so that all they have built may endure."

Adele looked at me wonderingly. "You should tell him," she said. "Tell him his dreams have found a son."

So I stayed, and told myself I was waiting for Walter; but when at last a knight rode in to Elmeslac, it was not the lord of the castle, but his neighbour, Roger de Mowbray.

Adele and I were in the hall, playing chess, and we looked up to find him watching us from the doorway. Laughing, he came forward and embraced us both, Adele for the love still between them, and me for the battle we had fought side by side.

"Where is the lady Albrea?" he asked.

"In Pickering," answered Adele.

"So much the better," said Roger. "The message I bring from Walter is as much for you as for her."

He joined us at the table, and Adele went to fetch crab-apple cider and a pastry filled with blackberries. As we ate, a shaft of sunlight was catching the reds and golds in a tapestry of Charlemagne and his paladins that hung on the wall above our heads.

"Thurstan still needs Walter at his side," Roger told

us. "Nothing has been settled."

"Did nothing come of the meeting in Caerluel?" I asked.

"The Church resolved its quarrels," said Roger. "Bishop Aethelwold is to be allowed to return to Caerluel; but as to the war, all David will give is a truce until Martinmas."

"Martinmas?" said Adele. "But that is barely a month away."

"For peace itself," said Roger glumly, "David makes demands..."

"Not more demands that Stephen will be honour-bound to refuse!" I protested. "This could go on for ever."

"What are they?" asked Adele.

Roger held up his hands. "All I know," he said, "is that Thurstan and Walter sat through the night talking with Bishop Alberic before he rode south to make his report to King Stephen."

"By the time they have finished," I said, "Jordan will be dead."

"Of Carham," said Roger, "there is good and bad news. The good is that Jordan still holds."

"How do you know?" I asked.

"By the bad. When David agreed to the truce, it was only if he be free to make war on all who still resist him in Northumberland and Cumbria. He named your father. He named Carham."

"He will not need until Martinmas," I said. "By now, Jordan will be starving."

Roger set down his cup and looked at me. There was a grim eagerness to his face. "Say the word, Simon, and I will gather my men and you and I will ride north, to fight our way to your father's side."

"Do that," Adele warned him, "and in one grand gesture, you will break the truce and get yourselves killed."

"Adele is right," I said, "and Jordan would say the same. He knew it might end this way."

Towards dusk, Roger rose to leave, and we went out into the bailey to watch him mount. I was just about steady on my legs. There was an autumn chill in the air, and Adele ran inside to find Roger a cloak. I watched Roger watch her go.

"You should marry her," I told him.

He looked at me reproachfully. "Until I come of age," he said, "my mother is ward of all my lands. She reminds me of it whenever I speak against her will. She would throw me out to get her way, and these are not safe times to put an inheritance in any doubt." He patted me on the cheek. "You are the one who should marry Adele. Walter would be overjoyed to have you for a son."

"But you have her heart," I pointed out.

"A part of it," said Roger. "She told me once that there are only two men she has loved since the day she met them. I was the second. The first was you."

When he left, Adele took my arm to help me back into the hall. I wanted to ask her there and then if what Roger had said were true, but it would not have been courteous. I decided to wait for signs, and by nightfall, I was longing for them, and the longing grew.

So I stayed on at Elmeslac, and Adele and I rode out hawking, and talked, and played chess, while the lady Albrea smiled on us. They were generous days.

When the last leaves had fallen from the trees, and when Carham if it held would be in the thirtieth week of the siege, Aimeric came to find me.

"Ready for the cold rains?" he asked. "Thurstan

wants us to ride north."

"Not before time," I said, and beside me, Adele caught her breath. She touched me lightly on the wrist.

"Eat before you ride," she told me. "I will go and gather you some winter clothes."

Aimeric watched my face as I watched her go, and with a face of angelic innocence, strummed an invisible lute.

"Keep your thoughts to yourself," I warned him. "She has never said a word to me of longing."

"You will be the last she tells," said Aimeric. "No maiden speaks her heart unless she is confident, or desperate. Why should she, for it leaves her defenceless?"

The look on my face made him chuckle. "Adele de Falaise," he said, drawing out the names as if to fit them to a melody.

"The twist is that I cannot ask for her," I told him. "I have to be sure I still have Carham, or to ask Walter for Adele would be to beg. It would be without honour."

Aimeric stared at me. "How very Norman," he said. "Remind me never again to sing to you of love."

"Love is what makes me care," I protested. "How do I know where my life is heading? I could bind myself to Adele tomorrow – and God knows, I would – but is it fair to bind Adele to me? She will need a strong husband to protect her when Walter is dead. For her own sake, she may have to do better than me."

"You may be right," said Aimeric, just when I was hoping he would contradict me.

There was no sign of Adele. I went to my chamber, and found she had packed my saddle-bag, and was sitting beside it on the bed.

"I will miss you," she said.

I sat down beside her and reached for her hand, but

she gave me a half-moon look from beneath lowered eyelids.

"Will you be riding west," she asked, "to that love of yours with hair gold as harvest-corn?"

I could not leave her thinking that, so I told her all there was to tell of Sigrid.

"So you see," I ended up, "she is a wife and a mother. She will never be mine."

Adele gazed at the rushes on the floor. "They do say," she murmured, "that often we need a love to open our hearts before we are ready for the love of our lives."

"You told me once," I reminded her, "that you loved many people, in different ways, but each as strongly. I know now what that means. There are loves that run deeper than first love."

She turned, her honey-coloured eyes searching mine.

"Simon," she began gently.

"No," I said. "Do not say it."

Her hand clenched in mine. In a moment she would turn away. Quickly, I raised a finger to her lips.

"Not yet," I whispered.

In an upper room of the archbishop's new palace, Thurstan and Walter sat by a fire of apple logs.

"We are sending you north," said Walter, "to bring Jordan home." His voice was flat, and their faces were expressionless.

"And Northumberland?" I asked.

Walter could not bring himself to reply.

"The troubles in the south are spreading," said Thurstan. "Stephen cannot help us, but he badly needs peace in the north; so badly, he is ready to pay heavily for it. He has sent us word that he is willing to grant Prince Henry the earldoms of Cumbria and Northumberland, all save the royal castles of Newcastle and Bamburgh."

"At a price," added Walter. "Henry must do homage, and acknowledge he only holds them by grace of the king of England."

"Has King David agreed?" I asked.

"Our envoy sets out tomorrow with the offer," replied Thurstan. "We are sending Abbot William of Rievaulx. You will ride with him." He looked at me questioningly. "You know something of David. Will he accept, or does it come too late?"

"Do we know," I asked, "if William FitzDuncan is still among David's trusted counsellors?"

"He was not among the dead on the field of the Standard," said Walter. "I know why you ask. He and his like will shout against any settlement. They will not want to give back Newcastle and Bamburgh. They will not want Henry to do homage for land he already holds by conquest."

"And for David to come to a settlement," said Thurstan, "is to admit that Stephen is king of England, and not a usurper. That alone may be more than he can bring himself to do."

"So everything still hangs on the brink of worse, and Stephen's offer is not the surrender it might appear," said Aimeric thoughtfully.

"It is the lesser evil," agreed Thurstan. "If David accepts."

He looked unspeakably weary. His robes looked as if they weighed more than his body. We had seen him struggle to hold Northumbria together, and we knew what it meant to him to fail. Walter looked as broken. They had no more to give. They were spent. This was what had become of the companions of the Sacred Blade.

"Has Aimeric told you?" I asked gaily. "We know

how to find the Sacred Blade."

Aimeric glanced at me with surprise, then caught my purpose. "It is true," he said. "It lies in one of the forty-five churches where Saint Cuthbert's body rested on the flight from Lindisfarne. We know them all. We have only to search them."

"I cannot send you back into danger," said Thurstan. "FitzDuncan may still be searching, and besides, I am not worthy to hold the Sacred Blade."

"You are, my lord," I insisted. "You did what no one else could have done. You raised Northumbria. English and Norman fought side by side. They will sing about it for a thousand years."

Thurstan and Walter looked at each other and laughed.

"It was the Sacred Blade," said Thurstan, "that raised Northumbria. What else could have given us the idea of the Standard? How else could two old Normans have known it was time to call on the saints of the Northumbrian past?"

"Then like King Oswy," I said, "you must found an abbey in thanks for your victory. What has become of the monks who fled from Calder?"

"So you remember them," said Thurstan warmly. "I am happy to say they are prospering. Roger de Mowbray has endowed them. The last I heard, they were building themselves a new abbey, not far from here, at a place called Byland."

Smiling, he gazed into the fire. "Yes," he said dreamily, "there is so much still to build."

24. THE SACRED BLADE

A BBOT William insisted on an escort of no more than three of his own lay-brothers. So we were six, and I was the only one of the party who carried a sword.

The abbot held fast to his vows. He had let himself be dragged into the world to do his duty to it, but he was determined not to say one single word more than he had to. At the hour of each holy office he called a halt and said his prayers by the roadside, even in the rain. As a result, we travelled slowly and sombrely, but that was no hardship. Neither Aimeric nor I felt very much like singing.

Otherwise, the road was a strange echo of our journey north with Thurstan, a year before. North of the Tees, we entered the Waste Land; but folk were returning to their villages, and winter wheat was shooting green through the soil. However cruel it had been, King David's Flood had done less damage than the Burning, when the Conqueror had the ploughs broken and the seedcorn destroyed and left the doors hanging open to famine and a plague of wolves.

It took us four days to reach the Tyne, where the blue boar banner of the house of Canmore flew above the ramparts of Newcastle.

Prince Henry himself was lord of the fortress. Because

FitzDuncan might be with him, I waited with Aimeric and the lay-brothers in the bailey, while Abbot William went to greet him. The abbot was back before we had even fed the horses. King David, he told us, was at Rocksburgh, and Prince Henry had given one of his knights the task of escorting us there.

His name was Rodulf de Melville, and he was the younger son of a Norman who held land in Angus. As we rode on into Northumberland, he looked around with interest and a glint came into his eye whenever we crossed a wild stretch without a castle. Off-handedly, I asked for news of Carham.

"It must still be defiant," he replied. "I have orders to take you by way of Redesdale and the pass to Jedburgh. The Till and Tweed valleys are unsafe for travellers."

"I was hoping to pass through Alnwick," I said. "How is Eustace FitzJohn these days?"

"Recovering from his wounds," said Rodulf. "He broke a shoulder at Cowton Moor."

Cowton Moor was the name of the heath by Allerton where we had fought the Battle of the Standard. So we were to remember it by different names, and as memories faded, it would be no more to the Scots than a lost battle at a place named Cowton Moor. They would have better things to tell their children.

FitzJohn had been lucky. He was still lord of Alnwick. In the chess-game, he had chosen the right side.

On the afternoon of the eve of Martinmas, we rode into Rocksburgh. The streets were crowded for the market that went with the great autumn feast and the castle was thronged with guests.

As soon as our arrival was known, Abbot William was taken to speak alone with the king. Aimeric and I exchanged a look of relief.

"At least David has learnt to hold his councils behind closed doors," I remarked hopefully.

We made our way into the hall, and were warming ourselves with mulled ale when Aimeric tensed and stared over my shoulder. Turning, I found myself face to face with Robert. He stood with his arms at his sides, waiting for me to speak.

"Do I know you?" I asked him.

"Only if you wish," he said quietly. "I owe you my life."

"Oh no," I said. "You owe it to Adam your brother. I would have killed you."

"For a time I wished you had."

It was not only the softness in his voice that was new. Something had changed in his face. The hatred had gone from his eyes.

"You were the one who broke friendship," I said searchingly. "It was not what I wanted. Shall we drink to the passing of a bad year?"

Eagerly, but still unsure of himself, he sat down beside us.

"What happened to you," Aimeric asked him, "after the battle?"

"I was my father's prisoner," said Robert ruefully. "He sent me south to King Stephen, like a rebel to be judged; but Stephen I found to be a knight of rare courtesy. He sent me back to my father, in thanks for his loyalty, and my father sent me here."

So that was it. Not only had his pride been broken, but at long last, Robert had had to cope with generosity and goodwill.

"And now?" asked Aimeric.

"Now I ride west to take up my lordship of Annandale. Annandale marches with Galloway, and my task will be to keep the men of Galloway to their own lands."

"We'll drink to that," I told him.

After supper, a steward came to take me to the king.

I was led through a maze of buildings and penticed walks that lay behind the hall to a large chamber hung with hunting-trophies. Wolfhounds lay stretched by the fire, and by the light of a stand of three candles, a clerk sat at a writing-desk. Behind him stood Abbot William and Hugh de Morville. From the way their eyes followed the pen, I guessed they had been haggling over the words being written.

David sat nearby, at a table, and he replied to my bow with a smile.

"No doubt you know the offer Abbot William has brought me," he said. "It is an offer I accept."

I searched his face for the slightest sign of victory or defeat, but there was none. In his way, he looked as tired as Thurstan and Walter.

"In accordance with the terms," he continued, "I will surrender Newcastle and Bamburgh, and Carham will be surrendered to me. Tomorrow at first light you may ride to your father. Tell him I come at noon, and I expect to find the castle gates open."

"Yes, my lord."

"Tell him also that he has won great honour by his defence. As a mark of respect, I will allow him to leave with his arms and his belongings, with banners unfurled, as befits an unvanquished knight."

That was courteous. I bowed again.

"So tell me, Simon de Falaise," he asked, "what do you make of the outcome of this?"

I gazed up at the rafters, wondering how honest one could ever be with kings.

"I hope, my lord," I said, "that now you have Northumberland and Cumbria, you are content."

"I am content for my son," he said, and paused. "I have lived with my father's work. He will have to live with his. Remember, as you grow older, that this was my doing, and not Henry's. Leave him unblamed."

There was true sorrow in his voice, and my heart went out to him. I looked, and met the kind eyes of David Margaretson. The exorcism was over. He was free at last of the ghost of Malcolm Canmore.

"By the way," he said, looking at me curiously, "Drustan gave me your message that I should give thought to my nephew. You may be happy to hear that I watch over him and listen to him with the greatest of care."

In the morning, Aimeric and I were ready to leave before the mists had cleared.

We paused for a blessing from Abbot William, who would be riding on to visit his brothers at Melrose. Robert walked beside us as we trotted through the bailey. At the gates he reached up, took hold of my bridle, and launched into a speech that came out so fast he must have been muttering it half the night.

"When you see Adele, tell her I wish her only the best. I know I asked too much and lost her love, but the blame for that is mine, not hers, and mine to carry away."

He let go of the bridle and stood back.

"If ever the winds blow you west," he added, "remember you will be welcome in Annandale."

I leaned down from the saddle, and in friendship we clasped the same hands with which we had tried so hard to kill each other.

"What did you make of that?" I asked Aimeric as we cantered through the burgh towards the ferry.

He laughed and pointed a forefinger at the sky.

"The road to wisdom," he said solemnly, "has some unexpected travellers."

The road to Carham, though, we had to ourselves. We splashed through the brook that had once been the border, and up onto the hummock crowned by the old church, to find the Scots striking camp. They were setting fire to their bothies, and the place stank as only a camp pitched for a night and then lived in for thirty-two weeks could stink. At first, I wondered how they had heard of the treaty, but then I caught sight of Rodulf de Melville. He grinned and waved us on towards the castle.

For it was still there, on its knoll above the Tweed. The sward before the gates was now a slope of churned mud, littered with broken weapons and shreds of clothing. The gates and ramparts were charred by burning, in one or two places so badly that the palisade was no more than a twisted comb of jagged black timbers; but there were guards above the gateway, and one with a grizzled beard I knew. Even from half a bowshot away I heard the oath to old gods that he muttered as he recognised us.

"Orm Sigurdsson," I yelled. "Go and wash your mouth out with holy water."

We reined to a halt before the gates, and I looked up to see Orm grinning down at me. He scratched his beard.

"Strange," he said. "It looks like young Simon, but he was always such a respectful and well-mannered lad. Perhaps I should take no chances, and tell my archers to turn him into a hedgehog?"

Before I could reply, the gates were swung open, and

we heeled our horses forward into the bailey. The garrison swarmed to greet us – the twenty or so that were still on their feet – and as I slid down from the saddle, I was caught by Jordan and crushed in an embrace.

"I suppose you can tell us," he said, "why the Scots are burning their camp?"

Uneasily, I told them of the truce, of how it was turning into a peace, and how the price of that peace was Carham's surrender. I was expecting Jordan to spit with disgust, but instead, he roared with laughter.

"There you are, lads," he said. "We are the ransom for Newcastle and Bamburgh, and we ride out with honour. Go and pack."

Only when his men had scattered to the halls and stables did he drop the swagger. He was thinner. Even Orm was thinner.

"So David wins," said Jordan. "I knew when no army had come by Michaelmas that we were lost, but I never thought Northumberland itself would be forsaken."

"Walter tried," I began, but he interrupted me.

"Spare me the story. If you care for sour ale or smoked beef, you will find plenty in the hall. I doubt we'll be taking it with us."

He turned and strode off towards the keep. I made a move to follow, but Orm stretched out a hand to hold me back.

"Later," he suggested, and turned to Aimeric, grinning and narrowing his eyes.

"I liked your song," he told him. "We might make a poet of you yet. If you can riddle me some Viking kennings, like a true skald, I might have a gift for you."

Aimeric took a deep breath. "Try me," he said.

"Name me a flood-elk," said Orm.

"A ship," said Aimeric.

"So it is," said Orm. "Name me cave-fire."

"Gold."

"So it is," said Orm, his eyes narrowing to the merest slits. "Now tell me the name of the rain-haired woman I love."

"Cumbria," said Aimeric.

"Three in a row," said Orm. "Wait here."

He stumped off towards the hall, and Aimeric let out his breath in a long gust of relief.

"That was impressive," I told him. "How did you guess them all so fast?"

"You may not know this," said Aimeric mischievously, "but I was once locked in a dungeon in Caerluel with Orm's brother Hoskuld. I forget whose fault it was that I was there, but I have him to thank for a headful of Viking poetry."

Orm returned, and thrust a newly-made lute into Aimeric's hands. Every leaf of the gourd had a different grain, and the lute had been waxed and polished until it shone.

"You'll have to string it yourself," he said, "and I'll need another look at yours before I can make the pegs."

Aimeric turned it in his hands, his mouth opening and closing. He held the gourd to his ear, tapping it with his fingers.

"This is beautiful," he said breathlessly.

"Aye," said Orm. "I thought you'd like it."

I had been looking round the bailey, trying to work out what was different about it, and I realised that apart from the hall, none of the buildings had roofs.

"What happened to the thatch?" I asked.

"We've been feeding it to the horses," said Orm.

"Well, I must go and gather my treasures."

When he had gone, I turned to Aimeric. "Sour ale or smoked beef?"

"I think not."

"Then perhaps we had better keep watch?"

We climbed the stairway to the ramparts and stood looking out over the corner of England I had once thought was to be mine.

"What do we do now?" I asked. "Do we ride south with Jordan, or do we melt into the land and begin our search?"

Aimeric made no reply. He was staring at the Tweed, lost in thought. Then he shivered.

"Simon," he asked, "do you remember the first riddle of all?"

I began to recite.

> *"Over me the thunderstorm,*
> *Search for me beneath the earth*
> *Where the water flows like mead ..."*

"Look at the river," said Aimeric. "I would say it flowed like mead." He raked his fingers through his hair. "I have just been remembering the litany of the flight from Lindisfarne. This is how it starts: '*Norham, Carham, Kelsow, Melrose ...*'"

"Carham!"

"Carham," repeated Aimeric, pointing to the church. "That is where Saint Cuthbert once rested."

Even as we stared, a party of knights rode up onto the hummock and dismounted by the doorway of the church. King David had come to accept the surrender of the castle.

Aimeric and I hurried down the stairway. The horses,

and there were far more horses than there would be riders, had been brought out into the bailey. Loki came trotting over and slobbered down my neck.

Aimeric spoke softly with Jordan, who beckoned to Arnoul.

"I have to speak with King David," he told him. "When the others are ready, bring them out onto the sward and wait for us there."

He rode out of the castle without a backward glance, Orm and Aimeric and I at his heels.

David and his companions were waiting at the top of the slope above the river, upwind of the reek of the burning bothies. Jordan dismounted and went down on one knee. He drew his sword and laid it at the king's feet.

"My lord, the castle is yours."

"It is yours to give," said David warmly. "You held it well."

He reached down for the sword and gave it back to Jordan.

"You and yours have my safe-conduct to the Tyne," he said. "Is there anything you need for your journey?"

"Only the hospitality we will ask along the way," said Jordan, "though I would value a moment alone in the church to pray for the souls of my dead."

"Take as long as you wish," replied David.

Jordan bowed, and walked towards the church, the rest of us trying to hasten after him without it looking as if we were in a hurry. Once inside, we closed the door. The Scots had used the church as a store, and the air smelt of malt.

Amongst the wall-paintings was an image of Saint Cuthbert praying on the shore, with two otters rubbing themselves against his legs. The altar was lit by a shaft of light that fell from the round-arched window high in the apse. Set in the paving of the floor was a slab the length of a man.

"Look at this," said Orm as we reached it.

Close by the slab, one of the paving-stones had chiselled on its surface a tiny but unmistakeable hammer of Thor.

"*Over me the thunderstorm,*" I recited.

"Here we are, then," said Aimeric, "in the cavern at the heart of the enchantment."

"I suggest we lift the slab," said Jordan. "With one of us to each corner it should come."

On our knees, we scraped with knives and fingers, loosening the earth that had been trodden firm around the edges.

"There is a hollow underneath," whispered Aimeric. "The stone is no thicker than a book."

Orm dug a hole at one end, worked the shaft of his axe into it, and levered with all his weight. The slab came up like a trap-door, and we seized the edges and staggered sideways until we had dragged it clear of its placement and could lower it to the floor.

I half expected a stairway to lead down into a crypt lit by magic, but what I saw was only a narrow trough between the blocks on which the slab had been resting. It was enough, for lying in the trough was a long, thin bundle of discoloured linen. It had the shape of a sword.

"Go on, Simon," said Jordan. "This has been your quest. You must be the one to draw the sword from the stone."

Reaching down, I gripped the bundle at one end. Through the damp cloth I could feel the shape of the hilt. My fingers wriggled round it, grasped, and I straightened out to draw the Sacred Blade from the earth where it had lain for so long.

It was so heavy it made the veins bulge along my wrist. Then, as I stood back and raised the sword into the shaft of sunlight, it snapped at the hilt.

The linen tore like a cobweb, and the Sacred Blade hit the ground with no more than a sodden slap. A liquid dark as blood trickled out of the twisted bundle.

"Rust," said Jordan quietly.

He reached down to pick up the bundle, and it came apart in his hands; a mess of rotten linen, rotten leather, and the dark shards that were all that remained of the blade of the kings of Northumbria. I pulled the linen from the hilt still in my hand, and found a lump of tarnished bronze. Set in the pommel was a clouded crystal of amber.

"Aye, it will have been monks who hid it," said Orm. "You cannot expect monks to know about the care of weapons."

Jordan scooped up the remains and threw them back into the trough, then he and Orm set the slab back in place.

"That hilt should fit in your wallet," Jordan told me. "All you can do now is take it to Thurstan. He will decide whether to keep it or throw it into the sea."

I tucked the hilt away and stood there desolate. I had been longing for this moment, and now I felt only emptiness when I had expected to blaze with power and purpose.

"So nothing has changed," I said numbly.

"We have been changed," said Aimeric, "and without the Sacred Blade, there might never have been the Standard, and without the Standard, we might none of us be here. Perhaps we can never hold the past in our hands, but we know now that we must keep it in our hearts."

"Words, words, words," I muttered.

Jordan gripped me by the elbow and marched me towards the door.

"Come on," he said. "I know what you need."

Outside, he led me to King David, who was standing with his companions discussing the smallness of the cavalcade that was trotting out of the gates of Carham to wait for us on the sward. The king turned to Jordan with a look of bewilderment.

"Is that your garrison?" he asked.

"One more assault, my lord," answered Jordan, "and we would have been overwhelmed."

"Then I am glad I never gave the order."

"My lord," said Jordan, "there is a favour I wish to ask of you. Grant my son his knighthood."

David looked at me thoughtfully.

"I know your son," he said. "He is worthy, though I believe a man should spend a night in a vigil of prayer before he makes his vow."

"He has lived through the past year," said Jordan. "That is vigil enough for anyone."

"Amen," agreed the king. "Simon de Falaise, place your hands between mine."

I went down on one knee and David's hands closed over mine.

"Will you vow," he asked, "to live with honour, to protect the Church, to help widows and orphans and all who need your strength, and to draw your sword only when justice demands it?"

There was not a word in the vow I could quarrel with. Meeting David's eyes, and with the hilt of the Sacred Blade in the wallet hanging from my belt, I made the vow with all my heart.

As soon as it was spoken, it felt right, and it meant that

when King David bade us farewell, we did not part as enemies. For when all was said and done, we shared the same fight, that of somehow staying true to ourselves in a troubled world.

We mounted and rode down to take the head of the cavalcade. I made to stay with Aimeric, but Orm came up and thumped me on the shoulder.

"I'll ride with the poet," he told me. "From now on, you ride with your father."

So I was at Jordan's side as we entered the valley of the Till, and Carham, with its castle and domain, fell out of sight.

Jordan gave a long sigh and frowned at me.

"Well, you have earned your knighthood," he said. "What are you going to make of it?"

"Who knows?" I said. "Our roads may be the same."

I could tell that pleased him, though he tried hard to look stern.

"Are you sure?" he asked. "I may lead you into trouble."

"True," I said, "but I'll take that chance."